Thirty Days to Thirty

Courtney Psak

Printed in the United States of America

First Printing, 2015

ISBN 9780996815918

CAMP Publishing

www.CourtneyPsak.com

Acknowledgments

I would like to thank you for taking the time to read Thirty Days to Thirty. I hope you enjoy reading it as much as I enjoyed writing it.

I would like to thank my husband Paul for helping me keep my sanity through this process, Bev Rossenbaum for her talented editing skills and to all of my friends and family for their love and support.

If you'd like to find out more about me and my next book, please check out my website Courtneypsak.com.

Chapter One

I glance at my watch and notice it's nine thirty at night, just another late night at the office. I've been killing myself at work trying to make partner by the time I turn thirty, which is now a little over a month away. I feel like I've gotten a handle on everything, and that's exactly when my boss Kimsley comes in.

"How are you making out?" he asks. I'm surprised to see him, as this is the latest I've seen him stay in a while. He's got his jacket off and his suspenders are hanging on for dear life.

"I'm good. I finished up your summaries and I was just going to go over a couple of case files." I stand and hand over a few folders, then search through another pile.

"Listen," Kimsley starts as he puts the files back down on my desk. He seems pretty uneasy and he's sweating more than usual. He pulls out a handkerchief and dabs his shiny head, not looking me in the eye. "The firm recognizes everything you've done for us in the past six years that you've worked here, and especially in the past six months."

This is it, I think. Finally my moment has come—they're going to offer me partner! I try to keep my composure as my legs bounce under my desk. I pull strands of my strawberry blonde hair behind my ear and try to keep my seemingly large smile under wraps.

"I appreciate that, sir," I say, trying to keep my expression stern.

"But as hard as you've been working, we aren't seeing the level of excellence that we had expected you to reach by now."

I feel my heart drop into my stomach and my eyes grow wide. You know when all of a sudden in a movie something happens that's not supposed to and you hear the sound of a record getting scratched? That's what I hear in my head. "I beg your pardon?"

"We're going to have to ask you to seek new employment," Kimsley finally says.

My fingers go numb and I suddenly feel myself getting hot. Thirty seconds ago, I was planning my gracious acceptance speech, and now I'm scrambling for my words. "What do you mean? I've done everything I can for this firm. If I haven't reached the level you wanted me to, maybe it's because I need to be given more challenging cases. I strongly suggest you give me a few more months to prove myself to you." Suddenly I realize he's already motioned to the security guard that I hadn't noticed standing outside my office to escort me out.

I'm defeated. All my hard work, all of my dreams, have been crushed just like that.

The security guard, who looks like the big guy from *The Green Mile*, hands me a box for me to pack my stuff. He's completely stone-faced and looking at me as if I'm a prisoner who's just been sentenced.

"I'm sorry, Jill, I really am." Kimsley looks genuinely upset, at least. With that, he walks out the door leaving me alone with the security guard. I'm only thankful no one's here to see this. I wait for a minute, watching Kimsley go. I try to will him to turn around and say he's made a mistake and he wants me back. But sure enough, he disappears into the elevator and the doors close. It's the loudest sound I've ever heard.

I'm experiencing a mix of emotions. I feel like I've lost not only my job, but my whole life. On top of it, I have an eight-hundred-pound man staring me down like I'm going to lose my mind and pull a Jerry Maguire.

When I get home, I put on my sunglasses to avoid letting the doorman see my bloodshot eyes.

"Good evening, may I help you?" he asks.

I realize I don't recognize him. He's an older gentleman with gray hair and a thick mustache. This is the first time in almost six months I've been home before midnight. He probably works this shift all the time.

"Hi, I'm Jill Stevens. I live with Brady Miller in apartment 902." I point towards the elevator.

"Are you his sister?" he asks. The marble floor seems to echo his voice. Realizing this is going to be a problem, I put my pathetic box of personal items from work onto the leather couch across from his desk.

I'm confused by his question. "No, I'm his girlfriend." What, is this sixty-year-old doorman judging me for living with a man I'm not married to? I'm starting to lose my patience with everyone. Besides, it's not like we aren't going to get married. We've been together for six years already. We both worked at the same firm; in fact, that's how we met. We both had the same goal to make partner by the time we were thirty, and fortunately that happened for him last year. This time it was supposed to be my turn, and then we were going to start talking about that next big step.

He gives me a concerned look as I attempt to fish my keys out of my oversized purse. There's some cursing involved and finally, I slam my entire bag onto the ground. Luckily, my keys are one of the many things that fall out. He has no choice but to let me pass, with a bit of an uneasy look on his face.

Like I need any more problems right now. I have to give him credit though. I'm sure my cheeks are flushed, and I'm wearing oversized sunglasses when it's dark outside. I wouldn't let me in either. I notice him reach for the phone, then stop. *Probably debating whether he needs to call the local mental hospital to see if they have lost anyone*, I think.

The elevator ride seems to take forever. I feel like my body weighs a thousand tons and the elevator is doing everything it can to pull me up.

When it finally reaches my floor, I start to well up again. What am I going to tell Brady? I haven't even thought that far. I've just been trying to process what happened. There wasn't a case I messed up, I did everyone else's work, I saved Kimsley's ass several times when I caught him screwing up his case files. In retrospect, I guess my goal should have been catching him with that strange woman who visits him, who isn't his wife. I bet I would've gotten partner that very second if I'd walked in on that.

When the elevator doors open, I get out and stare at the door for another few seconds when I hear a female voice. *Probably watching a movie.*

I turn the key and all of a sudden I hear a gasp and what sounds like scrambling.

"Babe, are you there?" I ask, a bit concerned now. Did someone break in?

"Uh, hi." Brady runs out of the bedroom. His face is red and his hair is a mess. He's wearing his boxers. Despite being very confused at the moment, I can't help but gaze at him. No one would ever believe he was a lawyer because of how good-looking he is. He has sandy-brown hair with deep gray eyes and an angular jaw. His whole body looks as if it were chiseled from marble. I can't help but think how lucky I am that a mousy klutz like me was able to charm a man like him.

"Were you sleeping?" I ask.

"Uh, yeah," he says. "What are you doing home early? I thought you had to work late again."

I do what I can to remain calm, but the words just pour out of me. "I got fired!" I drop my box and purse on the floor in front of me.

"What do you mean?" He sounds completely shocked.

"I don't know what happened." I try to walk towards the bedroom, but he offers to fix both of us a drink.

I sit down on the couch while he goes into the kitchen to make me a vodka tonic and pours himself a glass of scotch.

I start to tell the story and begin to fall apart. Everything I had spent years working towards was taken away so quickly ...

"I need to splash some cold water on my face," I say. "I can feel myself getting overheated and need to cool off."

"Don't worry about that now. You're beautiful." He grabs both my shoulders. Then he softens a bit and wipes a tear from my face and gives me that puppy dog look of his before pulling me in for a hug.

"I appreciate it, but right now washing my face might be the only thing that will make me feel better," I tell him, pulling away.

"Let's just get your mind off of this," he suggests. "Do you want to talk about what you want to do for the big 3-0?"

I look at him, unable to control my sobbing. I know he was trying to cheer me up, but what's cheerful about losing your job right before you turn thirty? Especially when you thought you'd be a partner and at least engaged by now.

"I'm sorry, that was a bad idea," he hugs me.

I pull away and this time he lets me go. "Do you want to go for a walk or something?" he calls out.

I ignore him. When I walk into the bedroom, it's dark. He must've been sleeping, but the television isn't on. Maybe he turned it off when I got in, I think. I turn the lights back on and see the bed is unmade. He was definitely sleeping. But, really? It's barely ten.

I head into the bathroom and, for the first time, take my sunglasses off and look at myself in the mirror. My face looks tired and worn. I can't remember the last time I really looked at myself. Do I always look this tired, or is it just tonight? I realize that rather than washing my face, a full shower might be what I really need right now.

I take the clip out of my hair and strip down, looking forward to feeling the hot water on my skin. Hopefully, the steam will take care of the swelling.

I give myself one more pitiful look in the mirror before I pull the curtain back to turn on the shower.

All of a sudden I hear screaming. It could be me doing the screaming, I've suddenly realized. I'm standing naked in front of Jenine, Brady's secretary.

Chapter Two

Her clothes look like they were thrown on at the last minute. Her skirt lining is facing the wrong direction and her button-down shirt is only half tucked in. Clearly she was trying to quietly dress behind the curtain. Meanwhile, I'm standing here in the buff, and let's just say my diet and exercise regimens have been somewhat lacking. I feel the urge to grab anything with which to cover myself. That leaves me trying to wrap a tiny fuzzy bath mat around my entire body.

"What the hell!" I can't help but scream as I see Brady running into the bathroom. "Really?"

"Babe, listen to me, it's not what you think," Brady tries.

"Oh, come on, really? This is straight out of every soap opera there is." My face is even hotter now and I have chills running up and down my spine.

"I'm sorry, Ms. Stevens," Jenine says, looking like a teenager who just got caught smoking by her parents. She's trying to smooth her hair and tuck in the rest of her shirt.

"Oh, please," I say in disgust. Then I look at Brady. "Don't tell me you didn't know about me getting fired, and on top of that, you do this? You're the worst boyfriend ever!"

"I didn't know you were going to get fired," he pleads, as if saying that was suddenly going to make everything okay.

"But you knew I wasn't getting partner?" I question, fishing for a hint. I'm keeping my back to the wall while trying desperately to reach for my robe. It's hard enough to have a serious conversation with someone, let alone when you're completely naked.

He opens his mouth, but closes it again, which proves to me he did know. He let me kill myself this whole time so he could sleep around with his temp.

"You two obviously need to talk. Is there anything I can get you?" she asks while combing her streaky hair through with her fingers.

At this point, I'm staring her down while at the same time trying to put on my robe without revealing any more of me than I already have. Though I have to admit, I'm in a position that makes it very hard to be intimidating.

"Right," she says. "I'll just get out of your way then." She has to slouch her way between Brady and myself who are both standing in the door frame. A few seconds later I hear a hard thud; it sounds as if she's just tripped over my box by the door. I try hard not to crack a smile and secretly hope she just chipped a tooth.

When she does leave, I make my way over to the kitchen and grab the bottle of vodka off the counter.

"I already made you a drink," he tells me, pointing towards the vodka tonic with a lemon twist.

I don't hear him. I'm already chugging straight from the bottle.

"Oh, okay then," he says, clasping his hands and slowly backing away.

I give him an evil glare; there are so many things I want to say to him. How I'd thought we loved each other, how I'd stupidly thought I'd make partner and he'd propose, but instead all I manage in between my gulps of my savior at the moment, a clear bottle of heaven, is "Pig head."

"Excuse me?" he says.

"You're a pig head," I say, not believing I said it once, let alone twice.

"Baby, it's not like I don't love you, but you've been ignoring me. I mean, I haven't seen you in over six months. It's like I don't even know you anymore." He says this in a whiny voice that makes him sound like a child, which is exactly what he is. "And I know that makes me selfish, but I've been starting to think."

"Good for you," I respond.

He looks at me for a second and continues on. "It's great that you're such a strong and independent woman with dreams of your own …"

I just shake my head and start to look up at the ceiling.

"I just think that I need to be with someone who needs me more." There it is, I think, the breakup sentence. Not that I didn't know it was coming, but I figured the presence of a twenty-year-old tart in the shower would give me the upper hand in this situation.

"No shit," I say, mainly because I don't know what else to say, but also because I need to still feel as if I have some semblance of control here.

"I think we should break up." Okay, I think, *that's* the breakup sentence. I feel as if I've just been punched in the face.

"And you probably want me to move out tonight." I try to hold back my tears. At this point, where would I go and what would I do?

"Not tonight …" He trails off.

Now, I know he lived here first and I moved in with him, but based on what he's put me through, shouldn't he at least be chivalrous enough to leave me the apartment? Then again, how would I pay for it with no job? "Wow, you take the cake," I say, as my head spins. He tries to follow me. "I should write an article about you for *Cosmo*. But I bet they wouldn't even believe me."

"Babe," he starts.

"No, wait, I should have you studied by a psychologist." I'm now walking around the kitchen in a circle. I can't tell if he's following me around the island or if he's trying to get away from me. I see him jump a bit when I walk past our knife set on the counter.

"I'm not saying I'm a saint, Jill, but I'm not the only one who's wrong here." He stops and puts his hands up in defense as I stop dead and stare at him.

I can feel my eyes burning as I look at him. I lose my job, walk in on him cheating on me, and he's going to tell me part of this is my fault?

"Well." I take a breath and swallow hard. I'm trying hard to stay strong, but the truth is, I've never been more hurt in my entire life. "Considering the fact that you're kicking me out on top of everything else I've just been through, I think it's only fair that you leave me alone tonight to give me time to pack and get the hell out of here." Clearly, there isn't anything to say. It's all out there. It feels like someone just took a huge knife and sent it right through my heart and then dragged it down into my stomach.

"I understand," he says in almost a whisper. His head is down and he won't look at me. I realize he'll never look at me the same way again.

I remain in the kitchen as he awkwardly packs his things for the night. He even has the nerve to pack the silk boxers I gave him for Valentine's Day. I know he's going to see the twenty-year-old tart, but at this point I don't care. It actually kind of frightens me how much I don't care. I'm jobless, homeless, unmarried, and about to turn thirty. "I guess this is what rock bottom feels like," I say while taking another swig.

Chapter Three

I'm standing in front of the old Victorian home I grew up in. It looks almost like a dollhouse you'd find in your grandmother's attic. It's a sandy color with dark brown shutters and a wraparound porch. I remember when we moved into this house when I was five years old. When I was little, I used to pretend I was a princess and this house was my castle.

My perspective has really changed since. I feel now as if this is where I've been sentenced.

I've just spent close to two hundred dollars to get here, and now, as the cab drives away, I feel my whole life is driving away with it. I'm back to square one.

"Honey!" My mother comes out the front door and opens her arms. "We're so happy you came home," she says as she meets me halfway on the front lawn.

"Thanks," I mumble.

"I'm so sorry about everything," she tells me, gripping me tighter. She has a much stronger grip than I remember. Maybe all of the Pilates she feels the need to call and tell me about are paying off. She looks good, though. She's clearly aiming for the Susan Sarandon look. Her curly hair, which I inherited but certainly don't embrace, gets tangled up in my mouth as she hugs me nearly to death, her silk blouse brushes against me, and I notice I've seen her in this outfit two out of the three times I've been with her this year.

"Mom, no offense, but could we not do this on the front lawn with Mrs. Mildred over there watching us?"

My mom looks over and sees her staring us down from the rocker on her front porch.

"Sure," my mother agrees, plastering a fake smile and wave to Mrs. Mildred while pulling away and leading me inside. At this point my father comes out to grab some of my luggage. "Glad to have you home, kiddo," he says, patting me on the shoulder.

"Oh, honey, it's just awful what's happened to you," my mother says as she ushers me inside. I notice her khaki pants come up to her rib cage. My mother always shops but somehow still manages to find the clothes that have been out of style for ten years.

"When your mother told me everything, I thought, she's been watching so many soaps, she doesn't know reality from fiction anymore," my father says as he leans down in his Hawaiian inspired shirt that overlaps his pleated shorts. Come the first sign of summer and he suddenly thinks he's Jimmy Buffet. He slips out of his Birkenstocks, while trying to lift my bags. I can see that the top of his head is burned, I'm sure from all of the yard work he's been doing.

"Seriously, what kind of man does that? I mean, that's just heartless. I have a right to call his mother." She opens the screen door with a little more force than necessary.

"Mom, you never even met him and you want to call his mother?"

"Well, have you ever met his mother?"

"No, because she's dead," I say in a deadpan voice, and walk past her into the front hallway.

"Well I guess that explains it then. Only a motherless son could act that way."

"Mom, be reasonable," I plead as I head up the stairs. The house smells like my mom's fragrance. It always has. It's like it's been baked into the walls. It never bothered me before, but today I'm pretty much choking on the scent, and I'm barely handling the steps with my massive hangover. I hold the bannister for dear life as I climb.

"Can I make you anything?" she calls out to me from the bottom of the stairs.

"No, I'm fine, Mom," I tell her.

When I reach the top of the steps, I suddenly feel a mix of emotions—nostalgia and depression. Not that I had a sad childhood or anything. I have a lot of great memories here. And it's not as if I haven't been home in forever; I was home just a few months ago for my parents' anniversary dinner.

Brady was supposed to come but he got held up with a case he had to work on that weekend. Do I even believe that anymore? Six years and he never once made an effort to introduce me to his father or try to meet mine. I guess I just always wrote it off as us both being really busy. Not to mention we had to keep quiet about our relationship for the first three years because we worked together. Office romances weren't all that accepted at our firm.

I look around the hall again. I start to feel depressed about how I'm about to turn thirty and I'll be living at home. This isn't exactly where I thought I'd be at this stage in my life ten years ago, or yesterday, for that matter.

"Move it or lose it," my father grunts as he practically knocks me over for blocking the top of the stairs. He throws my suitcases down on floor of the hallway. "What do ya have in there?" he asks.

"My entire life," I tell him.

He gives me a look that says I'm being overdramatic and continues to drag the bags to the end of the hallway until we reach my old room. I hear my mom from downstairs yelling at him not to scratch up the wood floors. Some things never change.

My room's a lot smaller than I remember. Then again, maybe it's all the useless crap I've accumulated over the years.

"I know it's a little tight, so anything you want to keep in the office for storage is fine for now," he tells me.

"Thanks, Dad," I say, looking down and slumping my shoulders. I still can't believe the situation I'm in.

Sensing my uneasiness, he gives me a sympathetic look and pats me on the arm. "It's good to have you back," he says. I feel the stubble on his face as he kisses me on the cheek.

I give a half smile as he leaves and I'm left with a pile of suitcases. I look at my twin-size bed and wonder how I ever fit in there. I take a seat on my bed and run my hands over the quilt. Nothing has changed about my room since high school. My lacrosse letters still are tacked up on my wall next to a collage of pictures with my friends. I realize I don't even really talk to any of them any more except for Liz. Liz was one of my best friends from high school. We did everything together, and then just as time went by we saw less and less of each other.

Impulsively, I pull open the cabinet door on my nightstand to find a scrapbook from high school. I open it and start flipping through the pages until I see our class graduation picture. *Wow*, I think, my eyes making a beeline. *Chris Matthews. I haven't seen him in over ten years.* I flip the pages and stare down at a picture of the two of us.

We had broken up senior year. He was smart, but completely unmotivated. Things came to a head senior year when I decided to take advance AP classes for college and he just wanted to live it up.

Then again, look at me now. Maybe he was right. What good did it all do me?

"Sweetie, I made you a sandwich. I'm sure you haven't eaten anything," my mom calls from downstairs.

"Be there in a second," I tell her. I close the book and immediately lose my train of thought, because I really am starving. Since last night's trip to hell, I've had nothing in my system but vodka.

When I get downstairs I see my mother has prepared a plate for me: a peanut butter and jelly sandwich with the crusts cut off, along with a bushel of grapes. Next to the plate is a tall glass of milk. I haven't had this lunch since elementary school. I realize this is probably the first time in over ten years she's gotten to feel like a mom, maybe even longer. I was always extremely independent, possibly because I was an only child. Also, my parents both worked.

Maybe that was why I always felt the need for a boyfriend? Maybe I subconsciously wanted the attention I didn't get from my parents. I make a mental note to tell that to my psychiatrist if this situation drives me to a mental breakdown.

Seriously, though, I don't blame my parents for anything. My father is a salesman for a manufacturing company and my mother is a nurse. They work super hard and always urged for me to do the same.

And I did. I just always wished for something bigger for myself. I wanted to be the daughter my parents could brag about.

"So do you want to talk about it?" my mom finally asks me, taking a seat next to me with a cup of tea.

"I'm not really ready to recap," I tell her with a mouth full of peanut butter. "I'm still trying to process everything."

My mother basically got the hysterical gist of it when I called her at midnight, crying, and all she could make out was "pig head ... boyfriend ... cheated on me ... fired ... homeless." She sat on the phone with me while I tried to pull myself together, and finally ordered me to pack up and get on the next train home.

"I understand," she says, sounding disappointed. "We can talk about what you want to do for your birthday coming up."

I look up mid-bite to stare at her.

"It's your thirtieth, it's a big deal," she presses.

Yes, I know it's a big deal. It's a big deal because that's when you're supposed to have your life together. "Mom, that's really the last thing I want to think about right now."

"Fine," she says getting frustrated. After a few minutes of silence, she leans forward as if to say something and then retreats.

"What's wrong?" I ask her, knowing I won't be able to avoid hearing what she wants to say.

"Well, I mean, aside from wanting to know what happened, I want to know what your plan is to get past this? I don't want you just sulking around the house for the next few weeks."

"Come on, Mom it's been twelve hours since my life fell apart. I can't get a full day to mourn here?"

"I didn't mean it like that," she defends herself, shaking her head as if I've blown things all out of proportion. "I was just reading this pamphlet about how to handle adult children living at home that I downloaded off the Internet." She stands up and pulls it out of a drawer underneath the phone. Then she hands it to me. I scan it over. "When the Empty Nest Becomes Full Again," I read. "I don't plan on being here that long," I say, handing it back to her. "Think of it as a two-week vacation."

She doesn't say anything. She simply shrugs and puts the pamphlet back in the drawer.

Finally, I give in and proceed to tell her what happened. My father, who's come in from the garage to get his keys out of the drawer, listens in and eventually joins us at the table.

"Those bastards," he contributes.

"Tell me about it," I say, looking down at my milk and swirling the liquid inside the glass.

"Can you sue them?" my mom suggests.

"For what, exactly? Even if I could, it's a law firm. You ever try to sue a bunch of lawyers?"

They're both silent for a moment and give each other nervous looks. It's obvious they're trying to be supportive but they don't really know what to say.

"It's fine." I try to convince them and myself. "I'm going to call a headhunter first thing Monday morning and I'm going to bounce back from this in no time. I'll start looking at apartment listings today. Everything will be fine." I stand up from my chair.

"I think you should at least stay here until you find another job," my mother says. "There's no sense in you getting an apartment somewhere and finding out your job is a far commute."

Stay here? I do a double take. I can't imagine doing that. "Mom, it's New York. No matter where I get an apartment, as long as it's in Manhattan, the commute will be doable." I stand up and dump the remainder of my milk in the sink and load my glass and plate into the dishwasher.

"Well, what if you don't get a job in New York?" she says, turning around in her chair to face me.

"Why wouldn't I get a job in New York?" I ask, confused, as I close the dishwasher and stare out the window. I feel my body turn to ice at the thought.

"Well, Jill," my dad says, "the job market is pretty bad, and as great as your resume and your education are, there may not be a lot of opportunities out there."

"All we're saying is maybe you've outgrown the city, and maybe now it's time to settle somewhere closer to home. Maybe you'll meet someone and settle down," my mom concludes.

"Really?" I say, shaking my head. "You're really giving me the you-aren't-getting-any-younger speech when I'm already at the lowest point in my life?" I start to storm towards the hallway. I really don't need to be hearing this right now.

"Sweetie, it's not that I'm trying to kick you while you're down, I'm just saying maybe it's time to start reassessing your life." My mom stands up to follow me.

"Thanks for the talk," I say, walking past her and back up to my room. I suddenly feel like I'm a teenager again as I slam the door to my room.

"Marilynn, she just got home. Go easy on her," I hear my dad defend me.

"Martin, I'm just following the pamphlet," she insists.

"Well stop reading," he says. "This is our daughter, not a case study."

Living at home with my parents in my thirties? Maybe I really am a case study. I barely made it out alive the first time, how the hell am I supposed to do it all over again?

Chapter Four

My parents know enough to let me cool off, so they don't say anything as I stomp around slamming things. I look around at what now seems like a prison cell.

I decide to be the ultimate teenager and blast my stereo. I soon find out the radio doesn't work, so I press play for whatever CD I happen to have in there.

Alanis Morsette's "You Oughta Know" starts to stream through the speakers, and I can't help but think about the irony. I leave it on as I unzip my suitcases. I open my closet and realize there's no room whatsoever for all of my things.

Frustrated beyond belief, I hurl everything I don't need out of my closet and onto the floor. I pull out my prom dress and my lacrosse uniform. Honestly, why was all this kept, anyway?

Then I aggressively pull out my suitcase clothes—which are still on the hangers because I was so mad, I actually just threw them in that way—and start to hang them up.

"There," I say out loud to my clothes in annoyance before I turn on my heel and promptly slip on my prom gown. I go flying into my wall, knocking my bulletin board off, and it nails me right in the head.

I lay there stunned for a moment.

"I know you're mad, but there's no need to storm around up there in a hissy fit," my mom yells from the bottom of the steps.

I want to yell back at her, but I choose not to. After checking to make sure my head isn't bleeding, I try to pull myself up, but sure enough, I just slip again.

My dad opens the door and sees me in a pile of pink pouf. Seeing I'm okay and not knowing what else to say, he just closes the door again.

I let out an exasperated sigh. I am surrounded by clothes and now random papers I had on my bulletin board. I pick up the calendar that fell next to me. It dates back to 2005. I shake my head. Yesterday I was a lawyer, and today I've been time warped to the millennium.

Suddenly I feel a deep, sharp pain. I realize I miss Brady. I want nothing more than to call him right now. It still seems unreal that he's no longer a part of my life.

Once I'm able to scramble up, I go over to my phone to see if he's even bothered to check if I got home okay or where I was even going, for that matter. Nothing. No text, no missed call. My blood starts to boil and my face gets hot. Six years together and he can be that heartless? I blink away a few tears and try to pull myself together.

Becoming frustrated once again, I put my phone on silent and shove it to the bottom of my purse in an effort to keep myself from checking it. "I don't care anymore," I try to convince myself. I don't want to care anymore, at least.

In an effort to forget about him for a while, I decide to distract myself and I head downstairs.

"What are you doing?" my mom asks when she sees me storm past her into the garage. She is reading the paper on the kitchen table, acting as if our fight never occurred.

"Throwing out all of the useless junk in my room," I tell her with frustration still in my voice as I grab a box of garbage bags.

"Like what?" she asks, following me nervously.

"My prom dress, for one," I tell her, continuing towards the stairs.

"Oh, honey, don't throw that out. You might wear it again," she says, stopping at the bottom of the steps and putting her hands on the railing.

I just stare back at her from the landing. I don't want to be sarcastic, but ... "When?" finally comes out of my mouth.

She shrugs. "You know, when you go to a wedding or something."

For a brief moment I imagine myself in a pink strapless ball gown at a wedding. It almost seems like a nightmare.

I decide my best bet is to ignore her, and I shake my head as I climb the stairs with the box of garbage bags.

I go for the bulletin board papers on the floor first. I don't even look at what I toss because I figure anything that's been there for over ten years is of no use to me now. One page happens to fall to the side of the bag. I lean down to pick it up and can't help but read it. "Thirty things to do before I'm thirty." I stare at it as I sit on my bed, trying to remember where this came from.

Then is hits me.

Senior year of high school our teacher and lacrosse coach Ms. Wannamaker was going through a bit of a thirty-year crisis. She acted as if her life was over.

I was now familiar with the feeling.

She told us to make a list of thirty things we wanted to do by the time we were thirty.

I start to read the list.

1. Learn to live without a boyfriend

2. Graduate from college

3. Get a job at a great law firm

4. Save a person's life

5. Get a makeover

6. Travel the world

7. Get over my fear of flying

8. Get on TV

9. Go skydiving

10. Write a book

11. Win one game of beer pong

12. Learn how to flirt

13. Dress out of my comfort zone

14. Kiss a total stranger

15. Learn another language

16. Make an ex jealous

17. Learn to drive a stick shift

18. Do more volunteer work

19. Sing karaoke

20. Ride a roller coaster

21. Learn to play golf

22. Become a wine connoisseur

23. Learn to cook

24. Become more organized

25. Learn to say yes before I immediately say no

26. Figure out my life's purpose

27. For once, go somewhere without a plan

28. Get a massage

29. Take up yoga

30. See a drive-in movie

I can't take my eyes off of this. Most of this stuff would have been relatively easy to accomplish, and yet I'd barely done any of it. I had graduated from Columbia and I had landed a great job, but that didn't really count since I no longer had it.

As my eyes move farther down the list, I get even more depressed. Number one hits me the hardest. *Learn to live without a boyfriend.* Clearly this followed my breakup with Chris, though my mind goes right to Brady.

I remember Liz's way of helping me through my high school breakup was telling me I needed to learn to live on my own and not depend on anyone but myself. Which is always easier said than done. Especially the older you get.

But I would try to apply her words to my current situation. "I definitely need to try to forget Brady and learn to live by myself for a while," I say out loud as if promising myself.

"Martin, the dishwasher is broken again," I hear my mom yell.

"You have to push it in all the way," he yells back.

"I did that; it won't work."

Well, the *living* part will be difficult, I think to myself.

I realize then how drained I am and collapse on my bed and slowly close my eyes. I try to make my mind go blank, but I can't help replaying the entire thing in my head. It's like an awful channel that I can't turn off.

Eventually, I wake up after a five-hour nap. I still feel awful. I've only been here for seven hours and I already need to get out of the house. I had tried to sleep, but I constantly kept hearing banging outside from whatever house projects my dad was working on and my mom yelling at him to keep it down. This repeated itself for about three hours.

Suddenly, I hear my cell vibrating at the bottom of my purse, and I immediately feel my heart jump out of my chest. It's Brady, I can't help but think. I race over to my purse, knocking my desk chair over and going down with it, hitting my head once again. I climb back up like I'm on *American Gladiators* trying to reach the top of the rock to hit the button, in this case, my phone. I eventually grab it on its last vibration before it goes to voice mail.

"Hello?" I ask nearly out of breath.

"Susan, is that you?" I hear my mom's voice.

I can't help but let out a frustrated sigh. "Jill? Is that you, honey?"

"Yes, Mom," I say very monotone. She does this to me three times a week.

"Why do you have Susan's phone?"

"I don't, Mom, you dialed my cell instead of hers."

"Oh, sorry about that."

"It's okay," I say, trying not to sound too disappointed that it wasn't Brady. I hang up the phone and look around, noticing how pathetic I must be that I reacted like that thinking my cheating ex-boyfriend was calling. I shake my head in disgust.

All of a sudden my phone rings again. I jump and immediately answer it.

"Hello?"

"Susan?"

"God, Mom," I say, collapsing my full body down to the floor.

I realize then I have to immediately get out of this house. I need someone other than my parents to talk to.

Chapter Five

"Holy crap, that's the worst story I've heard in my life," Liz says a few hours later as she downs her cranberry and vodka at the bar down the road, Charlie's.

She's still very much the same Liz I remember, and when it's just the two of us, I can forget she's a mom. She got married a few years ago and now has three kids. You wouldn't be able to guess it since she's wearing a lime green halter top that looks great with her dark olive skin. She also has on skinny jeans, which I could never, ever wear, but which look sensational on her. Her curly hair is pulled up into a messy bun. If I tried to go for that look, I'd just look like I never knew what a comb looked like. Guys keep checking her out, despite the three-carat diamond on her finger you can see from space.

"I know," I agree as I take a sip of my vodka tonic. Hair of the dog, I'm trying now. I'm wearing a black dress with a grey blazer over it. I don't have much in the way of casual clothes. Needless to say, both of us—me in my business clothes and Liz in her club gear—look a bit out of place here at Charlie's.

In fact, we're probably the oldest people at the bar. With it being summer, all of the college kids are home and clearly, this is the place at which to catch up with old friends. It's the place Liz and I always went to, but that was a different bar that has since been sold and recently reopened as Charlie's. The backwoods renovation doesn't help matters.

"You clearly need another drink," she says to me. She flags the bartender over to order two shots of tequila.

"What is this, spring break?" I say to her.

"She just got dumped," Liz says to the bartender, who looks very familiar. How do I know him?

"I'm sorry to hear that," he says with his head down so I can't see his face. "These are on me."

"Thanks," I say, glaring at Liz for announcing it to the world.

"Here." She starts to hand both shots to me.

"What are you doing?" I ask her.

"This one is a shot for the ex-boyfriend," she says, holding up the shot glass in her right hand. "And this one is for the ex-job." She holds up her left hand.

"I don't know if this is a good idea," I tell her.

"Do it. It'll be therapeutic. To hell with them both."

"I thought people burned pictures?"

"Yeah, well, we're drinking," she says.

I clink her glass and I down both shots.

"So how is married life?" I ask her, chasing the shots with water.

I see her take a deep breath. "I don't know. It's been pretty stressful lately. Tim got a promotion, which is great, but it means he now works eighty hours a week."

"Well, I would envy having a job to go to," I say, wallowing in my own self-pity.

"I wouldn't mind so much if it were just the two of us," she explains. "I like my me time, but with the kids, it's insane."

"I guess you're right," I agree. I don't want to make this conversation all about myself.

"By the time he gets home," she continues, "I'm nearly in tears trying to keep the boys from fighting, getting laundry done, and getting dinner ready."

"Damn, that is a full-time job," I say, I guess never realizing it before.

"Then on top of it, when Tim does get home, he completely shuts down. He tells me he's had a hard day and he needs a minute to rest," she laughs sarcastically. "A minute to rest, what I wouldn't give for that. With three kids under the age of five, there is no rest, honey," she says, taking a sip of her drink.

"Well, I'm glad you were able to take some time to catch up with me," I say, patting her leg.

"I was so glad you called, because the minute he walked in the door after 'golfing with a client,'" she shakes her head, "I got my butt out of there. If I didn't get a chance to blow off some steam, I was going to scream."

"So sounds like a pretty normal marriage," I laugh.

She laughs too. "I know, right?"

"So, want to hear something crazy? Do you remember Ms. Wannamaker's class?"

"Um, somewhat," she says, looking around at all the people. "Geeze, are these kids really twenty-one?"

"Well, I was cleaning out my room and I came across this." I pull out the list I have in my purse.

"Wow, I don't remember doing this," she says, sipping the water she just ordered to slow down. Guess she knows I won't be driving. "Learn to cook? Honey, you couldn't cook if Gordon Ramsey himself taught you."

I pull it out of her hands. "The point is, this was an assignment she gave us. Thirty things we wanted to do before we were thirty. Look at some of this stuff." I point. "Get a massage, ride a roller coaster. I mean, these are such simple things and I've been killing myself with work so much that I never took the time to do any of them."

"You've got time before you're thirty," she says. "Besides, it's a stupid list you made when you were eighteen. What's the big deal?"

"The big deal is I've become Ms. Wannamaker," I admit. "I'm going to become a spinster because I prioritized school and my job over everything else, and look where it got me."

"Booted out on your ass?" she says, swaying a bit in her chair.

"Thanks," I say sarcastically. "And I *don't* have time, I'm thirty in a month, practically."

"Oh, that's right," she says. "Then let's talk about your birthday. What do you want to do?" I sense she's getting sick of my pity party. But there's no way I want to talk about my birthday.

"Honestly, nothing. There isn't anything to celebrate at the moment," I say sulkily and slump in my barstool.

"Oh, stop being so dramatic. So your life had a bit of a hiccup. You're making it worse than it is because you're hitting thirty. What's the big deal with thirty?"

"Liz, is there anything you ever felt you missed out on?"

She thinks for a minute. "Never worrying if I was hooking up with a guy who had a venereal disease?"

I shove her only very lightly, but due to the number of drinks I've had, I almost send her over her stool. "That's the point I'm making. You regret nothing and are truly happy. My life is full of regrets, and I feel like I completely missed out on my twenties when I should have been doing all this stuff." I point to the list.

"So you have some regrets," she says. "Everyone does. Make your thirties about righting those wrongs. Make a list for forty things to do before your forty," she suggests, seemingly proud of herself for helping.

"I don't know," I hesitate. "I don't want to depress myself even more when ten years from now I come across that list and I'm a middle-aged cat woman living with her parents."

"I thought your mom was allergic to cats," she asks.

"You know what I mean, smart-ass."

"I think another drink will bring some inspiration," she says, waving over the bartender again.

I catch his eyes and suddenly it hits me how I know him. It's Chris Matthews, my high school boyfriend. I can't believe I didn't recognize him. His hair is a bit longer, but his eyes are still as piercing as I remember.

"Thank you for rescuing me from these damn college kids," he says to us. "I swear, if I have to pour one more car or Jaeger bomb, I'm going to lose it."

"Chris, is that you?" I ask, squinting. My vision is a bit blurry.

"Yeah." He laughs as if he knew who I was right away and couldn't believe it took this long for me to clue in.

"I'm sorry, my head is a mess right now," I say, feeling guilty.

"Yeah, getting dumped will do that do you," he says forgivingly.

Ugh, I still can't believe Liz told him I was dumped.

"So how have you been?" I ask.

"Can't complain," he says, wiping his hands on a towel. "Yourself?"

"My life is due for a bit of reconstruction," I say. "So what about you? Where are you working?"

As soon as I say it, I feel like an ass.

Thank goodness he laughs. "Actually, I'm a history teacher during the school year. I bartend and tutor in the summer."

"Nice," I say to him, nodding.

"Hey, you were in Ms. Wannamaker's class too, right?" Liz asks.

Great. Just when she told me she didn't remember anything from that class, she has to remember him in it? I know exactly where this is going, but I don't know how to stop it.

"Do you remember having to do this?" Before I can stop her, she pulls the list out of my hands, handing it to Chris.

"Believe it or not, I do, though I certainly don't know what I wrote." He turns to me. "You really kept this the whole time?"

"I just found it in my room today," I say, pulling the list out of his hand. "I-I'm just going through some stuff, and I realized I haven't done anything on this list."

"Well, sure you have," he says, pulling it back to read it.

"You finished Columbia, didn't you?"

"Well, yeah."

"And don't you work at a law firm?"

"Just got fired," Liz jumps in.

"You got fired and dumped?" he says, looking surprised, which depresses me to the max. Bartenders hear a lot of stories. Taking one aback is definitely a bad thing.

"You should write a country song," he tries to joke.

"She came home after getting canned and found her boyfriend's hussy secretary in their shower."

I glare at Liz. "Thank you for that."

"Whoa." Chris puts his hands up. "That takes the cake."

"And she's having some kind of thirty-year-old crisis," she adds as a side note.

"Liz, enough," I scold her.

She shrugs as if what I'm going through isn't her fault. "It's just a stupid list. Who cares if you haven't done anything? Nothing on it's huge other than the education and the job which you got," she says, trying to help.

"Actually, I disagree," Chris intervenes. "I think this list is very important."

Great, now I feel even more depressed.

"Your birthday's in August, right?"

"Wow, I can't believe you remembered that," I say.

"Mind's a steel trap," he says, tapping his head. "So you've got a little over a month. I think you should make it your goal to cross as many things off this list as you can. I know they're little things, but it'll be a great confidence booster."

"Getting a massage is a confidence booster?" Liz asks.

"Absolutely," he responds.

"Hey, bartender." Some clearly drunk girl in a halter top and white shorts is leaning over the bar.

"Give me a minute, don't go anywhere," he tells us.

"What are we doing here?" I ask Liz.

"What?"

"I came to talk to you, and I feel like I'm at an intervention."

"It's not an intervention. Maybe he's right. This list will be good for you. At the least, it will give you something to do while you look for another job."

Just then she stops and pulls her cell phone out of her jeans pocket. "It's my husband," she says rolling her eyes. "Hello?" She motions to me she's stepping out for a second.

I drink what's left of my vodka tonic, which is nothing but ice. As I am making slurping noises, Chris comes back with a fresh one. He lifts my head up, straw still in my mouth, and switches out the glass before lowering me down.

"Jill, you've done a lot of great things with your life," he says, leaning on his elbows to make eye contact. "Hell, you graduated from an Ivy League school and you're a lawyer."

"Was a lawyer," I correct him with my face still in my drink.

"You're still a lawyer. You'll bounce back from this," he says encouragingly. "Chin up." He puts his hand under my chin and lifts my head so I'm looking into his eyes. His eyes are so beautiful ...

"Jill, honey, I'm sorry, I have to go," Liz says, back with us. "One of the kids has some sort of rash and Tim thinks it might be the chicken pox. Do you mind if I drive us back now?"

"I can drive you home," Chris says. "I need someone to save me from all these pain-in-the-ass kids."

I'm still hypnotized by his eyes. "Okay," I say, getting the butterflies in my stomach I haven't had since high school.

The last thing I remember is getting into his car ...

Chapter Six

I wake up the next morning completely hungover and confused as to my whereabouts. I sit up in bed and feel my brain smack against the back of my skull. My head is pounding. I realize now that I'm back in my old room, and suddenly I remember why. I fall back onto the pillow with a moan.

When I do manage a shower and to head downstairs, I immediately make my way over to the coffee pot. I see out of the corner of my eye my parents are sitting at the kitchen table with bagels and juice. They're staring at me. I try to ignore them. My hair is still wet. I have no makeup on, and the last thing I want to hear right now from my parents is "Where were you?" When I looked at my phone this morning I noticed three calls from them last night and a text asking when I was coming home. I hadn't realized at thirty I would still have a curfew. Once the coffee's ready, I turn around to face them while I take a sip. I almost spit it out when I see Chris is sitting at the table with them. He is very cheery looking. He has a half-eaten bagel on his plate, which indicates he's been down here a while. Suddenly my mind starts to race. Did I sleep with Chris? Worse, did I bring him to my parents' house? I start to cough uncontrollably. Suddenly a crystal clear memory from last night—of Chris on top of me—flashes through my mind.

"How are you feeling, dear?" my mom asks, spitefully cheerful.

"Fine," I say, trying to stop from choking while I join them at the table. My body is shaking, whether from the alcohol or nerves, I'm not sure. I can't believe I'm sitting in my kitchen with my parents and my one-night stand.

The room is suddenly quiet, which makes me even more anxious.

"So Chris was nice enough to check on you this morning. He brought over bagels," my mother says in a tone that says she's disappointed in me.

Great, so they don't know. He must have snuck out and come back. I breathe a sigh of relief. I'm a grown woman, but you still can't help but always feel like a teenager around your parents.

"That was very nice," I say to him with a half smile before burying my head back into my coffee cup. I'm pretty embarrassed. One-night stands aren't really my thing, even if he was my boyfriend ten years ago.

"So I was telling your parents about your list," he says. Just then I notice it sitting on the kitchen table.

"Great," I say sarcastically.

"Honey, I think it's a wonderful idea for you to try to complete this list," my mom says.

"I could help you with the golfing thing," my dad adds, pointing to it on the list.

"And I can help you learn to cook," my mom says. "She used to burn popcorn every single time without fail, and the best part is, we had a popcorn sensor she refused to use," she tells Chris.

I don't know why my mother always makes the effort she does to get under my skin. I turn to glare at Chris after her. What has he done? Why is everyone ganging up on me?

"Anyway, I've got some yard work to do, and you've got your gardening, right?" My father gestures to my mom to indicate they should leave us alone.

"Oh, yes, every Sunday," she says, getting the hint and standing up. "Chris, it was lovely chatting with you. Feel free to come by anytime." She grabs his chin and kisses him on the cheek.

"Sure thing, Mrs. S," he says.

When they've finally left, I take another long gulp of my coffee. "Thank you for not telling them about last night," I say.

"What do you mean?" he asks.

34

Does he really expect me to spell it out for him?

"I mean, sneaking out so my parents didn't know you were here," I say.

He bursts out laughing. "Wait—you think we slept together?" He laughs again, pushing his chair out a bit, which makes a squeaking noise on the tile.

"Did we not?" I ask, confused. "I have this recollection of you on top of me."

"You got really drunk last night, and I gave you a ride home. You weren't capable of standing so I took your keys and carried you up to your bedroom. I fell on top of you when I slipped on a garbage bag you had on the floor. That was it, though. I would never take advantage like that," he says, almost sounding hurt.

"Now I feel really embarrassed," I say, looking down.

"Don't. You're going through a rough time. I get it. You thought you were going to make partner and spend the rest of your life with this guy."

I swallow hard. "I told you that?"

"Yeah, you told me a lot of things last night," he says, leaning in with his elbows crossed.

"Oh, no," I say, putting my head in my hands. "I hope I didn't say anything bad."

"You couldn't even if you tried. And what you did say was a hundred percent correct. I do have very sexy eyes."

With that, I slump my head on the kitchen table.

For the next few hours I sit on the couch in my sweats watching the travel channel nursing my hangover. Maybe Chris was right. Maybe I should try to accomplish it. I pick it up off of the coffee table in front of me and start to read it. *Write a book.* Well, I certainly can't accomplish that in a month. I get discouraged and toss it back down. Then again, maybe I could start a blog? I grab my mom's laptop off of the kitchen table and bring it back over to the couch.

Hi Everyone I start. I immediately delete that. *So here's my life.* I delete again. *My name is Jill and I was fired and dumped in the same day right before my thirtieth birthday.* That'll draw in some readers, I think. I'd certainly want to read about someone's horrifying pain to feel better about myself. I take one more big stretch before I write about my story and my list.

So here it is, world. I'm going to try to accomplish everything on this list before I turn thirty in thirty days. Will I travel the world? Save someone's life, or figure out my life's purpose? Probably not. But I'm going to give it a shot and see what I can learn from this.

After twenty minutes, I check back on the comments section. No wonder people get so addicted to this stuff. I see I already have one comment.

Good luck Jill--Cyber Sally

I hear my phone buzz on the brown leather couch and feel under the throw I have over me until I find it in between the couch cushions. I read the info: "Sexy Eyes."

"Oh my God," I say out loud. Did I really put Chris in my phone like that? And why is he calling me? I want to let it go to voice mail but decide I'm just too eager to know why he's calling, so I answer it.

"Hello?"

"Hey, how's your list coming?"

"It's good," I say.

"Which one are you working on?"

"Umm …" I trail off.

"I'm coming over to help you."

"Wait, what?" I notice dead silence on the other end and realize he's hung up. Immediately I throw the blanket off of me and quickly race upstairs to freshen up.

I throw on a pink blouse and white shorts when I notice I haven't shaved since, well, who knows when, and I quickly grab a disposable out from underneath the sink in our hallway bathroom.

"Damn it," I yell as I nick myself while balancing my one leg on the sink while the other hand is brushing my teeth. I quickly grab some toilet paper, which of course doesn't tear off, and blot my leg. Scrambling around for a hair tie, I continue to wrap myself up in toilet paper.

The doorbell rings and I jump. I spit out the toothpaste in my mouth and pinch my cheeks a bit to give them some color. I smooth away the wisps of hairs sticking out the side of my head and try to smooth them back into my ponytail.

"Chris, so good to see you again," I hear my mom say downstairs. "Please go right up."

I walk out of the bathroom and notice the trail of toilet paper still attached to my leg. I quickly yank it off and close the bathroom door behind me just as he reaches the top of the stairs.

"Hey, long time no see," he says, giving me a quick peck on the cheek.

"I know," I say, feeling this odd sensation in my stomach when his lips touch my cheek. Am I that starved of affection that a kiss on the cheek suddenly does it for me? I immediately suppress the feeling as I follow him into my room.

"Nice room you got here," he says, looking around. Based on the garbage everywhere from my fit of rage yesterday, I assume he's being sarcastic.

"I just moved back yesterday," I defend myself. "Besides, you don't know how hard it is to move back into your old high school bedroom at this age."

"I do, actually."

I stop and look up. "Are you living at home now?" I try not to sound as shocked as I am.

"Not exactly a bachelor pad," he responds.

"So what happened with you?"

"Well ..." He takes a breath and sits next to me on the bed. I feel his leg brush up against mine and I get this weird feeling I can't describe. Good thing I shaved my legs.

"I brought you two a snack." My mother walks in with cookies and milk. Now I really feel like I'm twelve. I quickly shift on the bed away from him.

"Thanks, Mrs. S., your cookies were always my favorite." Chris smiles as he takes a bite. My mom smiles and closes the door behind her.

"You're such a momma's boy." I can't help but laugh.

"No, I'm not," he argues, with chocolate chips stuck to his teeth.

"You so are," I say. "'Thanks Mrs. S. Gee, your cookies are swell,'" I say mockingly.

He gives me a playful shove. "How else will I get into your bedroom alone unless the parentals trust me?"

I back away. "Chris, like I said," I begin, "I'm not ready for a relationship."

"I know, I know. I'm just joking." He rolls his eyes.

Why all of a sudden flirting? I wonder. I'm not quite buying his "just friends" line. Does he really still have feelings for me after ten years? Or does he feel living at home hurts his game and me living at home leaves no room to judge?

"So what exactly are you keeping this for?" he says, holding up the calendar. He starts flipping through the pages and stops on the month of May.

"Prom with Chris," he points out. I feel my face flush. I wrote it in red with hearts around it.

"Okay, I'm not sure I need you to help me clean my room," I tell him while taking away the calendar, slightly embarrassed. I stand up as if to show him out.

"Why not? It's fun," he says, drumming his hands on his thighs.

"Nobody thinks cleaning is fun," I retort.

"It's fun for me. It will help me find out who the 'real' Jill Stevens is," he says with air quotes.

I roll my eyes. "Enough with the air quotes."

"So where's the infamous list?" he says, spinning around to face me.

"You'd be very happy to know that I started a blog," I say, proud of myself.

"Really? That's awesome!" he says, genuinely enthused.

"I had 'write a book,' but I didn't think that was at all possible, so I decided to write a blog about my list and trying to accomplish it."

"That is such a great idea, what's it called?"

"Thirty Days to Thirty," I say, slightly embarrassed.

"I can't wait to read it," he says. "Is today the thirty-day mark?"

I nod my head biting my lower lip. I'm already starting to doubt myself.

"Well, I'm officially enlisting my services to you," he puts his arms out.

"What do you mean?"

"I want to help you," he shrugs.

I stare at him. "Why do you want to help me?"

"I don't know," I notice him blush a bit.

"Really?"

"I just—I just always watched you kill yourself, but I hardly ever saw you happy."

"What do you mean?" I cross my arms rather accusingly.

"You were always stressed out. I want to see you put that effort into something that will make you happy, no matter how big or small it may seem."

I stare at him for a second. I feel this weird spark between us. I clench my jaw as I see him looking at me. I decide to change the subject. "So what about you?" I ask. "Anything on your list that you have or haven't accomplished?"

"I don't remember my list," he says, smiling as if hiding something from me.

"Sure you do. I can see it in your eyes," I follow him back to my bed to sit. "Come on, spill," I say sitting cross-legged now and propped against my headboard facing him.

He looks down at my leg and makes a weird face before pulling some leftover toilet paper off of my leg. I feel my face get hot, and I quickly take it from him pretending as if nothing has happened.

"Well, I wanted to travel the world," he says, lifting one leg onto the bed and letting the other hang.

"Did you do that?" I ask, gripping my pillow in front of me. It immediately reminds me of Liz and I sitting like this on my bed exchanging gossip.

"Yeah, I did, actually. After we broke up, my dad was pushing for me to get a job or an internship the summer before school started. He and I were constantly fighting everyday, so we worked out that I would pack up and go to France for the summer."

"Wow," is all I can manage. "Some punishment."

"Not exactly," he laughs. "I lived in Paris and backpacked around Europe on the weekends. It was a win-win. I got to see the world, while my dad thought it would look great on my resume and get me to grow up a bit."

"That sounds amazing," I say to him. I would never have had the guts to do it. I would have been worried I'd miss out on an important internship opportunity or something.

Suddenly his cell goes off and he picks it up. "Hey, no problem, I'll be there in a few." When he hangs up he says, "Sorry, I have to go," without further elaboration.

"It's okay," I tell him, slightly disappointed to see him go. "I think I can manage the list myself like a big girl."

"I'll be back to check on you," he says, pointing his finger at me.

"What are you, my parole officer?" I counter.

"Yes, as a matter of fact," he says as he stands up. "Seriously, though, I had fun today."

"Me too," I say, realizing I'm grinning like an idiot.

"I'll call you later?"

"Um, sure," I say, feeling uneasy. What am I doing here? I just got out of a relationship, but I can't help but feel that's where this is headed and rather quickly.

I walk him to the front door and when he leaves, my mom gives me a big grin.

"What?" I ask her, trying to keep my own smile under wraps.

"Nothing." She smiles and walks back into the kitchen. I roll my eyes at her and head back upstairs.

"What the hell happened to this bathroom?" I hear my dad yell. I immediately turn around and slink back downstairs.

Chapter Seven

I definitely feel something here, but the one thing my list had right was I needed to learn to live on my own. I had to stop jumping from relationship to relationship. At this moment I feel completely lost. I'm getting weird vibes from Chris, but strangely enough, I feel guilty about them because of Brady. As much as he hurt me, I can't help but miss him.

I decide to distract myself by calling Liz to tell her about how I've decided to tackle this list, but really to gush about Chris.

"He's still so in love with you, he's like a puppy dog," Liz tells me on the phone. I switch the phone from one ear to the next as I sit back down to reread my blog to her.

"He can't be. We haven't seen or spoken to each other in almost ten years," I tell her.

"So? All these old feelings are coming back. There was so much chemistry between you two at the bar last night."

"That wasn't chemistry—that was alcohol," I say, rolling my eyes. "This just all seems a bit weird to me. I mean, really, why is he helping me?"

"Because he loooves you," Liz says through the phone. "Michael, stop hitting your brother," I hear her yell. This happens so often I've learned to just keep the conversation going.

"You know he still lives at home?" I say. "It almost sounds like he never moved out of house. This was the reason we broke up in the first place, because of how unmotivated he was." I'm not sure why I'm saying this. Am I saying he's not good enough for me? Like I'm one to talk …

"So maybe you two can move in together," she says.

I can tell she's really not listening to me. It usually happens after ten minutes. She has the attention span of a cocker spaniel. Then again, with three kids, who doesn't?

"Look, I'm sorry. I have to go, but I'll talk to you later."

"Okay, bye," I say, a bit disappointed.

The next morning, I try to finish organizing my room. This is the first day I've woken up with energy in who knows how long. Probably because it's the first time I've had a decent amount of sleep that wasn't assisted by alcohol.

"Do you need help?" I hear my mom ask. She's peering through the door as if I'm a Tasmanian devil and she's using part of the door as a defense in case I start throwing things. To be fair, I am. I have the garbage bag hanging on my doorknob and I'm taking things out of my dresser drawer and throwing them in that general direction.

"No, I'm okay, thanks." I close my top drawer with a solid slam.

"When did you ever wear this?" she says, picking up a pink lacy tank top I had thrown in her direction, not realizing it.

"I don't know," I shrug.

"Well, I certainly hope you didn't wear this in high school, you would've looked like a hussy," she says, holding it up.

I take it out of her hands and put it in the garbage bag. "I just wore it underneath clothes," I tell her. Really, I wore it underneath clothes when I was home.

"Well, I found this and thought it might help."

I turn around as my mom tosses me a French learning disc from Rosetta Stone.

"I got this for you when you took up French in high school, remember?" she asks.

"Yeah." I look at it.

"Pop it in while you're cleaning, maybe you'll pick up a few things."

"Thanks," I smile and do just that.

"Au revoir," she says as she walks down the hall.

I head over to my ancient stereo, and after forcibly pulling out the CD tray, I place the disc in the device.

After an hour of listening to the disc and cleaning my room, or should I say putting a small dent in the massive cleaning job that really needed to be done, I decide to return to the list on my desk.

"Okay," I say as I pull out a red pen to cross off what I've done so far.

~~Graduate from college~~

~~Get a job at a great law firm~~ *though maybe we change this to getting a job in general*

~~Write a book~~ *Writing a blog*

~~Become more organized~~

I continue to read through the list.

Learn how to flirt

Learn another language—working on it, poorly.

Take up yoga

I pick up the phone and call Liz. "Want to go to yoga with me?" I ask.

"I have a sitter coming by to watch the kids while I run errands anyway, I'll pick you up in ten," she says immediately. "I've got a great place I go all the time." One of the great things about Liz is she never needs a reason for doing something; she's just always game for anything.

I wish I was like that. Probably should have put that on the list ….

"So are you an avid yoga-goer?" I ask her while we drive there. Her car is a gorgeous white Porsche SUV, but it smells of peanut butter and jelly sandwiches, along with goldfish crackers.

"Are you kidding me? Uh, yeah. I have three kids. I need some time during the day that's quiet."

"I feel kind of weird doing this," I admit to her while looking out at the road. "I'm always stressed. I don't think I know how to be calm."

"Why is that?" She turns towards me.

"I really don't know." I say, "Too busy, I guess."

"Then you obviously need this," she says.

We pull up to a white stucco strip mall with a generic sign that says Yoga on it. "Some Zen-looking place you've got here," I tell her sarcastically. She ignores me as we head inside.

"Hi, is there room for two in your next yoga class, by any chance?"

I look around. The place is very white and minimalistic. I'm guessing it was a hair salon before it was a yoga studio. There's tile everywhere. The only thing Zen about the place is the dim lighting.

"Hi, Elizabeth, we do, and it will start in about ten minutes. Feel free to go in and get warmed up."

I follow the woman and Liz down the hall to a dance studio. This wasn't what I pictured. The place has floor-to-ceiling mirrors and a hardwood floor. Not exactly comfortable, though the wood floor's better than tile, I guess. The floor-to-ceiling mirrors mean I'm going to be self-conscious. Too late, I remember I can barely touch my toes.

"Maybe this isn't such a great idea," I whisper to her. I already feel claustrophobic; it's too hot in here.

"Nonsense. Fern is teaching the class, and she'll help you relax."

"The woman's name is Fern?" I say, less quietly. "Why am I not surprised?" I add under my breath.

I suddenly hear someone clearing her throat. "Good morning, people. For those of you who don't know me, my name is Fern and I'll be your yoga instructor." She's a tall, skinny woman who has a milky white complexion, which is shocking for the middle of the summer. She has wild white hair that seems to do whatever it wants.

Shoot, I hope she didn't hear me.

She gives everyone a minute to get settled. I sit down until I see everyone going to the closet and pulling out rubber mats. I sheepishly follow the crowd to get one.

In that time, Fern has turned off the lights, leaving nothing but the hall light peering through the glass circle in the door. She turns on her iPod to nature music.

"All right now, everyone take a deep inhale," Fern says, instructing us to raise our arms above our heads. "And exhale," she says as we follow her motion and try to touch our feet. I can't help but look around at everyone else, for whom this seems to be effortless. Fern stands up and walks towards me. "Keep your head down," she says, pressing on my neck. Then she gets behind me and pushes down on my spine. I'm feeling so awkward and tenser than ever, as she completely molds herself on top of me.

"Um, excuse me," I try. "Ow."

"Relax, this doesn't hurt," she tells me.

"Yes, it does," I argue.

"Shh." Liz glares at me.

"Just relax," Fern repeats in her calming voice. I take a deep breath, more in frustration than for the sake of relaxation.

"Now into downward dog," she says. I have no idea what this is so I watch everyone around me and try to manipulate my body into a triangle.

"Vinasa," she says.

Vin what? I think. I watch everyone lower themselves into a pushup position and back into that dog thing. I am so lost and half a second behind everyone else.

"Now you are a tree," she tells us. I see everyone balance on one leg. "Your arms are the branches to your life. Extend your life and your opportunities."

I'm trying not to laugh, but this seems a bit much. Liz hits me. I try to concentrate on my breathing to keep myself from giggling.

Before I know it, we're in some cat-cow pose that has us arching our backs on our hands and knees. I feel more like a stripper crawling on a stage.

"Now you are a cow," Fern intones. "You are giving milk to your baby calf. He is suckling the milk from your swollen udder."

At this point I can't stop laughing. What is wrong with this woman?

"I'm sorry, but I believe I'm going to have to ask you to leave. You're disrupting my class," Fern finally snaps. She puts her hands on her hips and stares me down.

"Oh, uh, sorry." I try to keep a straight face as I awkwardly roll up my mat and place it in the closet. I then have to go across the classroom with everyone staring at me. Eventually Liz gives in and comes with me.

"I can't believe you," she yells at me when we get outside.

It takes a second for my eyes to adjust to the sunlight. I squint and hold my hand up to block the sun. "I'm sorry, but how am I not supposed to laugh? The woman is telling me my stomach is a swollen udder as I feed my baby calf. I mean, what is that?" I say, standing on the passenger-side door of her car.

"So Fern is a bit extreme, but so were you," Liz argues, unlocking the car, while still speaking to me over the hood. "Did you really have to burst out laughing every time she said downward dog?"

"It sounds dirty and hence it was funny," I tell her, opening the passenger door and stepping in.

She sighs in exasperation, pulling her door open. "You're ridiculous, and now I'll never be able to show my face in that place again."

"Oh, stop being so overdramatic," I tell her, putting on my seat belt. "So I guess the yoga thing isn't something I can cross off of my list, huh?"

"Not unless you buy a DVD you can do from home, because I sure as hell will never be seen with you in a yoga class again."

"What the hell are you doing?" my dad asks me the next day when he comes home and finds me doing a vinasa.

He scares me and I wind up slamming my face into the carpet of our living room. "Ow," I say before sitting up and looking towards him. "I'm taking up yoga," I say as if it's no big deal.

"Oh honey, that's on your list, isn't it?" my mom asks as she puts the groceries down on the kitchen table. "You know I'm not too bad myself, I could help if you want."

"Really?" I ask, surprised.

"Of course," she says, taken back by my reaction. "And what we could do is play the Rosetta Stone disc at the same time so you can learn French simultaneously."

I jut my lower lip out as I nod. Not a bad idea. "Thanks, Mom," I say as I position myself into downward dog and try a vinasa again.

"Oh dear, what the hell is that?" she says shaking her head.

After half an hour of trying various poses, I decide that I'm not going to be able to relax, since I can't seem to quiet my mind. Brady and even Chris are surprisingly popping into my thoughts. I quickly check my e-mail to see if my headhunter has found anything yet. I take a deep breath when I see that my in-box is empty.

I distract myself by writing up my yoga experience in my blog. A few minutes later, I see a response from Liz.

This story is putting it mildly, you were way worse, but best of luck ☺- Liz

I let out a smile and decide to call her. My phone's cell service is horrible so I use the house phone.

"I'm starting to get nervous about my job situation," I admit to her. "What if I don't find anything?"

"You'll find something," she assures me. "So I've been thinking," she changes the subject. "A makeover would really be the best thing for you right now. What better way to get your confidence back than by revitalizing your whole look? And you'll be able to cross something off of your list, too."

"I'm not sure," I say.

"Learn to say yes before you say no," she says, quoting my list.

I finally give in. She squeals in excitement. "I'll pick you up in an hour."

I look at myself in the mirror. "Good bye, Jill Stevens."

"Stop being so dramatic," she scorns.

"Okay, fine," I say, rolling my eyes. "I agree I probably do need this, though I'm feeling a lot better than I did last week. I'm even thinking a little less about Brady."

"That's good," she says. "The bastard still hasn't called you yet?"

"Ugh no," I say annoyed, falling back onto my bed. "I want to call him, but I wouldn't know what to say."

"Maybe you should try calling him anyway. If you can't think of anything to say then just hang up."

"You two are grown women, what the hell are you thinking?"

"Mom?" I say sitting up. "What are you doing listening to my phone conversations?"

"I was trying to call Susan and I heard you on the phone. Jill, you are not going to call that man, I forbid it, and you, Liz, you shouldn't be encouraging unhealthy behavior like this."

"Sorry Mrs. S," Jill suddenly falls into her teenage self.

"Mom, you can't tell me what to do anymore," I argue.

Just then my mom bursts into my room and grabs my cell off of my dresser.

"What are you doing?" I say, still holding the house phone to my ear. I follow her into the bathroom.

"This is for your own good," she says as she throws my phone in the toilet bowl.

"Are you psycho?" I start to yell.

"Yea, I'm going to go," Liz says uncomfortably and clicks off.

Chapter Eight

"Roberto." Liz holds both of her arms out and air kisses a man wearing a purple silk shirt and white pants. His black hair is slicked back. Enough said.

"Lizzy, you look stunning." He holds out her arms as he checks her out.

I have to refrain from groaning. Where does he think we are, Los Angeles?

"Roberto, I would like you to meet my friend Jill. I'm trusting you with my life to give her the best makeover you can."

He lowers his eyes to check me out. "Breakup?"

"Um, you could say that," I say a bit uncomfortably.

"Well, sweetie, come with me and we'll make sure that man regrets he ever dumped you."

"What makes you think I was dumped?" I pull away.

The problem with gay men is they see through it all and are unapologetic about it. After he stares me down, I finally give in.

"Okay, you're right," I tell him as he makes a bitchy noise that signals to me he's always right and leads me to his chair.

"So what happened?" he asks as he fluffs my lifeless hair. I haven't had anything done to it in years other than the occasional cut.

"I don't really want to talk about it," I say.

"Roberto, she's been dumped and fired. Make this makeover spectacular," Liz says as she texts on her phone.

Seriously, I'm going to have to kill this girl.

"Dumped and fired? You poor thing!" He squeezes my shoulder. "Lenny, bring out the champagne. We're going to need it," he calls.

Eventually, after a half hour of foiling and a nice buzz on the champagne, Roberto presses again. "So tell me about your drama," he says as he combs my hair down and starts to cut.

I take a deep breath and finally give in. "Well, I was working a hundred hours a week at a law firm so I could make partner, and then right when I expected them to promote me, they fired me instead."

"Mm, mm, child, that's just wrong," he says, pursing his lips and shaking his head. "But maybe it's for the best. If you were killing yourself and not getting appreciated, well, you don't want to be at a place like that, am I right?"

"I suppose so," I say with a sigh.

"You hear that?" he yells over towards his manager who just walked by. He responds with an eye roll.

"And this guy," he continues, "was the breakup before or after the job ending?"

"Same day," I say.

"Shut up!" he says, turning my chair around so he's facing me. "Did he know you got fired?"

"I caught him cheating on me with his secretary when I got home."

"That slut!" he yells.

Everyone stops and looks at us. "People, we have a major crisis here. We need more champagne!" He snaps his fingers.

After two hours and a slight buzz, I'm spun around to see my new look.

My hair has been Chinese straightened and I've been given side swept bangs, soft blonde highlights, and a drastic bob cut.

I'm kind of stunned. It's a big change. And I've never worn this much eye makeup before. I don't know if red lipstick is really my thing …

50

"You look gorgeous!" Liz comes in the door after being outside on the phone for the last hour. I was constantly looking for her to help me, as Roberto wasn't exactly listening to a single request I made.

"Thanks," I say, running my fingers through my hair.

"Stop making that face," Roberto says. "I know it's dramatic, but trust me, you look good."

"Roberto, you're a lifesaver," Liz tells him, kissing him again on both cheeks. "Now off to buy you some new clothes to go with this look," she tells me as she pulls me out of the salon. I think she fears I'm ready to finally react and she needs to get me out of there before I blow.

When we get outside, I see her car is packed with groceries.

"I needed your help in there and you went grocery shopping?" I'm still running my fingers through my hair uneasily.

"I have a family to feed, and a babysitter for only a few hours," she says, unlocking the car. "Tim says all we ever eat is chicken fingers and macaroni and cheese, but what does he expect? We have three picky eaters, we have to give them what they want in order for them to eat something."

"Why don't you cook a separate meal for you both?" I ask, getting back into her car.

"I tried that once and we wound up eating a salmon salad with a side of mac and cheese and chicken nuggets," she says, pulling the car out of the parking lot.

I'm so busy staring at myself in the mirror, I don't realize we're already on Greenwich Avenue.

"I don't even recognize myself. I can't believe this is me." I have to say, as uncomfortable as I am with the change, it's certainly better than the face I stared at the other day—the tired, worn face with signs of premature wrinkles—just before discovering our shower guest.

"Now you're going to complete the look," she tells me as we pull into a parking spot.

I'm a little hesitant. I love the clothes Liz wears, it's just that I'm sure I could never pull them off.

My fears come to a head when she brings me into one of the fanciest boutiques in Connecticut, where both the prices and styles prove way out of my league.

Liz immediately picks up a tight-fitting green dress and hands it to me. "Try this on," she orders me.

"Liz-" I try to object.

"Dress out of your comfort zone," she reminds me. I roll my eyes and grab the dress out of her hands. She's got to stop quoting the list. "Do you have the damn thing memorized already?" I ask in frustration.

She just smiles and shrugs while taking a seat on one of the white vintage chairs outside the dressing room. I turn on my heel and huff my way back towards one of the dressing rooms.

When I put it on, I'm a bit surprised by how good it does look on me. It makes my edgy new haircut look even better.

I step outside to Liz, who whistles at me.

"Now that is the type of thing you should always be wearing," she says, pointing her finger at me.

"I wrote dress out of my comfort zone, not my price range," I tell her.

"Then consider it part of my early birthday gift to you," she tells me.

"Liz, no," I argue.

She shakes her hand at me. "Not another word."

An hour later, since we had to reprieve the sitter, we're walking out of the store and I have a whole new wardrobe. I paid for the dress and the rest of it after all, rationalizing that since I was living with my parents, I had some extra money.

"Jill, is that you?" I look up to see Brad Stevens. I had crushed on him in high school. He was a senior when I was a freshman. He looks just like he did back then. He has very broad shoulders and a thick head of brown wavy hair.

"You look great. How are you?" he says.

"Um, good," I say a little nervously, shifting back and forth. I don't exactly want to get into my whole situation now, though I'm tempted to explain the makeover ...

"She's great," Liz takes over.

"Liz, right?" he asks, turning towards her.

"Yeah." She's already about to lose her patience.

"How've you been?" he says, sticking his hands in his pockets, trying to be polite.

"Great, couple kids, married, you get the idea," she says. "We have to get going, but we'll be at the Madison tonight if you care to catch up."

"Um, sure, I'll see what I can do," he says.

With that, Liz gives him a fake smile and pulls me away.

"Bye," I say awkwardly.

"Bye." He smiles as he makes his way towards the front door.

"What was that about?" I ask her when we're safely in the car.

"I was saving you," she states as she puts the key in the ignition. "You're not going to tell your sob story to a guy you crushed on in high school right now."

She knew me too well.

"We are going to go to the Madison tonight to show off your hot new look, and you're going to flirt with him there."

"I've never even heard of the Madison," I tell her.

"It's the most expensive chic bar in our town, though still cheaper than those in the city," she explains.

"Why haven't we gone there yet?" I ask her, thinking about the bar we went to the other day that we were way too old for.

"Because it's full of pretentious snobs, which is the perfect place for your coming-out party."

I look at her.

She rolls her eyes as if she can't believe I don't see what she means. "Stop all those people right in their tracks. You'll show off how great you look and you will not tell anyone your sob story."

"Right," I tell her. I think for a second. "So what do I say?"

"You say you're newly single, you're a lawyer, and you're home for a few days. That's all." She motions her hand across her neck, much like a director would when he yells cut.

"So I need to lie to everyone?" I ask.

"It's not lying, it's flirting," she says.

I shake my head at this explanation. "What makes you the expert? You've been married your whole life." Liz never went longer than a month without a boyfriend in high school, and in college she met Tim freshman year and that was it for her.

"Exactly, which means I'm the best person to give advice to you because I'm looking at things from a different perspective. The same way you're the best person to talk to about my marriage."

"So how is your marriage, by the way?" I ask.

"I don't want to get into that," she says, shaking her head.

"Whoa, what's going on there?" I press her.

"There's nothing wrong," she says defensively. "It's just—I just feel like maybe I did miss out on a few things in my life," she admits finally.

"Miss out on what?" I ask her. "Being single sucks. I have to completely change who I am so I can get a guy to talk to me."

"That's not true." She sounds offended and, remembering all the hard work she put in to making me over, I regret saying it the way I did.

"I know." This is me backpedaling.

"The makeover is supposed to help you get your confidence back," she says sternly.

"I know," I say. "I'm sorry I said it like that."
When she doesn't say anything I say, "What's wrong with Tim, though?"

"Tim's fine." She shakes her head. "The kids are fine too ..." She trails off. "It's just these past couple days with you, I realized how much I miss you. We never see each other anymore, and I know that's my fault."

"It's not your fault. Well, not all of it." I shift in my seat to face her. "I worked all the time," I tell her.

"Yeah, but even if you didn't, I was never around. I spent my whole life being about my boyfriend or husband, now it's all about my kids, I feel as if I don't even see my husband anymore, and I just miss my life," she says, frustrated.

Suddenly I realize Liz, too, has issues. Maybe she's so into this because it gives her a way to live vicariously through me.

"Well, I think you can still live," I say. "When's the last time you and Tim went out?" I ask.

"I can't even remember," she says. "He works all the time."

"Well, how about you and Tim come out together with me tonight. He'll be able to read the guys and tell me which ones are worth talking to," I tell her.

"What about the kids?" she asks.

"We'll drop them with my parents. I'm sure my mother's heartbroken she isn't getting grandchildren anytime soon, so at least she can play with yours." I laugh.

Liz laughs too. "You're right, I think we do need this," she says.

"Good, I'll let my mom know."

Chapter Nine

When I get home, I get quite the reaction from my family on my whole new style.

"Well, isn't that a fun look," my mom says with a plastic smile.

"It's very, um, different," my dad adds.

"I let Liz take over, but trust me, I'm letting it grow out," I assure them as I blot off the bright red lipstick. The problem is it looks like he applied the long lasting kind, so I'm really just smearing it around my mouth, with the results that I look like a vampire who finished a meal.

"Just promise me you don't become slutty," my mom says.

"Mom!" I yell at her as I remove the rest of my makeup.

"I'm just saying that dress says something."

I roll my eyes. "I'm not going to become the town hussy, so don't worry. It's not like I have a place to bring anybody back to." I wave my arm to show them to look around.

"Well, I just don't want you to make any bad decisions tonight. With all the upset you've been through, I don't want you to put yourself in a worse position."

I look over at my dad who has his head buried in the paper.

After an hour of stomping around while my mom chases me with a shawl, Liz and Tim finally come to rescue me. I kept the dress on but compromised with a black blazer, and I removed the excess eye makeup and toned down the lipstick.

"Better," my mom says, smiling, as if I did it for her.

"Trust me, you look hot," Liz insists as we settle into the Madison. The place is all black with a white bar and white furniture. The music is kind of clubby, geared to our age group. "Doesn't she, Tim?" Liz elbows him.

Tim's face shows his nervousness. It's pretty funny to see a tall muscular guy get bossed around by Liz, who's all of five-foot-nothing.

"Absolutely," he says, clearing his throat and wiping a bead of sweat off his large forehead. I can sense the tension between them, like they just put a fight on hold. "This guy over here's been checking you out," he says, pointing. I assume he's doing this to quickly get the heat off him, but Liz agrees and I turn around to see who it is.

"Oh, wow, that's Chris," I say. He must have read my blog post about coming here. Once we catch eyes, he makes his way across the crowd to the booth where we're sitting.

"Wow, I didn't even recognize you at first. You look stunning," he says.

"Thanks." I smile. "It's a little much," I say, running my fingers through my newly shortened hair.

"Not at all. It looks great on you." Chris proceeds to introduce himself to Tim and says hi to Liz.

"So, fancy meeting you here," I say. "Do you come here a lot?"

"If that was a pickup line, it was the worst one ever," he laughs.

"I know," I say sheepishly. "So who are you with?"

"Um, some friends over there, coworkers." He points towards the back of the bar. I don't really see anyone I recognize.

"What about you?"

"We're practicing our flirting," Liz breaks in.

"Really," he says, sounding amused.

"Oh my God, he really came," Liz says, hitting me on the leg.

"Who?" I ask, turning.

"Brad, he really came," she nearly squeaks. "He's at the bar. Quick, go get me a drink," she says, sticking a twenty-dollar bill down my dress like I'm a stripper, and downing the last of her wine.

I give her a reluctant look.

"Go!" She shoves me. I awkwardly get up and watch Chris take a long pull of his beer.

"Well, I don't want to mess up your game," he says. "This is number twelve on the list, right?" he asks.

I nod my head in embarrassment. He actually remembered.

"Well, I'll leave you to it," he says, standing up. He gives me a quick peck on the cheek, and I feel that sensational spark again. "Have a good night."

I can't help but feel extremely guilty as I walk up to the bar. But why should I? I told him I'm not ready for anything. Before I can think any further about it, Brad comes up to me.

"Hey, there you are." He smiles.

"Good of you to come," I say anxiously. Gosh, I wish I didn't suck so much at this.

"So what have you been up to?" he asks.

"Since high school?" I ask.

He laughs. "I guess."

"Um, I'm a lawyer now," I say, praying he doesn't ask where.

"That's great," he says. "I'm in real estate."

"How's that going right now?" I ask him. These questions are so vague. I'm really dying here. On top of it, I feel like all eyes are on me. Both Liz and Tim are staring me down, and I can see Chris glancing over every once in a while.

"It's doing okay," he says. "Can I buy you a drink?"

"I'm okay, thanks," I say. There's a bit of an awkward silence. "So you live around here?" I ask.

"Yeah, only twenty minutes away," he says. "How about yourself?"

"I'm living in the city, but I'm thinking I might need a change," I say.

"Well, let me give you my card." He pulls out his wallet and ruffles through a few receipts. After a few minutes he looks up. "It looks like I'm out of them right now. If you're looking for anything in the area, just let me know."

"Sure," I tell him, though I don't know how without his number. Then there's a long pause.

"Anyway," he says finally, "I have to run, but it was good catching up. I'll talk to you later."

Before I can say anything else, he's out the door. Wow, that was painful.

I sulk back to the booth where Liz and Tim are sitting. They seem to be having a good time, hopefully resolved whatever issue they were having, which is good. I vow not to put a damper on their night.

"That looked like it was promising," Liz says, nudging me.

"Well, turns out it was more business he was looking for, not pleasure." I sigh.

"Eh, he's not that cute, anyway. Besides, I think you're nervous because we just got here and you're self-conscious. Now, Tim's driving for a reason, so drink up," she tells me. "Back to the bar."

"What am I supposed to do?" I ask her.

"Go make out with someone random."

"I can't just do that!" I say, shocked.

"It was on your list," she insists.

I roll my eyes. "Yes, it was on my list when I was eighteen because I had only kissed one boy in my life and I didn't want it to be anyone else in our school. Therefore, I thought it had to be a stranger."

"Back to the bar," she says slower, as if I didn't understand her the first time. When I don't respond, she nudges me.

I take a deep breath and do as she says. After ten minutes of waiting on a drink, I catch eyes with Chris again, who's talking to a group of guys. He looks like he's about to come my way, when all of sudden I hear someone introduce himself to me.

"Hi, I'm Mike."

I look over, a bit surprised, "Jill," I respond. He's pretty cute, has the look of a baseball player, with broad shoulders and a cleft chin. His eyes are a light blue, which go well with his light hair. I'm not sure what I think of the tight black tee shirt with the big arm muscles, but it's worth a shot.

"Nice to meet you," he says. "Can I buy you a drink?"

"Oh, sure," I say this time.

"Two tequilas," he yells.

"Oh, I don't know if I can get into tequila tonight," I tell him.

"Oh, you'll be fine," he says. "Cheers," he says when the bartender gives them to us. Then he clinks my glass and we take the shot.

"How did you get these so quickly? I've been waiting ten minutes," I say, wiping the corner of my mouth.

"Oh, I know the bartender," he says. "Stan, what's going on?" he yells. "Get this lady her drink!"

Stan comes over with my cosmopolitan and wine for Liz. "Sorry about the wait," he says, smiling at me and pounding fists with Mike.

"Oh, it's fine." I try to brush it off.

"You know better than that," Mike says jokingly to Stan.

"Really, it's fine, thanks," I say.

"Another shot when you get a second," Mike tells Stan.

I want to leave, but I look over and see Liz and Tim enjoying themselves and I don't want to sulk back to their table. I think about looking for Chris, but I don't see him. Finally I give in.

"All right," Mike says, handing me my second shot. I take a swig and slam my glass on the bar. "Easy there, killer," he says.

"So where are you from?" I ask him.

"I live around here," he says. "I'm a local cop."

"Oh, how do you like that?" I ask.

"It kicks ass. You can do whatever you want."

"Uh-huh," is all I can manage to say to him.

"What's your deal? What do you do?"

"I'm a lawyer," I tell him. Looking around anxiously for someone to rescue me.

"That's awesome," he says. "You and me could make a pretty good power couple," he says.

"Yeah," I say, finishing off the rest of my lime.

Before I can even remove the lime, Mike jumps me and suddenly his tongue is down my throat. I'm taken aback but part of me loves the thrill. I kind of feel like I'm in college again, not that I ever did this in college, I just

60

watched other people do this. We make out for few minutes, and finally he pulls away.

"That was awesome," he says.

"Yeah," I say, taking a breath and a swig of my drink.

"I mean, really, cougars are such great kissers."

I nearly spit my drink out back into my glass. "Excuse me?"

"Oh," he says, "I didn't mean to be insulting. That was supposed to be a compliment."

"I'm not sure if the question now is how old do you think I am, or how old are you?" I say.

"I'm twenty-two," he says.

"And do I dare ask how old you think I am?"

He hesitates for a moment. "I figured thirty-five."

"Huh," I say. Well, this certainly has gone well. I just became a cradle robber, and he thinks I'm thirty-five. I polish off my drink as he tries to backtrack.

"Hey, there you are." Chris comes up and puts his arm around me. "I want to introduce you to someone." He pulls me away and I don't look back.

"Sorry, you looked like you needed help," he says when we reach a safety zone.

"In the worst way," I tell him. "Thanks."

"So everything okay?"

"Yeah," I say, starting to feel those two shots. I can't believe how foolish I feel. My eyes begin to water, but I try to keep it in. I sit down at a random ottoman. "The good news is I made out with a stranger, so I can cross that off of my list. The bad news is I'm a cradle robbing slut." I put my head down in my hands.

"Excuse me?" he asks, partly laughing and partly shocked. He takes a seat next to me and puts his hand on my back.

"Look at me," I say, sitting up. "This isn't me. I don't want to be this person. I don't like wearing tight clothes, I don't like chopping all my hair off and wearing a ton of makeup, I don't like flirting, and I don't like kissing strangers."

"Hey," he says softly. "It's a lot to handle, but you had this on your list for a reason. You wanted to know that you could do it and you did. Now do you regret anything?"

"I regret making out with a twenty-two-year-old," I say. "I don't know how Brady does it."

He tries not to laugh.

"Shut up," I hit him.

"But do you still want to make out with strangers?"

"No," I say.

"And did you before?"

I shrug my shoulders.

"Trust me, you got it out of your system, and now if you want to grow your hair out, wear sweat pants and not a stitch of makeup ever again, you can."

"Yeah, that'll draw the boys in," I say sarcastically.

"You'd be surprised how sexy a girl is as long as she's confident. It doesn't matter what you look like or what you wear, it's all about how you carry yourself."

I look at him. "Thanks for cheering me up," I say. Nudging him. I know I certainly wouldn't have gotten that advice from Liz. She would insist I stuff my bra more.

"Hey, we have to get going." Liz comes up to me. "Sorry, but it's almost midnight, and I don't want to leave the kids too late."

I nod as I stand up. "Thanks for the advice, Chris."

"No problem," he says, leaning into kiss me on the cheek. "Have a great night," he whispers in my ear. I feel my whole body shudder. Oh, this is going to be really hard to stay away.

Chapter Ten

The next morning, I wake up with a bit of a high. As uncomfortable as last night started out, I actually had a great time. I was so proud of myself for actually accomplishing flirting and kissing a stranger. It makes me feel oddly confident. I find myself obsessing over it before I finally force the thought out of my head and decide to be productive and write.

As I finish wrapping up my entry, I notice several comments from my last post.

"It's so great that you are getting out there but BE SAFE! - Love Mom."

Damn Dad for telling her about this blog.

"This is really inspiring. I just went through a rough time myself and I think this list idea is a great way for me to bounce back. Thank you for the help."

I look down at the name and I realize I don't recognize it. I even go as far as looking on Facebook to see if it's a friend who got married and has a different last name. The same goes for the next one.

"I believe you are going to accomplish this! Best of luck."

Then I read the next one—again, someone I don't know.

"This is by far my favorite blog to read. I love hearing about your adventures. Keep up the good work. P.S. I think that guy who's been helping you has a major crush— give him a chance."

I feel my face flush when I read that last one. I'm not familiar with blogs so my hope is only I can read the comments and no one else. I'd be devastated if Chris read that.

I can't believe I'm actually inspiring people! I feel very uninspiring myself. Sure, I'm a bit more relaxed than I've been in a while, but inspiring? Not so much. Feeling as if I have a duty to my readers, I hit play on my disc player and listen to the French teacher's voice stream through the speakers. At the same time, I pop in my Yoga at Home DVD and dutifully recite my French words out loud while doing the tree pose. Unfortunately, I'm too preoccupied with thoughts about Chris to focus, and I wind up falling into my closet. Okay, so maybe I'm not getting as good as I thought.

Maybe tomorrow will be better, I think, giving up on the French and yoga for today after only a few short minutes. *Crawl before I walk*, I rationalize. I pull myself out of my closet and turn off the stereo. I'm drawn back to my blog and look at my list again.

Ride a roller coaster.

I shiver a bit at the thought but take a deep breath. I just made out with a stranger. I think I can ride a roller coaster.

I call up Liz to see if she and Tim want to take the kids to the park.

"We'd love to, if I can get him to leave work," she says. "I just don't know if you'll fit in the car with the kids."

"It's okay. I'm thinking about calling Chris to join us."

"Are you sure that's a good idea?" she says after a few seconds of silence.

"Why not?" I ask.

"There's nothing wrong with him—I like him a lot. Love him, actually. I just know he really likes you and I don't know if you're ready for that."

"He doesn't like me." I blush. "He's just been a great help through this. He knows we're just friends, and besides, I need someone to ride the roller coaster with me because I know you won't do it."

"Okay," she says, "I'm just saying."

I ignore her and call Chris. I have all the confidence in the world to call him, but suddenly I feel my stomach clench. I don't want to lead him on. But to be fair I've been saying this whole time I don't want a boyfriend right now. I can't feel guilty if I've been open and honest about that, right? Finally I get the nerve to just do it.

After only two rings he picks up.

"Yeah, that would be fun," he says immediately. "I'm wrapping up with a student and I'll come pick you up in an hour," he says. I hear what sounds like an intercom saying something in the background. Maybe he's tutoring at the school, I rationalize.

Once we get to the park, I watch as poor Liz and Tim try desperately to get ahold of their three sons, who, as soon as they're let out of the car, look like those scary jack-in-the-boxes you can never get back into their boxes.

Chris assists by picking one of them up and throwing him over his shoulder while Tim and Liz grab the other two, who are running through the parking lot. Tim is reaching for one kid, while his BlackBerry is permanently glued to his right hand.

"Hey, Chris, that's not fair," says Chad, the one Chris is holding.

"Well, Chad, maybe if you weren't so ticklish," Chris says, pulling him into his arms and tickling him.

Chad goes into a laughing fit.

They seem very familiar with each other. "You two know each other? Or do you randomly assault children?" I ask jokingly.

"Chris is my tee ball coach," Chad says upside down, since that is how Chris has him hanging.

"Yeah, this one can smack it out of the park," Chris says, putting him back down on the ground. "Of course," he adds putting his hands over Chad's ears, "first he has to learn how to run from first to second."

"I heard that," Chad says. "And that was one time," he complains.

"I know, buddy, I'm kidding." He pats him on the chest as we walk across the parking lot.

"I knew I knew you from somewhere," Tim says, finally looking up from his phone.

"Honey, you didn't realize?" Liz asks surprised.

"That's cuz you're always working, Daddy. You never get to see me play," says Chad.

Liz gives Tim a cold stare. Tim looks completely stunned and hurt.

"It wouldn't kill you to try to make their games every once in a while," Liz says as if she intended on mumbling, but that didn't really work out.

"I work late so I can pay for everything, including all of your nice things at home and tee ball," Tim retorts.

"I'm so sick of that excuse. I never asked you for all of the fancy house stuff. You do it more for your own ego."

Both of them stop dead when they seem to suddenly remember they're in public, and Chris and I exchange glances. I decide to grab Michael and Anthony from them and we all keep walking.

"Liz," Tim continues quietly, though not quietly enough, "we've talked about this. I need to pay my dues now so that not only will I have time for their games, I'll actually be able to coach them."

"What, when they're teenagers, Tim?"

"Are Mommy and Daddy mad at me?" Chad says to Chris.

My heart breaks a little and we try to walk out of verbal range of Liz and Tim.

"Not at all, buddy," Chris says. "They both love you so much, they're fighting over who loves you more."

This seems to go over well with Chad, who agrees.

"What about me, huh?" Tim says to her. "You think this makes me happy? You think I enjoy working eighty hours a week, and the second I come home every day, you're nagging me to fix something, or discipline the kids. Then I sit down and eat the same three meals, because our kids are picky and therefore that's all we can eat."

What do you want from me, Tim, huh?" Liz retorts. "I spend the entire day doing laundry, keeping the house in order, and keeping the kids entertained while cleaning up after them so you can come home to clean shirts and a clean home. I handle all of the bills and excuse me if I'd love a half hour every once in a while that we can just be us. You never want to catch up on our day, you never even ask me how I am. It's like you come home on autopilot and then go to bed to do it all over again. How do you think that makes me feel?"

By this time we've reached the ticket booth, which seems to silence Tim and Liz, at least for now. I'm really thankful that Chris is here; otherwise, it looks like the way things are going I would've been the most awkward third wheel ever.

66

It's a trade-off, I guess. Liz got to be a stay-at-home mother at twenty-five, but her husband has to work twenty-four/seven to support them. So what's better really? One stay-at-home parent or two who work full-time you never get to see like mine? Tim is a network television executive. He heads up a morning show which, unfortunately for his family, airs six out of seven days a week.

Once we get into the park, the tension starts to break and the kids squeal in excitement.

"Michael, Anthony, Chad, you make sure you stay close to us," Liz yells to them. "I tell you something," she then says to me, "once I had twins at twenty-five, I should've stopped there."

"I can't believe they're almost five already," I say.

"And Anthony's going to be two," she adds.

"I gotta hand it to you. Maybe if I had a few kids, my life wouldn't be such a mess."

"I have three kids, Jill—my whole life is one big mess." She laughs as she chases after Anthony, who's trying to keep up with his brothers.

"So you want to face your fear now or build up to it?" Chris asks as he puts his arm around me.

"Um, build up to it," I say, feeling slightly uncomfortable with his arm around me, but at the same time, I've never felt safer. I feel this strange sensation course through my body.

"I wanna ride the Ferris wheel!" Michael points to the ride.

"That sounds great. I want to ride the Ferris wheel too," I tell him as I crouch down and grab his hand.

All the boys pile into one box and say it's kids only, leaving Tim, Liz, Chris, and I to fend for ourselves in the next one.

"No horsing around in there," Tim tells them sternly.

They respond by sticking their tongues out at him.

"I can't get respect from anyone in my house," he says shaking his head and looking back down at his phone.

After the kids are settled, the Ferris wheel moves a bit for the next box to load and they scream with laughter.

"This was a great idea," Liz tells me, though I can tell she's putting on a front. "Tim, really, when was the last time you were able to get off work and take the day like this?"

"Not since before the kids," he says, putting his phone away for the first time.

We all take our seats in the box.

"Then I'm glad we were all able to do this," I add. "You're getting some great family time, and I get to cross stuff off my to-do list."

"Why is riding a roller coaster such a big deal, anyway?" Tim asks.

"I guess it's about facing my fears. I was always so afraid of rollercoasters because I always think the worst. What if something bad happens? What if the ride fails?"

"You have to say that to me while our kids are on a death trap," Liz says, grabbing her husband's arm.

I laugh at her. "This isn't nearly as intimidating," I say. "I don't know; I always watched my friends go on the scary rides and I always wanted to try, but my fear always got the best of me."

"Well, after what you've been through, I bet this roller coaster will seem like nothing," Liz says.

"Well, we'll see about that," I say.

As soon as they're let out of their cage, Michael, Anthony, and Chad run to the bumper cars, giving Liz a heart attack, as we're still waiting to come down.

"Stay where you are or we will leave this park immediately," Liz yells.

All three stop dead in their tracks.

Once we get out, Chris and I run to catch up with the kids.

"Me first," Chris says, cutting in front of the boys when we're in line for the bumper cars.

"Nuh-uh," Michael says. "I was here first."

"Well, I didn't see you," Chris messes back.

"Tell him that's because he's an oversized ogre," I whisper to Michael.

"Yeah, you're a big ogre, and that's not our fault," Michael says.

"Relax, you little gnome," Chris responds.

"I want to ride with Mommy," little Anthony says.

"I want to ride with Mommy," the twins yell as well.

I can't help but look over at Tim, who seems a bit heartbroken but is trying not to show it.

"Well, I don't know about you, but I think your dad here is the ultimate bumper car driver. He's the best in town, and I'm going to ride with him," Chris declares.

"Nuh-uh, he's my dad I want to go with him," Chad says.

Liz gives Chris a smile.

Chris's phone then starts to ring and he immediately picks it up and walks away. "Everything okay?" I hear him ask. I look over at Liz who shrugs. After a few minutes he comes back, shoving his cell into his pocket. He doesn't mention anything about the call. I want to ask, but it's not like I'm his girlfriend or anything.

"Everything all right?" I settle for.

"Yup," he says. "Who's ready for some bumper cars?"

After a few more rides, Chris finally decides to taunt me. I'm surprised it didn't start sooner.

"Okay now, who wants to watch Aunt Jill here ride that big monster roller coaster?" Chris asks the boys.

"Using the kids as artillery? Very nice," I say.

"I do, I do," they all yell.

"Well, it looks like Jill here might be too chicken, so I think we need to tickle her until she agrees."

"No," I yell at him. Before I can say anything else, Chad, Michael, and Anthony all start to tickle me, but really, they're just poking me. Liz is cracking up. "So much for parenting," I say, faux glaring. "Okay, okay, I surrender," I tell the boys.

"Yeah!" they cheer as they jump up and down.

I head over to the line, dragging Chris with me. When I hear the first rumble of the coaster flying above us, I can't help but scream.

"Relax, drama queen," he tells me.

"You know what, you have to be scared of something," I tell him. "What is it?"

"I'm not afraid of anything," he says puffing his chest out and flexing his muscles.

"Seriously, that's a lie," I tell him.

"Fine." He looks around. "You promise not to repeat this to anyone?" he says, leaning in towards me.

I nod.

"Especially the boys?"

"Michael, Anthony, and Chad? Um, Okay, kind of weird."

He takes a deep breath. "I'm terrified, I mean really scared, like scream like a girl scared, of spiders."

"You're such a liar!" I hit him.

"I am, really," he insists.

"Okay, so you haven't realized a spider's been crawling on your shirt this whole time?"

"Ahh, where?" He jumps and starts to hit his shirt. After he's convinced himself it's off, he looks at me.

"Wow, you really do scream like a girl," I tell him.

"That hurts," he tells me.

I roll my eyes and walk ahead of him.

"Seriously, was there a spider on me?"

"Relax, drama queen," I say mockingly. I go from laughing to stone-faced when I realize it's our turn and my legs have turned to Jell-O. "I can't do this," I tell him.

"Yes, you can. We're the next ones up."

"No—uh, I can't."

"Jill, you need to stop freaking out here, it's just a ride. A twelve-year-old got off in front of us."

"I, uh—don't feel well."

"That's a lame excuse," he says.

"Come on, Chris, this is really scary for me."

When it's our turn to get into the seats, I grip his shirt.

"Just relax and don't think about it," he says, leading me into the car of death.

I start to breathe heavily. I feel like an idiot because everyone's looking at me like I'm some kind of freak.

"Come on, lady," the snotty sixteen-year-old operator says to me. Should I be trusting a teenager to operate this thing? I mean, with his hormones all out of whack, he could see a cute girl and forget to turn the ride off …

Finally I shut my eyes and sit down. Chris assists me with my belt.

"There. Now you're not going anywhere," he assures me.

Suddenly the coaster jerks violently and I can't help but scream.

I have to say the most torturous part of the experience is the thing chugging up to the top. It's literally like walking the plank. You know once you get up there, it's all over.

Then, before I'm about to black out from how high up we are, the coaster picks up momentum and we're flying across the tracks. I'm screaming bloody murder as I find Chris's hand to grab for dear life. After the first loop, I finally stop freaking out and realize this is actually pretty fun. Now I'm screaming in excitement. I see Chris look over at me and smile, but when I turn to him, my hair covers my face.

I can't believe I was ever scared of this before; this is so much fun. Then with a sudden jolt, my face goes flying forward slamming my entire mouth into the bar in front of me.

Chapter Eleven

"That wasn't so bad, right?" he says to me once we've gotten off the ride and are now walking towards the exit.

I stare at him while holding a bunch of paper towels to my mouth. When I got off the coaster, everyone jumped like I was a zombie about to attack them. One mother even ran away with her kid. The snot-nosed teenager pulled a bunch of paper towels out from behind his stand.

"Happens to one in every five people," he says, not really caring.

"Come on, you were having fun until you cracked your face."

I can't help but smile a bit, even though it hurts. "I have to admit, that was a lot of fun." I laugh, trying to smooth my hair out. "Oh my gosh, what a thrill. I'm still shaking."

"Oh, this I gotta see," he says, stopping me in front of a shed.

"What's this?"

"Oh, they take your pictures on every roller coaster and you can choose to buy it or not."

"They take pictures of you?" I say. "That has to be the cruelest thing I've ever heard of."

"Oh, nice." He starts laughing. I scan through the photos on the monitors until I find us. Chris is making a goofy face and smiling while I have my mouth as wide open as it can go, and full of blood. Seriously, you can see my tonsils in this picture. Then I see my eyes are popping out of my skull.

"Oh my gosh, this is horrible," I say, putting my head down afraid someone might recognize me.

"I'd like to purchase that, please," he says, pulling out his wallet from his back pocket.

"Why would you do this to me?" I ask him while tugging on his arm.

"Because it's too good," he says, putting the money down and taking the picture from the man. He opens up the folder one more time to show me before closing it again. I make a face of disgust.

"I appreciate your sympathy," I tell him.

"For you," he says, handing the photo to me.

"Why did you get this for me?" I ask, confused. I figured my bitching made it clear I never wanted to see this again.

"Because it's a memory of your first ever roller coaster. It's a very important feat."

"Sure." I laugh, looking at it again.

"Don't you feel just a little more confident now?" he says, putting his arm around me again.

"You know something, I do," I tell him. "Hell, I'm even going to go as far as posting this on my blog tonight."

"I will see that you do," he says. "So are you tired now?"

"Exhausted, actually, this day really took it out of me. Not to mention my gums are bleeding."

"Well, you did what you came here to do. Now let's go home."

We say our good-byes to Liz and Tim who are trying to get their kids to willingly leave the park and head towards Chris's car.

"So I know this sounds strange," I say, buckling my seat belt. "But I still feel like I don't know you all that well."

"Really?" he says, surprised as he starts the car and we drive away.

"I know that seems stupid. I mean, I know your childhood, I know what you do now, but it's like there is this big ten-year gap that I don't really know anything about."

"Well, when you put it that way, I guess I could say the same for you," he says. "What do you want to know?"

I want to ask why he's still living at home, but something keeps me from asking that, at least right away. "Is your favorite color still red?" I start with.

He laughs for a second. "That's what concerns you with this ten-year gap? That my favorite color has changed?"

"I don't know," I laugh.

"Well, you're right. My favorite color is now yellow. And the minute I came to that realization, I have to say something, my whole life changed. It's like my life flashed before me and I realized that if I didn't change my favorite color my whole life was doomed."

I burst out laughing and he does as well. "Okay, your turn. You can ask me."

"Hmm," he thinks for a second. "I pretty much know a lot more than you think, because you really spilled your guts to me that first night," he laughs.

I roll my eyes.

"I guess, um," he starts to think again. I notice that his face turns serious.

"Why did we break up in the first place?" he says, looking at me.

I feel my face get hot and I shift in my seat. "I don't know, we were kids really, we didn't know what we wanted," I start. "I guess it was mainly because our lives were going in separate directions, you know, off to different colleges ..." I trail off.

"Really? It didn't have to do with me being a slacker?"

"I'd say more of me being a workaholic."

He smiles as if I'm saying that to be nice, but to me it was the truth. The rest of the ride is pretty silent.

"All right, well, here we are," he says pulling up to my driveway. "Thanks for inviting me," he says.

"Thanks for coming," I reply. "I would've never ridden that scary thing without you." I give him a quick pat on the knee and jump out the car. I panicked since I don't know how to react with him, especially when we are saying our good-byes. Normally I would kiss him on the cheek, but I was nervous he'd view that wrong. When I get inside, I shake my head at myself.

When I get upstairs, I can't wait to get into my sweats and lounge around the house. I have my mom take a look at my mouth.

"You just have a gash on your gums, but you should be fine," she says. "Hardly any swelling, and your teeth are good. I'll pick up some cream at work to keep it from getting infected," she runs her hand along the side of my head.

"Thanks," I say, thinking back to when she would look at all of my cuts and bruises after lacrosse games.

I hear my phone ring and see it's Liz.

"So you manage to wrangle the kids?" I say when I pick up the phone.

"Yes, we survived," she laughs. "I just put them to bed, actually. They crashed in the car on the way home. I hope you don't think the night is over," she says.

"I just spent all day with you. Aren't you sick of me?" I fall onto the couch and turn the television on.

"Uh-uh," she says. "You want to get over your real fear? We're going to do some karaoke."

"No," I tell her. "Shouldn't you stay home with your husband given the fact you say you never see him?"

"He's working," she tells me. I sense annoyance in her voice. "Learn to say yes before you say no," she quickly changes her tune.

"You need to stop quoting my list," I tell her.

"Karaoke, karaoke, karaoke," she chants.

"Fine." I hang up on her.

I meet her at Charlie's, which, it turns out, has a karaoke night. It's not lit very well, which is promising, I think. This time we are dressed more appropriately.

I notice this place draws the strangest crowd. There are middle-aged men singing, and then the college crowd is more gathered around the beer pong and arcade games.

"Isn't this place great?" Liz says, putting her arm around me.

"I'm so confused right now," I tell her. "What is this place, exactly? It looks like a whole different bar from last Saturday."

"It's a mutt bar tonight," she says.

"What's a mutt bar?"

"It's a mix between old geezers and college kids."

"Great," I say sarcastically.

"Yeah, well, I read your blog and found out this place has a karaoke night. By the way, I can't believe you posted that roller coaster picture of yourself. Not a good look for you."

"Thanks." I laugh.

"I also know how much you love beer pong," Liz adds, pointing towards the end of the bar.

"Last time I checked, you sucked too," I tell Liz.

"I know, which is why I called Chris."

"Really?" I say nervously, looking around.

"Yeah. I'm in love with him now, so if you're not ready for him, I'll take him," she says.

"Today was great, don't get me wrong, but I'm nervous about things moving too fast with us. I mean, you were right, it's too soon."

"Where's that confident peacock I saw this afternoon? After that roller coaster, you were ready to take on the world."

"Yeah, and then reality set in," I say.

"Well, it's hardly swollen."

"I look like I have herpes," I can't help but say.

"Well, the one guy that doesn't think that is Chris, and here he comes," she points.

"Hey." I turn around and smile. "Long time, no see."

"Hey." He smiles back. "Where's Tim?" he asks.

"That day at the park meant three days of working with no sleep," Liz says.

"Aw, that's a shame."

"At least the kids won't bother him. They've been passed out since we got back."

"So, ready to start singing?" Chris asks me, rubbing his hands together.

"The kids aren't here to help you with that now," I tell him.

"I think we should start off with a friendly game of beer pong," Liz says.

"I hope you're good, because I suck," I tell Chris.

"I'm sure you'll be fine," he says.

"So do you get to play on the nights you're working here?"

"Yeah, every once in a while I get a game in," he says, high-fiving a couple of kids at the arcade.

We sign up on the board and watch a bunch of college kids try to distract the ones on the other team and give each other high-fives every time they get a cup in. They are all wearing college hoodies that I'm assuming represent the school they go to. Part of me is eager to get in on the fun while the other part of me feels as if I'm a chaperone.

"Hey, mind if we get in on this?" Chris asks the winner.

"Sure thing, gramps," one kid says.

"I got experience with this, my man," he says while setting up the cups. "I was sinking these balls while you were still in your diapers."

"Yeah, whatever," the kid says back.

"You really have the ability to relate to all children," I tell him.

"What can I say? That's why I'm a teacher. So do you want to start?" He holds up a ping-pong ball for me.

"Um, sure," I say, taking the ball from his hand and staring at it like it's an alien.

Finally I release it and it goes flying past the cups, and the other team, for that matter.

"Whoops," I say.

"It's okay, you just need your sea legs back," he says as he sends his ball flying right into the top of the triangle.

"Wow, that was pretty good," I say nodding my head.

"Liz, did you know Chris would be this good?" I ask when I see her emerge through the crowd.

"I don't know. He's a boy and boys seem to be good at this game. I just took a guess." She hands Chris and myself a shot. "To loosen you up a bit."

The other team retaliates and sinks both of their balls into different cups. Chris hands me one of them.

"Once you have a few of these, you should be more relaxed and it should help your aim."

"Impairing your vision helps?"

"What can I say? It makes the hole look bigger."

"That's what she said," one of the college kids laughs. We both look at him and shake our heads laughing.

After a few rounds, the guys are beating us, but Chris is holding us afloat. After a few, he's right, finally the hole does start to seem easier to hit. I close one eye, aim, and bam. "Hook, line, and sinker," I yell.

The guys all just look at me. What, they can trash talk and I can't? "What?" I ask.

"Nothing," Chris laughs.

"Honey, no," Liz tells me, positioning herself on a barstool. I notice the guys stop for a moment to admire her doing this.

"What are you perves looking at?" she says, causing them to stutter and pretend to fix their beer cups.

The game starts to get more intense; we are even with two cups on both ends. "Booh-ya," Chris yells as he sinks the cup and now we are down to one.

"It's all up to you," he tells me, rubbing his hands together.

I take a deep breath, aim, close my eyes, and shoot. It literally feels like slow motion. Either that or I've had too many. Then to my surprise, it actually goes in.

"Oh my gosh!" Chris yells.

"And boom goes the dynamite," I scream.

"Seriously, enough with the trash talk, you suck at it," Liz comments, looking around, embarrassed.

Chris picks me up and swings me around. I feel like Rocky when he wins and everyone runs up to him. Only here it's just Chris, as Liz seems totally bored.

"Okay, karaoke time," Liz says, pulling me away. "This will make things more interesting."

"I-um-no," I stutter.

"You know, Liz," Chris says. "I think you two should do a duet together."

"Oh my gosh, yes!" I say, grabbing her arms. She is giving Chris the bitchy stare down.

"Come on, please?" I beg.

"Well, in order for it to count on your list, it has to be just you."

"I believe it only specified she needed to sing karaoke. Nothing was ever mentioned about her being alone," Chris says. "Besides, I helped her with beer pong. Now it's your turn to help her with singing."

"And here I thought I liked you," Liz tells him with a smirk.

We do one more shot at the bar to get our nerve up and I manage to pull her on stage. I suddenly realize that although the bar isn't well lit, the stage sure is.

I suddenly get a jolt of fear.

I look over at Liz who is about to bail on me, and I have to then put all of my concentration into keeping her on stage.

Then the pang of the eighties keyboard comes over the speakers and the words for "What a Feeling" from the movie *Flashdance* roll across the screen. *Liz, you bitch,* I can't help but think.

"At first when there's nothing but a slow glowing dream," I sing. Then I nudge Liz.

"That your fear seems to hide deep inside your mind."

I immediately forget we are in front of a crowd and I start dancing to get her to laugh. Eventually we get such a kick out of each other that we wind up singing the song like we're in sixth grade again at a sleepover, singing into our hairbrushes. We're kicking and waving our arms like Jennifer Beals in the video.

"What a feeling, bein's believing, pictures come alive, you can dance right through your life. Take your passion and make it happen, what a feeling …."

Suddenly the roar of the crowd brings us back to reality and we can't stop laughing.

"I can't remember the last time I had that much fun," I tell her, after we practically fall off the stage towards a booth off to the side.

"Me neither," she agrees.

"Man, I miss high school," I say.

"Me too," Liz says.

"Me three." Chris joins us, sitting down with a round of beers.

"Seriously, why do we have to grow up and face life's disappointments? I want to go back to when we feared nothing," I say.

"Hey, do you remember that time when some guy dressed as the school mascot during class pictures and shot water balloons at the crowd?"

"Oh my gosh, that was hysterical. Principal Harvey, this, like, eighty-five-year-old man, started chasing him with his cane."

We burst out laughing.

"Hey, was that you?" I ask. "As I recall, they never found out who that was."

"I have no comment," he says, taking a sip of his drink.

"Oh, you did!" Liz points at him.

"Hey, how about the time the lacrosse team had a game on Sunday and afterwards we all got together at your house and partied till three a.m.," I tell Liz.

"Oh yeah, Wannamaker was pissed." She laughs. "She made us run five miles at our practice the next morning. Then Kelly was so hungover she tripped over the fire hydrant and twisted her ankle."

We burst into laughter. I literally had tears in my eyes. "Oh, that was so worth it," I say.

"You know, I still can't handle the smell of rum because of that night?" Liz tells me.

"That was the only thing in your parents' house."

"Cheap rum at that."

We start laughing again.

"How about when I brought both of you girls to prom?" Chris brings up.

"Oh yea," Liz says. "I forgot all about that. You were so sweet to do that," she says patting his forearm.

"Sweet? Are you kidding? I looked like the biggest pimp there, my popularity points went up after that," he laughs.

I suddenly realize that I feel like me again. This is what I've missed out on all this time. Just being out for a few drinks with friends, reminiscing about good times while creating new memories.

I have to say it feels good to be back.

Chapter Twelve

"Hey, kiddo."

I jump in my desk chair. I'm in my pajamas stalking my blog. It's only been a day since my last blog entry and I've gotten a bunch of new followers.

"Dad, you scared me," I tell him. He scares me even more when I turn around and see him in multicolored plaid shorts and a pink polo shirt.

"Sorry about that," he says. "I was going to go for nine holes and your mother reminded me that was something on your list, so I thought maybe you'd like to come out with me and I could teach you?"

I smile. "That would be great, Dad. Thanks."

As I get ready, I start to get excited. It will be nice to have a bonding experience with my dad, I think. And developing a closer relationship with him might keep me from developing any (more) weird complexes about men.

"I'm not sure if I have any golf stuff to wear," I yell to him while I pull my hair back.

"That's all right. You can just borrow stuff from your mother."

A half hour later, I'm standing in front of the country club, humiliated. Turns out my parents had matching golf uniforms. I'm sporting a multicolor plaid skirt and pink top to match my dad. I have on a hat and big sunglasses to avoid anyone recognizing me.

"Bill, how are you?" We're in the clubhouse and a man has come up to my father to shake his hand. He looks like your stereotypical country club golfer. He's wearing a yellow polo with white shorts and yes, a sweater tied around his neck. I haven't seen anyone dress like that since *Caddyshack*.

"Stephen, how's it going?" My father returns the handshake. "This is my daughter Jill," he says to him. "Jill, this is Stephen Young."

"Ah, nice to meet you," I say, shaking his hand. *Stephen Young as in I have a bitchy daughter named*

Sarah Young who I went to high school with?

"I think you may know my daughter Sarah," he says to me.

Damn it. "Yes I do," I say, praying he doesn't go and tell her I dressed to match my dad.

"You know, she actually works here? She's an event coordinator for the club." I see him step out into the hallway and flag someone down.

Oh my God, please tell me this isn't happening.

"Sarah, you remember Jill from high school," he says, reintroducing us. Sarah looks the best I've ever seen her. I thought the rule was pretty, mean girls peaked in high school. Apparently this one is immortal.

"Yes." She eyes me up and down, barely holding back a smirk. She has her long blonde hair pulled into a sleek ponytail, and a string of white pearls around her neck.

She's wearing a white dress with a gold belt and has a nice even suntan. She looks stunning. I hate her.

"Well, we might want to get going, Dad, maybe to the club store so I can get my own golf outfit," I say.

"Nonsense," he says. "You look great." He nudges me to emphasize the fact that we're in matching outfits.

I try hard not cry.

"Okay, we'll let you get to it," Stephen finally says. "Good luck out there."

"Thanks. You too." My dad shakes his hand again. "Such a nice family," he says as we walk away, picking up both of our bags and heading towards the golf carts.

"Yeah," I say with a fake smile.

"You're not keeping your head down," he repeats to me for the umpteenth time.

"Dad, I realize that. I'm trying to fix it, but my coordination is doing otherwise," I say through clenched teeth. We're only on the third hole and already I'm about to kill him. I take another swing. This time I do make contact, but the ball veers directly to the left into the woods.

"Wow, did that even go a little ahead of you?" he asks. He says it in a joking way—he's trying to loosen me up—but his "jokes" only make me more tense.

I take a deep breath as we go on what seems like a much-less-fun Easter egg hunt to find my ball.

"Don't worry about it, honey," he says finally, "we'll play best ball so you can just drop a new one near me."

"Fine," I say with my fists clenched tightly around my driver. Why the heck did I ever want to learn golf in the first place? It's hot, I'm all sweaty, and this game seems to take forever.

"Beverages?" A woman pulls up in a cart.

"Absolutely." My dad smiles as he walks over to her.

The young brunette driving the cart, who looks like she's barely eighteen, hops out of it and opens the cooler in the back.

"A couple of waters," my dad says, pulling out his wallet. "Honey, do you want a Bloody Mary? It might loosen up your swing a bit."

My ears pop up. I can have a Bloody Mary while playing golf? *Maybe this will work out,* I think to myself.

When we get to the middle of the green, I'm forced to sit through another one of my dad's instructional monologues. At least my drink makes this situation more tolerable.

"Okay now," he says to me. He's positioned just like a real coach, with a wide stance and his hands crossed. I'm reminded of when he coached my tee ball team when I was eight. "Feet, hip distance apart. Lean on your front leg—not that much. Keep your front elbow locked—not that stiff. Relax."

"Dad"—I try to relax my stance—"how can I lock my elbow but stay loose? That's contradictory."

"Every part of your body should be relaxed except your elbow," he tells me.

"What does that even mean?" I ask him in frustration. I don't know what else to do at this point except pick up my drink and take a swig.

"Come on, loosen up. This is supposed to be fun," he says, taking my Bloody Mary out of my hands. Then—whether it's to make me laugh or piss me off, I'm not sure—he runs behind the golf cart and ducks down.

"Very funny," I tell him. With that I take a swing, which actually sends the ball straight and onto the shorter grass closer to the flag.

"Great shot," he tells me. "See what happens when you're relaxed?"

"You're right," I tell him. "Drinking can be fun."

He gives me a disapproving look. "Why don't you go ahead and shoot my ball, too. That way you'll get more practice in. I'll bring the cart up to the flag."

"Sure," I say rather confidently. I line myself up, swing, and—"Ow," I hear my dad yell.

I look up a half a second later, since I was told to keep my head down. It appears as if my ball went directly to the right of me and hit my dad right in the back of the head. He went down like a sack of potatoes.

"Oh my gosh, are you okay?" I try not to laugh but I know he's fine. I help him sit up and we both look at each other and burst out laughing.

"You're better than your mother, at least." He rubs the back of his head while he laughs.

"Where did she hit you?" I ask, still laughing.

"She hit the porta-john when I was in it. Scared the crap out of me," he adds.

This makes me laugh even harder.

Our laughing subsides when we notice the group of people at the tee waiting on us. We gather our stuff and move onto the next hole, still giggling.

We scurry up to the hole to putt.

"Remember, head down," my dad says, kneeling in front of the hole. "Aim right here." He points to the left of the hole.

"Really?" I question.

"When you get down low, you can see the green is uneven. It'll pull your ball to the right." He motions with his hands to show me.

I just shrug as I take my swing.

On the first try it goes right in.

"Unbelievable!" he yells, putting his arms up as if it's a touchdown.

"Holy cow!" I say, jumping up and down.

He runs over to hug me.

"You know, with a little more practice and training, I think you could be good at this." He smiles as he pats me on the back, and for the first time today, I don't find the gesture to be condescending.

"So why was this on your list, anyway," he asks while we pull away in the golf cart.

"I'm surprised you're even asking. You constantly nagged me that you wanted me to learn. You said it would be good for the business world."

"Oh, I guess you're right," he says. "Did you ever feel you needed to learn it, once you started working as a lawyer?"

"Not once," I laugh. "But I'm glad I'm learning now," I reassure him.

The rest of the day goes much more smoothly. My dad was actually right. As soon as you relax, you do much better.

"You know, sweetie," my dad says to me as we drive to our final hole. "I know life sucks right now, but you'll get through this." He gives my hand an encouraging squeeze.

"I know," I tell him. I knew this speech was coming, but it sucks because we've actually been having so much fun.

"And I just want you to know that I've really seen a great improvement in you in this past week."

"Thanks." I feel slightly offended, but I think I know what he means.

"And I don't just mean since you moved home, I mean in your life. I've never seen you this happy."

I give him a smile.

"I know your mother and I always pushed you to work hard and be the best you can be, but I think we were wrong to push you."

"What do you mean?" I ask. "Doesn't every parent want success for their kids? That's what I was trying to do—be the best."

"Well, don't get me wrong, we wanted what was best for you, but I think between us pressuring you and you pressuring yourself, you sacrificed a lot of growing up."

I feel sick. It was bad enough I felt that way, but to find out other people—the ones who had pushed you your whole life—agreed …

When he realizes I haven't said anything, he continues.

"Don't get me wrong, we're so proud of you and everything you've done, but just seeing how happy you've been just doing these things you've never done before and now you've finally just relaxed and are finally doing something for yourself …"

"But my whole life has been about myself! That's the problem!" I say. "My whole life has been about prioritizing me, and in the process, you're right, I sacrificed my social life and plenty of other things."

Now it's my dad's turn to look confused.

"Dad, I never see you. We've never spent any time like this together because I'm always working. I missed out on being your daughter," I say, starting to get really upset.

"Now, don't say that," he tells me and stops the cart. "You've been the best daughter in the world, and we couldn't be more proud of you. You can regret a lot of things but don't ever regret that," he says. "Your mother and I love what a hard worker you are, but some of the harsh reality is that life can kick you in the teeth and you just have to make sure when that happens, you surround yourself with the people that matter."

"Still, I'm sorry Dad," I say.

"Don't apologize," he tells me. "If anything, I'm sorry. I should've been there more to tell you to go out and have fun. My problem was when I was a kid, I was a slacker who just cared about partying, and not that I don't love my job, but I think if I'd pushed myself I would've been happier with where I am now from a career perspective. That's why I pushed you."

"Guess you and I have to work on that balance thing," I tell him.

"Yeah." He laughs. "But the good thing is, it's never too late to start."

Chapter Thirteen

When we get back to the house I can hear my French disc being played on the stereo. This raises my curiosity. I follow the sound into the kitchen, where I see my mom has organized it to look like she's about to have a cooking show.

"What's all this?" I ask her.

"I'm not going to lie. I'm a little jealous that you two got to bond and your father was able to help you with your list," she says. "So I decided that I'm going to help you learn to cook." She puts her arms out to show me everything she's done. Mixing bowls and measuring cups are filled to the brim with ingredients.

"Great!" I try to be enthusiastic. The truth is, I'm exhausted, sweaty, and really just want to order a pizza. I also know I can't hurt her feelings.

"I know what a challenge this could be for you, so I decided to help by pre-measuring all the ingredients."

This is going to be rough, I think. I convince her to let me just shower and say I'll come back down when I'm a little more refreshed. I also decide this is a good time to write up my blog for the day and try to psych myself up for this. Why did I ever even put this on my list in the first place? Sure, I guess learning how to cook yourself a meal is a pretty basic thing you should know, but the truth was I had tried this before and was never good at it. I make my way back downstairs and pretend to be enthused.

"So what's with the French?" I ask.

"We are making beef bourguignon," she says proudly in a French accent.

I lose my excitement immediately. "We couldn't start with, maybe, spaghetti?"

She puts her hands on her hips. "I think you can do a little better than that, Miss Over-Achiever."

"Touché," I respond. "Although not trusting me with the measurements doesn't say all that much."

"Well, you were never a chemist, Jill."

I roll my eyes. "Mom, can you not point out every one of my flaws?"

"Honey, I'm not trying to make you feel bad. You have a lot of great strengths and qualities. This isn't one of them."

I immediately fall back into old habits. All through my childhood and adolescence, the second she told me I wasn't good at something, I felt the need to prove her wrong. "You know I got an A in chemistry, right?" I return.

"Well, you needed a tutor," she says while pulling the aprons out of the pantry.

I can't help but let out a sigh. "God, nothing is ever good enough for you."

This causes her to stop dead in her tracks and look up at me. "Beg your pardon?" she says.

"This is why I am the way I am. Everything I did was never good enough. I spent my entire life trying to prove myself to you. I get an A in chemistry, and because I needed a tutor, what, my A didn't count?"

"Jill, that was over ten years ago. Does it really matter?" She tries to laugh if off like its nothing, but my blood is boiling.

"Yes it matters, because it's exactly that kind of thing that made me insecure. My whole life, I was always worried about what you thought. I gave up on so much so I could show you I was worthy of your respect."

"Good enough for what, Jill?" She's angry now and has thrown down her towel. "What are you not good enough for? What made you think you ever had to prove anything to anyone? Don't for one second think I kept you from anything."

"What are you talking about?" I say, frustrated. "You treat me like a child all the time."

"You want me to stop treating you like a child? Why don't you start acting like a grown-up? Lesson one: take responsibility for your own problems and stop blaming the world. You want to be an adult? Why don't you start doing your part since you're living here. Your father and I work all week; you can't once go food shopping or do laundry?"

"That's it!" I roar. "I can't take this anymore!" I storm back upstairs. As I reach the top, I see my dad hiding in his office.

"Why is she like this all the time?" I yell to him.

He smiles weakly and puts on his headphones while he pulls out an airplane model he's been working on.

"Great, now you, too." I continue to stomp to my room. He never gets involved. Anytime I fight with my mom, he hides. I slam the door to my room.

I need to get the hell out of this house, I type in my blog. It's like a diary— very therapeutic. After I finish pounding out my frustrations re: the cooking disaster, I'm surprised the keys on my keyboard aren't broken.

A few minutes later I see a message below my post.

Give your mother a chance. Remember we only want what's best for you —Dad

I let out a sigh as I slump back into my chair.

As I stare out the window, I start to think about what she said. Whether or not I think she was the catalyst for my problems, they were still my problems that I perpetuated myself. Only I had the power to change things and make them better.

But does she have to be so damn blunt all the time? I already have Liz for that.

I start to feel guilty and eventually decide to take another shot.

I open my door slowly, but it makes a loud creaking noise. The rest of the house is quiet, with the exception of the television I hear downstairs.

I take a deep breath and descend the staircase, not knowing what to expect, exactly. If my mom hasn't calmed down just yet, she's likely to throw a mixing bowl at me. When I find her on the couch with a cup of tea, I assume the dust has settled.

"I'm sorry, Mom," I say, still standing in the hallway. I'm still terrified to move any closer until I can judge her response.

"I'm sorry, too," she says, turning to me. I take that as an invitation to sit on the couch.

"I just get frustrated with myself, and I shouldn't have blamed anything on you."

"I know," she says, taking a sip of her tea. "I don't mean to be so hard on you all the time," she says. "The truth is, I think you're so great in so many ways, I feel if I criticize you, it will keep you more grounded and level-headed. The last thing I want is a pretentious daughter."

That would be my mother's rationale. It makes me laugh a little. "It's not that I don't appreciate everything you've done for me," I say carefully, "it's just that I wish you would only offer advice when it's asked."

She's quiet for a second. "I suppose you're right," she says. "But then again, I haven't seen you in so long, I guess I had a lot to unload on you."

"Again with the guilt and criticism," I say partially laughing.

"Sorry again," she says, rolling her eyes. "It'll be hard to turn off the instinct, so you're going to have to be patient with me."

"As you're going to have to be with me," I say. "I don't know what it is with us, but anytime you start on me I revert to my fifteen-year-old self."

"And trust me, that wasn't your most shining year."

I roll my eyes at her.

"Baby steps," she says correcting herself.

"I know I might regret this," I say. "But will you help me learn to cook?"

She smiles and nods.

"What is all this?" I ask when we're back in the kitchen. I point to a bowl with strangely colored meat.

"That's bacon," she says.

"If that's bacon, then what's that?" I ask, pointing to what I thought was bacon.

"That's bacon rind," she says.

"Two types of bacon and beef. Well, this will certainly be heart stopping."

"Stop being a pain," she says, handing me a recipe sheet. "I got this from Oprah."

"Remove rind from bacon and cut into lardons. What's a lardon?" I ask.

"Quarter-inch sticks," my mother says as she rinses off the cutting board.

"Are we really following an Oprah recipe here? I mean, the woman isn't exactly Julia Child."

"This is a Julia Child recipe."

"Then why did you tell me it was Oprah's?"

"Well, she got it from Julia," she says.

"So if we make this, can we say it's our recipe?" I ask her.

"Sure. Why not?"

I realize I'm being a bit short and difficult so I stop myself from talking.

"Put the bacon in the pan," my mom tells me. "Make sure to simmer it."

Why would you simmer bacon? I think. I go to place it in the pan and turn on the stove.

"Now dry the stewing beef," she tells me, handing me a paper towel.

"What am I supposed to do with this?"

"Dry the stewing beef in paper towels," she reads.

I sigh and start to press the paper towel to the meat. As I pull it away, I see bits of the cheap towel are stuck to the beef and I have to try to pull it all off. I guess this is what happens when you don't spring for the dollar-ninety-nine brand. Eventually I give up and leave some of the teensy bits on there. It's not like it is going to kill me. At least, I hope it won't. Just then, I hear the bacon screeching. I turn around and there's oil bubbling everywhere. I frantically turn the dial down. The bacon looks completely burned and shriveled and it's supposed to be too thick to shrivel.

"Oh," my mom says. "I turn around for one second ..."

"You're supposed to be helping me," I snap at her. "And not speaking to me like that!"

"It's fine," she says, looking at the recipe. "Just throw the meat in there."

I take a hunk of it and slam it on top of the bacon.

"Not the whole thing; you have to slice it!" she yells.

With the oil still spitting, it's too hot to take it back out of the pan without getting burned, so I grab a large knife and start to stab at the meat.

"Stop," my mother yells, horrified.

"Okay," I yell back. I go to pull the knife out, but it's now stuck in the meat. I try again and the meat comes right out of the pan and falls onto the floor. Finally my dad comes in and removes the pan from the hot area on the stove. We all stand in front of the meat on the floor, staring at it helplessly.

Dad just pats me on the back. My mother looks at me like I've just ruined a piece of artwork she spent her whole life creating.

"Sorry," I say as I cringe.

"Honey, I love you, but some things just can't be taught," she says, removing her oven mitts and tossing them on the counter.

"Mom, what did we just talk about?"

She softens a bit. "I'm sorry, you're right. This was a hard recipe to start with. We should've done something easier."

"Sweetie, it's okay," my dad says to her. "I really wanted pizza anyway."

I still want to try to move in a positive direction with my mom. "I've got a great idea. This might have been a little too much for me to handle, but why don't I pick up the makings for pizza?" I feel bad for ruining my mom's hard work, even though starting with beef bourguignon was a ridiculous idea.

She has her arms crossed, but a smile creeps across her face. "I'll make you a list," she says.

I come back from the store a little while later. I have flour to make dough from scratch, mozzarella, pepperoni, and a frozen pizza I stick in the garage freezer in case this goes awry.

Once I'm back in the kitchen, my mom claps her hands and reaches into a cabinet. "I finally get to use my pizza stone!"

"What the heck is a pizza stone?" I ask, putting the groceries on the counter.

"All right," my mom says, "I'll get the bottle of wine."

My father whispers to me. "Maybe once we get some wine in your mother, she won't be as stressed out."

I try to keep a straight face but a smile creeps across it. Time with Mom has turned into more bonding with Dad.

"Don't you two gang up on me," she says, taking a wine glass out of my dad's hand. "Okay," she says, once she's taken a sip, put the glass down, and pulled out an oversized mixing bowl. "Time to make the dough."

A Dean Martin track replaces the French music we were initially listening to. Before we know it, all three of us are drinking wine, singing "That's Amore," and dancing around, covered in flour. I can tell my mom's spirits have finally lifted and she is just having fun with us. I can't remember ever having this much fun with my parents before. This is the first time ever that all of us have just let loose. Our crust turns out to be a mess, thick on one side and way too thin on the other. The cheese hasn't melted evenly, and the pepperoni was sliced too thick. But we all made it out alive and had a great time. The pizza was even edible, which is a great accomplishment for me.

"Would you like to help me with some brownies for dessert?" my mom asks when we're done eating the pizza.

"Sure," I say, jumping up from the table and heading to the cabinet with a new found lightheartedness. I like this new carefree me, and I think everyone else does, too.

It is then that I realize that is isn't just me who needed to loosen up. It was my parents as well. For the first time ever, I look over and see them looking into each other's eyes while dancing to the Dean Martin track.

While the brownies are baking, my mom and I clean up the dishes and the disastrous kitchen.

"Thank you for helping me learn to cook," I tell her while I'm drying the dishes.

She looks up from the sink and smiles at me. "It was just nice to be able to help you, for once. You were always so independent, as soon as you could walk you wanted nothing to do with me."

"It's not that I didn't want anything to do with you," I say, feeling guilty. "I just wanted to do things for myself."

She nods her head, "I was the same way."

"Truth is, I'm clearly not perfect, and I do need help from time to time, and I appreciate you helping me. I wish it hadn't taken me falling on my ass to realize I need that."

She stops her scrubbing and looks up at me. "It's okay, sweetie. It's easy to take things for granted sometimes. Just know that we will always be here for you, no matter what."

I lean in and give my mom a hug. "Thanks," I tell her.

"Movie's starting," my dad yells from the living room.

"Just in time for brownies," my mom yells back. She looks at me, hits me with the dishtowel, and tells me to join my dad.

I settle on the floor in front of the couch and take a sip of wine. I look over and notice my phone has a text message from Chris.

I have a surprise for you tomorrow. I found some other stuff to cross off your list. Pick you up at eleven.

I feel butterflies in my stomach as I read it. I think about how Chris, despite not seeing him in so long, like my parents, is still there for me no matter what. I know this goes against my list, but maybe I should be considering this relationship. Who knows, maybe whatever he has planned will completely break down my guard?

Chapter Fourteen

It's the next morning and I'm literally sitting at the top of the stairs, from where I can see the outdoor walkway. I jump up and run into my room when my dad comes out of his bedroom behind me. Damn, I didn't realize he was up here. He gives me a puzzled look as the doorbell rings while I shoot into my room.

I hear him let out a sigh as he goes and opens the front door.

"Jill," he calls up a minute later—a bit sarcastically. "Chris is here to see you."

"Oh, hey." I come out as if I've just been getting ready in my room the whole time and not anxiously pacing.

"Ready to go?" he asks, as his runs his fingers through his hair. He's wearing a flannel print button down and jeans. He looks great, I can't help but think.

"You bet," I say as I wave good-bye to my dad and we close the front door. "So what's the surprise?" I ask.

"You'll see when we get home."

"Oh, are we going back to your house? I could have driven over," I said.

"No, it's fine," he says, opening the car door for me.

When we get to his house, he makes me put a blindfold on.

"You're kidding me, right?"

"Nope." He smiles as he ties it too tightly around my eyes.

"Ow," I complain.

"Sorry." I hear his car door shut a few seconds later before mine eventually opens. He leads me out of the car and directs me up his walkway. I suddenly trip and feel myself fall into the bushes on the side of his house.

"Oh, crap. Sorry," he says, quickly pulling me out of the bushes. I take off the blindfold in frustration.

"Sorry," he says still holding my arm. I try to be mad but I can't help but laugh. He laughs as well and pulls a twig out of my hair.

"So much for trying to be cute," he says, shaking his head as he fumbles with the doorknob.

"It's okay," I say. "It was a cute attempt."

He flashes his smile at me and I feel a pull in my stomach.

When we get inside, I'm overwhelmed by the smell of raw onions.

"Ew," I say. "What's that?"

"Ta-da," he says.

I see he's displayed a raw turkey, onions and other vegetables, stuffing mix, and gravy on the counter.

"What's all this?" I ask.

"This is a turkey dinner you and I are going to make."

"I don't know if you read my blog last night, but I don't do well with cooking."

"I did read your blog, which is why I wanted us to do this. You see, I happen to be a gourmet chef."

"Really?" I say doubtfully.

"No, not really," he says. "But I know my way around the kitchen, if you know what I mean." He deepens his voice and winks. I try not to smile, but I can't help myself.

"I don't want to ruin all of this," I say pointing to the display.

"I told you I'll be there to help you," he says, putting his arms on my shoulders. "Okay." He grabs two aprons out of the closet and throws one at me.

"You really wear an apron when you're cooking?" I ask.

"Yeah, why not?" he says.

"Just wondering." I smile while tying my apron. I look up and burst into laughter when I realize Chris is wearing one of a woman in a bikini and it says "kiss the cook."

"What?" he says, pretending as if he doesn't notice.

I shake my head as I look over at a picture of Chris with his parents.

"Wow, your dad lost a lot of weight. He looks great," I say.

I watch as he oddly stiffens. "Ugh, yea," he says, looking down as he ties his apron.

I sense some discomfort, but then I remember what a tough relationship he had with his dad. They always butted heads when we were teenagers. I was actually over at his house once when his dad had asked him if he bothered to fill out any college application forms, which he hadn't, and the two of them had a big blow out. I can't say I blame his dad; he wanted Chris to be more motivated. The same way I did.

"So where are your parents today?"

"They left for Boston to visit my grandparents," he says, leaning over the sink and looking out the window.

"And what type of grandson are you that you couldn't go too?" I ask.

"I wasn't invited," he says, looking down into the sink and running the water. "They're picking my grandparents up and going on some cruise for the week."

"Oh, I see," I say, thinking about some alternate motive he might have. "So what's all this for?"

"I told you, we're going to cook," he says.

"I figured that." I roll my eyes at him. "But who's going to eat it all?"

"We will. Hope you're hungry."

I give a laugh that turns into a snort.

"Did you just snort?" he asks me.

"No," I say.

"Yes you did," he says, pointing a spatula at me. "I never knew you were a snorter."

"I do not snort," I tell him.

"You do, though." He starts poking me in the stomach with the spatula.

"Stop!" I snort again while laughing. "Damn you."

"Is that your real laugh?" he asks.

"No," I say.

He pokes me again with the spatula as I try to not laugh, and I wind up snorting again. Chris seems amused by this and continues poking. Finally I get him to stop.

"I can't believe that's your real laugh," he says.

"Shut up," I say.

"No." He hesitates for a second. "I mean, I can't believe that I never heard your real laugh."

I start to realize he's right. Anytime Chris has tried to get me to laugh, I've been angry or stressed and distracted. The way I've been my whole life.

"I can't believe it either," I say to him.

"Well, we need to get you laughing more like that because it's the cutest thing I've ever heard." He pokes me again.

"Stop it—really," I say to him, smiling.

"Okay. Let's see how far you'll go to learn how to cook."

"What do you mean?" I ask him.

"Well, the first step to making a turkey is cleaning out the giblets."

"Meaning? What are giblets?"

"They're the insides of the turkey."

"Ew," I say, horrified. "They leave those in there?"

"Yeah, just to mess with people," he tells me. "So are you willing to go the distance?"

I hesitate for a second. Then I think in my head, one, this is a part of cooking, and two, I need to learn to say yes even if it's to something like this. I walk over to the counter where Chris has laid out some rubber gloves. I slap a pair on like I'm just about to go into surgery.

"Give me the turkey," I say.

Within twenty seconds, I'm literally crying. "Ew, what is this? Oh my God!"

"You can do it," Chris encourages.

"It's so squishy." I can't help but make a face. I have no idea what I'm touching, but it is not pleasant at all.

"Stop feeling around in there and just pull it out," Chris laughs.

"I can't," I say.

"Finish him!" he jokes.

I finally pull them out and nearly lose my breakfast when I see what they actually are.

"You're fine," he says rubbing my back. "You did great."

"Thanks," I say, wiping my forearm on my forehead.

"Congratulations, it's a boy," he laughs. I push him with the hand I just removed the glove from.

"You're such a jerk."

"Hey, can you grab me a mixing bowl? They're up in that cabinet," he points.

"You mean this one?" I pull out a ceramic bowl that Chris must've made in kindergarten. It's completely uneven and says "I Love Mommy" on it. "This is seriously the cutest thing I've ever seen."

"All right enough," he says, taking it and putting it back.

"What other incriminating stuff do you think I'll find?" I say, teasing him as he chases me around the kitchen. I make my way towards the refrigerator. Sure enough, there is a magnetic strip of all of Chris's elementary school pictures. "So cute that they still have these here," I say, picking one up and looking at it. Just as I do, I notice a note fall onto the kitchen floor. I pick up a prescription note and read the border on it.

"St. Francis Hospital?"

"Okay," he says taking the picture away, but unaware of the note in my hand.

"Chris, what is this?" he looks over my shoulder and then I see him stiffen once again.

"That's for my dad," he finally says.

"What's going on with your dad?"

He pulls on his neck. "He's battling a brain tumor."

"What?" I ask, completely shocked. "Chris, why didn't you tell me?" I have to admit I'm hurt he kept something like this from me.

"It's just that I've talked about it for four years now, it's all I talk about, and I just wanted to have something in life that didn't involve me talking about it."

I try not to take offense to it, but it still stings a little. I'm obviously not important enough to talk to about something as big as this, but then again, I'm the one saying let's just be friends. I'm the one that put that boundary up. Right?

"Are your parents really on a cruise right now?" I ask.

He looks down and shakes his head. "They're at a hospital up in Boston. They wanted a couple of experts there to examine him. I wanted to go, but my grandparents are up there too, and my mom didn't want all of us to overwhelm him."

"Chris, I'm so sorry," I say, hugging him. He pulls away.

"It's fine," he says, looking at the ground. "I know he'll be fine."

"We don't have to talk about it any further," I tell him.

"Great, then let's gets started," he says, trying to go back to being his perky self.

Chapter Fifteen

Five hours later, I'm wiped out. Chris and I have baked a turkey with stuffing and several other dishes. I peeled, boiled, and mashed potatoes, shucked and boiled corn, made gravy from scratch, and baked a pumpkin pie. He was a good teacher—extremely patient. I would watch him slice an onion, and then I would mimic his actions, a much better teaching method than my mom's. Now I'm hot and sweaty, with flour on my face. I fall onto his leather couch when he finally gives me a break. Thank God I didn't have on my list to learn to run long distances. Chris would've had me running a marathon without any training.

"Well, wouldn't you know it, you had it in you," he says, rubbing his hands on a dishtowel and tossing it onto my face.

"Yeah, you're quite the pain in the ass," I tell him, removing the dishtowel to wipe my hands.

"Hey, you did it, right?"

"Yeah, it looks like I did." I smile, looking at the turkey and everything else displayed on the kitchen table. "Now who's going to eat it?" I ask.

"Well—" He takes a look at his watch. "You have approximately thirty minutes before I take you somewhere where you'll find out."

"Huh?" I ask, pulling myself off the couch. "I'm disgusting looking," I tell him. "I need to shower."

"Well, you can use my bathroom then," he suggests.

I hesitate for a second. I hate using other people's showers. I don't have my own hair conditioner that keeps my hair from frizzing, and boy's body wash I feel makes me smell like, well, them. It's either that or I smell like a turkey, so I decide to shower. Thankfully, Chris warned me to be prepared for various activities, so I also packed a royal blue sundress with heels I wore to my company's 4th of July picnic. I grab my bag out of his car and head upstairs to shower.

Forty-five minutes later, I realize we're at the local park. It looks like there's some sort of event going on.

"Annual Boys and Girls Club Dinner," I read out loud on a banner that's streamed across the road between two telephone poles.

"And you just cooked for it," he says.

"Me?" I ask.

"Yeah, so now not only have you learned to cook, but you're donating your hard work to charity." He says, "Something you might have mentioned on your list."

"Huh," I say. "I can't believe you thought to help me out like that."

"It was no big deal. I work this every year, meaning it's my second time," he says. "It's actually a lot of fun. The kids are really nice and appreciative."

"How old are they?" Old enough, I hope, to know if I've somehow poisoned them, and to be able to get to a hospital immediately.

"They're in middle school. Most of them are my students."

"So what is the Boys and Girls Club?" I ask.

"It's kind of like a summer camp. We do everything from educational programs to athletics. A lot of these kids' parents work. It's a great place for them to go in the summer and be active. If they didn't have it, a lot of them would be with a babysitter who'd sit them in front of a TV all day."

"It sounds great," I say honestly. "I wish I'd had something like that. Would've been better than staying with that crazy old bat Mrs. Mildred next door, who made me watch marathons of the *Golden Girls*."

As soon as we get out of the car, the kids run up to Chris.

"Mr. Matthews," they all yell.

"Hey." He smiles.

"I hit my first home run," one of the kids tells him.

"Just now?" he asks him enthusiastically.

"Yup." He smiles.

"All right! Nice job, man," he says, tipping the brim of his hat. "See what happens when you keep your head down like I told you?"

"Will you come play with us?" one of the other kids asks. He's dressed in full-on baseball gear with the pants and a shirt from, I'm assuming, last year, and punching his fist into his glove, eager to get back out there and play.

"I will, but we gotta bring all this food over to that picnic table first. If you all help, the quicker I can join you," he says.

All of them cheer. "Everyone, this is Jill. She cooked all of this awesome food for you," he says.

"Is she your girrrrl-friennd?" one boy says in a mocking tone.

"She's just a friend," he says, looking slightly embarrassed.

"Mr. Matthews and Jill sitting in a tree k-i-s-s-i-n-g," they all start to chant.

"All right, enough, enough," he breaks in, handing a filled piece of Tupperware to each kid.

"You certainly have a way with kids," I say, smiling, as we walk towards the picnic table and the rest of the volunteers.

"Well, I am one myself," he jokes.

"That's true." I smile.

"Jill, do you want to play with us, too?" a little girl with blonde braided pigtails asks when she approaches me.

"I'd love to, but I don't have a glove," I say, thinking about the sundress and heels I'm wearing.

"I've got one for you." She smiles and runs over to a plastic Rubbermaid box and pulls one out.

"Great," I say, trying to sound enthusiastic.

"You don't have to you if you don't want to," Chris tells me.

I'm not very familiar with baseball, but I also don't want to be a stick in the mud.

"Oh, it's on," I say.

"Yeah," the little girl cries. "You can be on our team. It's boys versus girls."

"All right, let's do this," I say and high-five her. When she runs away I stand up and give Chris a terrified look.

"You'll be fine," he smiles.

"I wish I'd known—I wouldn't have worn a dress," I say, nudging him.

"Well, I didn't know we were going to play baseball," he tells me. "You think you can manage?"

"I'll be fine," I tell him. "So they didn't play baseball last year?"

"Nope, last year we played soccer."

I can't help but roll my eyes. Boys just don't get it sometimes.

"Okay," I say to the girls as we huddle. It's me, one other volunteer who looks likes she's in her late teens, and a bunch of twelve-years-olds. "Does anyone have any advice for me?" I ask. I'm definitely at a disadvantage in a dress. Everyone else is in gym clothes.

"I think you should just tell Chris you like him," one girl says.

"I mean about how to play the game," I say, trying not to blush. Children have no filters; they say exactly what's on their minds. So how obvious must I be? I can't help but think.

"Oh. Well, just stand in the outfield, and if the ball comes to you, chase it, and we'll tell you where to throw it," one of the girls tells me.

"Okay, sounds good," I say. We clap our hands together and run out to the center of the outfield. Well, everyone else runs. I hobble and soon realize it's probably just best to take my shoes off. I toss them over to the foul line. The glove is too small for my hand and I desperately try to shove my fingers into it. *There goes that manicure,* I think.

Sure enough, the first hit goes flying into the air right towards me. I watch it as it's coming, coming, then I lose it in the sun and suddenly I feel a hard thud. Before I know it, my head is slamming into the ground.

"Ow," the crowd says collectively. I force myself to get up, and I quickly throw the ball—not very well—to the second baseman.

Once the ball is out of my hands, I feel the top of my head throb. I put my hand over it and can already feel the bump starting to swell. I don't know what's bruised more, my head or my ego.

"Are you okay?" Chris runs towards me once the play's done.

"I'm fine," I tell him, waving him back.

"Guys, easier on her, okay?" he tells them.

"I can take it," I yell back with my hands on my hips.

I try not to stress over the grass stain I now have on my dress. Instead, I hit my glove and my fist together—the universal sign for "let's go."

Fortunately nothing else comes my way for the rest of the inning, and we're called in to bat.

"Are you sure you're okay?" one of the women asks. "I'm a nurse and you look like you got nailed pretty bad."

"I'm sure I'm fine," I tell her, "but thanks."

"Thought I'd give you some tips on how to hit." Chris turns up behind me.

"Don't you have to be out there warming up?" I ask him.

"I'll be fine," he says. "I don't want you to embarrass yourself again," he adds teasingly.

I give him a mean look.

"Okay," he says. "First, you're going to hold the bat like this." He stacks his fists on top of each other on the lower part of the bat. Then he juts his elbows out, indicating to me how far apart they are. I note he has the bat about an inch and a half above his shoulders. I mimic his position with the second bat he hands me.

"Good," he says. "Now, you'll swing like this. Lead with your wrists and just follow through …"

Once again, I mimic him, but I guess he isn't far enough away from me.

I hear a grunt as he drops his bat and grabs for his shoulder, falling to his knees.

"Oh, I'm sorry," I say, putting my hand over my mouth and dropping the bat. "Are you okay?"

I see his eyes are a little glassy, but he takes a deep breath.

"Nice, I think you'll be fine," he says, trying to shake it off. Then he gets up, pats me on the shoulder, and runs onto the field.

After a few batters have been up, I get called. I pull my hair back and shove a dirty helmet over my head.

The girls cheer for me as the boys yell at Chris to strike me out.

Chris points towards his eyes to indicate he's watching me.

"Really intimidating," I yell to him. I kick my feet on the dirt like a bull ready to charge.

In slow motion, the ball heads my way. I swing as hard as I can and miss it completely.

"Keep your head down and watch the ball," he says.

"If one more person tells me to keep my head down …" That was all I heard golfing with my dad.

Another pitch comes my way, and this time I'm too ahead of the ball.

"I'm not going to say it," he tells me.

"All right already," I say in frustration.

The third pitch comes down the line, and this time I'm determined. I watch the ball leave Chris's hand and it makes its way towards me. At the last second I shut my eyes and hear a ping. I've made contact with the ball. I immediately drop the bat and start to run. It isn't until I make it to first, though, that I realize I've hit the ball directly into Chris's stomach and he's keeled over on the pitcher's mound. Everyone's running towards him.

"Oh my gosh, are you okay?" I say to him.

"Fine." I can barely hear him as the wind was obviously completely knocked out of him.

"I'm sorry," I say.

"Nice hit." He coughs. I can't help but laugh at this, which leaves me to snort yet again.

He looks up and smiles at me.

"Looks like we make a pretty awesome team," he tells me as we drive home. "I've never seen a more banged up couple."

"Yeah, sorry about that," I say, noting he just called us a couple.

"It's okay. It was a solid hit, which shows you did what I taught you."

"Those kids really are great," I tell him.

"Yeah, they've got a lot of spunk."

"Everyone there just seems really nice," I add. Other than that one kid, of course, who told me my hair made me look like the cowardly lion.

"Well, they all loved you, kids and parents."

"Thanks." I smile. "So how often do you work at this club?"

"Um, I don't really have a set schedule, but I try to go at least three times a week to help out."

"Well, I wouldn't mind going with you every once in a while. Next time I'll be better prepared," I say, realizing that I'll never be able to wear this dress again.

"Absolutely." He smiles.

Before I realize it, we're pulling into my driveway. I forgot this park was only a few blocks away from my house.

"So do you want to come inside?" I ask.

I see him look at his watch. "I actually have to get going," he says without further explanation. It frustrates me that he doesn't really seem to open up with me. Then again, it's probably involving his dad, which he already made clear he doesn't want to talk about. "Thanks again for everything," he tells me.

"Thank you," I say. "If it weren't for you, I wouldn't have anything crossed off my list."

"It's nothing." He smiles modestly.

"It is, though. It really means a lot to me. I'm sure you have better things to do."

"Well, I enjoy spending time with you." He starts to lean towards me. I know what's going to happen, but for some reason I'm not stopping it. Once our lips press together, I feel a spark I haven't felt—even with Brady— since we dated years ago. Then it hits me: Brady, losing my job, the whole reason I'm back here. What am I doing? I just got out of a relationship. It's only been two weeks, and I'm making out with Chris? I'm not ready for this. And besides, I have to learn to live without a boyfriend. I quickly pull away and run out of the car into my house without looking back.

"Honey, come downstairs. We decided to watch *Titanic*."

"Do we really have to?" I say. It's been a long day, but I'm still freaked out about what just happened with Chris. I haven't bothered to tell Liz because she saw this coming and tried to warn me. I've spent the last few hours mentally debating how I'm going to handle this. I do enjoy Chris's company, but I just can't put my heart out there again. I still need to heal. And to learn to live without a guy. And to get a job, my head keeps spinning.

"It's classic movie night," my mom calls up to me, bringing me back to the present. "Oh, we can watch *An Affair to Remember* or *Sleepless in Seattle*? I have a huge collection."

My mom has been doing this classic movie thing for years, but I was always in my room studying. I realize I've never, in fact, seen any of the movies in her classics collection.

"How about *Breakfast at Tiffany's*?" I finally call back. No use feeling sorry for myself.

At the thirty-minute mark, my dad falls asleep and my mom's already crying. Like mother, like daughter, I think. It's not even sad. Well, maybe the fact that the heroine's living on her own and depending on other people for money is kind of sad, but then again, so is living at home.

As the movie goes on, I realize the heroine is looking to escape her former life. I suddenly realize that's what I want to do. I don't really want to go back to being an overworked, overtired lawyer with no real connections to anyone. I love the way I've been living lately—well, except for the living-at-home part—and I want a life and job that I'm equally happy with.

The question is, what kind of life and job are those?

By the end of the movie, wherein our heroine, Holly Golightly, gives up her plan to marry a millionaire to be with the not-so-average Joe, I know what I have to do.

As soon as the credits roll, I stand up to grab my cell phone.

"Look at you, you aren't even crying," my mom says as she dabs her eyes.

"Not anymore," I say as I walk out of the room.

When I get upstairs, I have Chris's number dialed.

"Hey, Chris," I say, my heart skipping a beat.

"Hey, great to hear from you," he says. "Look, about this afternoon, I'm sorry—"

I cut him off. "You mind if I kidnap you?"

"Kidnap me?"

"Yeah. I have a surprise for you, too," I tell him.

"Of course," he says.

"Can you take off for a few days?"

Chapter Sixteen

The next day I borrow my parents' car and pick him up.

There's silence for a while. I'm not sure what to say so I try to just pretend nothing's happened.

Chris decides to take a stab at conversation. "Jill, I want to apologize for yesterday. You told me you've been through a lot, and I get that. It's just that I guess with all the time we've been spending together, I don't know, I guess old feelings I thought were gone came back again."

"Don't apologize, I'm sorry. You've been nothing but great and you make me really happy. I'm not sure why I insisted on fighting it." I know I said I need to learn to live without a guy, but I've also recognized the fact that I need to stop shutting the world out. I shouldn't settle for just any boyfriend, but I also shouldn't ignore an opportunity for someone great to be there for me. Chris is a good guy and I really do like him. It would be stupid for me to run from that.

I go for his hand and he reciprocates with a smile and interlaces his fingers with mine.

About an hour and half later, I still haven't told him where we're going. Finally the sign for Martha's Vineyard comes up.

He looks at me and smiles. "Become a wine connoisseur, huh?" he asks.

"Yeah," I say. "I thought I could cross it off my list, but also kind of thank you for everything."

"Have you ever done this before?" he asks.

"Nope, but I always wanted to."

"Me neither. I've always been more of a beer drinker."

"Well, maybe for once I can teach you a thing or two."

"What, about drinking wine?"

"Yeah, I have some knowledge, though I'm not by any means an expert. Which puts me ahead of you, for once."

He laughs at this as we pull up to the ferry.

"So why would any eighteen-year-old put this on her list of things? Not that this isn't cool," he saves himself, "but at eighteen, you know nothing about wine. I remember sneaking your parents' schnapps with you. We thought we were so cool just because it was alcohol."

"I know, it's kind of weird," I admit. "The truth is my dad is in sales and one night over dinner he was telling my mother and I how he landed this huge deal all because when he took the clients to dinner he understood wines. Anyway, he told me that it really makes a big difference when it comes to making an impression on clients. I know very little, like red wines are good with meats and dark sauces, while white wine is better with fish and lighter dishes."

"It's a good start," Chris agrees. "More than most people would know."

"Anyway, I wanted to have a better understanding, but once I got my job, they really buried me behind my desk. I never really had any clients, especially ones that I would need to impress by my wine knowledge, and once again, just another thing I never got around to."

"Well, I'm glad we are here now," he smiles.

"Me too," I smile back. "I really appreciate you doing this with me."

"Anytime," he says, reaching for my hand. I feel my face get hot as I start to blush.

When we're on land, I drop the bomb. "So I booked us into a nice bed and breakfast." I try to gauge his reaction. "Was that the right thing to do? I put us in a room with separate beds, just in case."

He smiles and brings me in for a kiss. "This is great," he reassures me. I feel my stomach drop in excitement.

When we enter the blue Victorian house, I suddenly fall in love. Everything about it is so homey, I feel like I'm visiting a relative's home rather than a hotel. The place is full of charming antiques and all the guests look as if they're there for a fun gathering.

"Check out the garden," I say, looking out the window of our bedroom once we're checked in. There's a koi pond and a little bridge that goes over it and benches around it.

"This is really nice," he says, putting him arms around me. I can't help from stiffen.

"So I made dinner reservations." I pull away slightly and he gives me a look.

"Sorry, I'm just getting used to all of this," I say, crossing my arms.

"It's okay, we'll just take things slow."

"Thanks," I say.

It's such a nice summer night, we decide to walk to town. Everything is so quaint. It's a nice change from the crazy city life. And from the suburbs with their strip malls.

I lead us to a French restaurant that looks like it's been here for over a hundred years.

"Nice," he says.

"Thanks. I got a few recommendations." I leave out the fact I was up all night researching restaurants, wine tours, and bed and breakfasts.

We take our seat and the maître'd hands us menus.

"So are you going to get the foie gras?" he asks me in a French accent.

"What's that?"

"Duck liver, really big in France."

"No thanks," I say.

"Well, if you want to travel the world, you have to learn to try new foods," he tells me.

"How about you order it and I'll try some."

"No thanks, I hate foie gras," he says.

"You're such a jerk sometimes." I hit him playfully.

"Well, I definitely say a bottle of wine to kick it off," he says.

"Shall I choose?" I say, pulling the wine list from him. I kind of like that he doesn't know anything about wine.

"Shall I start you off with something to drink?" the waitress asks us.

"Yes," I say. "We'd like a bottle of Chablis," I say.

"Very well," the woman says, taking the menu and walking away.

Chris starts to laugh.

"What?"

"It's pronounced sha-blee," he says.

"What did I say?" I ask stubbornly.

"Cha-Bliss."

"Oh, what do you know," I say, waving my hand at him.

A few minutes later the waitress comes back with the wine. "Your Chablis," she says the same way that Chris corrected me with. I purse my lips and squint at him. I take a sip and make a face.

"Not to be rude, but I think this has gone bad," I say.

"Allow me," Chris says. The waitress pours him some. I watch as he raises his glass to his nose to smell, then holds it out and swirls the wine around the glass. Then he gives it a taste. "It's good," he says to her. "It just needs to breathe," he then tells me.

"I thought you knew nothing about wine," I say to him, a little put out.

"Well, I may know a little. I mean, what else do you do in France when you live there for a summer?"

As the night goes on, we get a bit tipsy, but we have a blast—we don't stop laughing.

"Okay, so this couple over here," he says to me after we've already done a couple rounds of "What's Their Story?"

I take a sip of wine and look over.

"I think, she's an escort and he's her client," he whispers. We both start laughing.

"Why do you think that?"

He shrugs. "Well, we're in a quaint little town, and she's dressed in a black spandex dress and stilettos. Also, she doesn't seem interested in him and he's drinking like a fish."

"Wow," I say. "Maybe it's like *Pretty Woman* though, she just wants to shop but no one will let her. The stuck-up town of Martha's Vineyard will not let the woman shop!"

We both start laughing again—and barely stop until hours later.

After we stumble back to the house, I grab onto the door handle and motion to Chris to be quiet by holding my index finger over my lips and making a very loud shushing noise. We both start to giggle like we're fifteen again, sneaking into one of our houses after everyone's asleep. All goes according to plan until I slip on my heel and I fall up the stairs. Luckily, Chris catches me, but we burst into fits of laughter. When we hear something coming from one of the rooms, we quickly race into our room and shut the door.

"That was a close one," Chris says.

I'm not even thinking about my problems. All I can think about is Chris. I walked up to him, wrap my arms around him, and kiss him, rather hungrily, actually.

"Ow," he says, "my tooth."

"Sorry," I say, still laughing. I try to kiss him again, but he says, "Jill, you told me you want to take it slow, and I want to respect that. You doing that—as much as I like it—doesn't help." He looks me up and down.

"I don't care anymore," I say, kissing him.

He pulls away. "But you do," he says, "and I can't take advantage."

"I understand," I say, feeling slightly embarrassed. "How about we just make out like we used to do at high school parties?"

He thinks for a second. "I'm okay with that." He smiles.

Chapter Seventeen

I wake up to the sound of birds chirping. For most people, this would be pure bliss. The reason they would come to a place like Martha's Vineyard—to get away from the city and be one with nature. But I have a major hangover, and I just want to kill those damn things.

"Make them stop," Chris says next to me, rubbing his eyes. Both of us are still in our clothes from last night and on top of the covers. We must have fallen asleep mid-make out.

"Coffee," is all I can manage.

We slowly pull ourselves out of bed and get ourselves showered (separately). When we make our way downstairs to the dining room, an older couple in their sixties is making breakfast. The smell of bacon is intoxicating and the amount of it just as much so.

Chris and I make a beeline for the coffee, which is on a sideboard, then sit down at the table with our plate and reach for the bacon with some eggs on the side. Compared to the other couples, we look the most disheveled and hungover. By the looks we're getting, you'd think they were about to stage an intervention.

"Y'all enjoying your time here?" the woman of the house asks. She's a cheery woman with oversized seventies glasses and a blond perm.

"Yes, thank you," Chris says, sipping some orange juice.

"So what's on the agenda today?" she presses. Does she not know when you're hungover no one should talk to you until you've had your coffee?

"I figured we would go to town, rent bikes for the day, and go to the beach," I say.

"Oh that is such a lovely idea." She smiles. "Well, enjoy your day."

"We will," I smile.

After the bacon, coffee, and two aspirins have settled, we decide to face the bright, sunny day.

"I can't remember the last time I was this hungover," Chris says, digging into his pocket for his sunglasses once we're outside. "It's like being in high school again."

"I know," I say, "with a bigger allowance."

"So how's everything going with your parents?" Chris asks me. "You know, the whole transition of living at home."

I take a deep breath. "It's different," I laugh. "My mom and I have a tendency to really butt heads a lot. She has a hard time staying out of my business."

"All parents are like that," he says.

"I remember you used to have it out with your dad," I recall. "Are you two better now or worse since you're still living with them?"

He doesn't say anything for a few moments, and I'm worried that I hit a nerve of some sort. "We've gotten along much better now," he says, without further elaboration.

"Well, I hope it picks up between my mom and me, because right now it seems as if it would take some sort of miracle."

"Whatever you do, just don't take them for granted. Both your parents, despite how much you fight, they really do care about you."

"I know, Mr. Rogers," I laugh.

"I know it's lame," he smiles a bit while kicking a rock on the road, "but eventually you'll come to the realization that your parents aren't always going to be around forever, and you should make sure you appreciate the time you have with them."

"That was pretty deep," I tell him.

"Yeah, well," he says shoving his fists into his pockets.

"Have you become a full-fledged momma's boy now?" I laugh.

"No, it's just I learned to recognize what to be grateful for, you know?"

I nod my head. "I guess you're right. I guess it wouldn't kill me to have some patience with my mom."

At the bike shop, Chris goes for more of a mountain bike while I go for the big comfy seat with a basket in front.

"Okay, Grandma," Chris says laughing.

"We'll see who's laughing when your butt goes numb," I retort. "Besides, the basket is for the wine we buy."

"And the bell?" he asks, ringing it.

"To warn people there's a drunk girl on a bike," I say without hesitation.

After Chris settles with the owner, we take our bikes and make our way towards the beach. I get lost in how beautiful the countryside is.

"Is this it?" Chris points to the upcoming sign.

"Yup," I call out and we both follow the path. "This is so beautiful— the dunes and the ocean."

"When's the last time you went to the beach?" he asks, getting off of his bike.

"Probably when I was eight years old," I say, thinking back. My family didn't really do vacations all that much. Everything always revolved around work.

"Wow, really?" he asks, surprised. "What about the senior trip?"

"I didn't go, remember? I had my Columbia interview that first day of the trip."

"Would you have gone if you hadn't?"

I look down. "At that time, probably not," I say.

He puts his arms around me. "Well, at least we're here now." I can smell his cologne as he rests his head on my shoulder. After a few seconds, he grabs the towels out of my basket and we set ourselves up near the lifeguard stand. The beach is pretty packed, but it still seems peaceful. No one's blasting their stereos or yelling; everyone's just enjoying their own quiet time.

Chris immediately settles down onto one of the towels and takes off his shirt. I can't get over what great shape he's in. I hesitate for a second, then I go sit on the towel next to him.

"Are you going to take your cover-up off?" he asks as he rubs sunscreen on his shoulders.

"No, I think I'm good," I say.

"Come on, really? What do you have to be afraid of?"

Finally I give in and lift my oversized dress over my head.

"Ow, ow," he yells.

"Stop it!" I hit him, worried he's going to attract attention.

"You look great. What do you have to be afraid of?" he asks.

I shrug.

"You really need to build up your confidence. That's what all of this is about, remember?"

"I know," I say.

"You should go do a strut," he says.

"Excuse me?" I ask him, laughing.

"A strut. Get up and walk down to feel the water. Hang out for about a minute and then walk back. You'll be amazed by how many guys check you out."

"What are you, my pimp now?" I laugh.

"Swear to God, it will make your day."

I take a deep breath. "I'm not going to strut," I say, "I'm just going to feel the water."

"Whatever you say," he says, putting his sunglasses back on. He still has a smear of sunscreen on his cheek so I go over and wipe it off of him. I end the wipe with a little slap. "That's for trying to pimp me out," I say, and I walk away with a little attitude.

I have to admit, it's fun. The closer I get to water, though, the more exposed I feel, I look down at myself in nothing but a tiny yellow bikini that Liz made me buy. I stand up a little straighter to elongate my torso. It isn't until I reach the water that I start to notice those around me. I feel like people are looking, but Chris could have just put that thought in my head. For all I know, I'm hanging out of my top. I make a quick check just to be sure. Nope.

I think he's right. I do see guys looking at me. I've never noticed that before. Of course, I haven't been strutting around in bikinis. It's a fun rush, but I start to get embarrassed so I quickly head back to my towel. At which point, I look up and notice the lifeguard's looking too! Huh. When I get to the towel, I immediately sit back down. I feel guilty, as if I just did something wrong.

"See what I mean?" he says.

"I don't know what you're talking about," I say, putting on my sunglasses and lying down.

"Seriously, you won't admit you saw guys checking you out?"

"There were some glances, but I wouldn't call it 'checking out.'"

"What would you call it then?" He sits up.

"I don't know. It's like what I do when other girls walk by. I look at them and think, oh, I like her shoes."

"You think guys are looking at your shoes?" he asks. "We aren't in the West Village here."

"I doubt they're thinking just that, but maybe they see this bikini and think, I'd like that for my girlfriend."

"Yeah, that's what we're all thinking," he says sarcastically. "Though we do say that when we get caught."

"So what are you men thinking about then?" I ask.

"Do you really want to know?" he asks.

"Probably not," I say, lying back down.

After a nice morning at the beach, we take our bikes and head back to the B&B to change for a wine tour.

"So are you having fun?" I ask as I apply my makeup in the mirror. He just walked into the bathroom.

"I'm having a great time," he says, pulling a towel off of the shelf.

"I'm glad," I say. "Because I was thinking—" Suddenly my mind goes blank as Chris proceeds to strip down.

"Because you were thinking what?" he asks, turning on the shower.

"Uh, I, uh, I forget," I say.

He shrugs and steps into the shower, pulling the curtain closed.

"Oh my God," I whisper to myself in the mirror.

When we do leave for the wine tasting, my mind is completely elsewhere. Why did I ever break up with Chris? He's gorgeous, funny, smart, and encouraging. What was wrong with me?

"Are you okay?" he asks when we are on the tour.

"Yeah, I'm fine." I smile as we walk through the tour of grapevines. All the history and scenery is interesting and beautiful, but I'm ready for the tastings. I'm starving since I haven't eaten since breakfast.

Finally, it's time. We take a seat across from each other and stare at our plates. The room is all stone with a wooden ceiling and beams. An old rustic-looking chandelier is hanging above us. All we see, though, is the food. There are pieces of bread on each plate with spreads smeared on them.

The man proceeds to read off which wine to drink with which piece. The first one is the one with a dark spread. I pick it up to smell it and make a face. Our tour guide has a French accent and I can't understand a word he's saying. I try to follow along and drink when everyone drinks, but I can't bring myself to eat whatever's on top of this.

"What is this?" I whisper to Chris.

"Try it," he says, taking a bite.

I take one more whiff and take a small bite because I'm so hungry. I almost throw up in my mouth. I desperately try to find a napkin, but they gave us cloth napkins that I don't want to spit food into. I try to very casually get up with the aim of going to the bathroom. My mouth is full so I can't exactly ask directions, so I just have to guess. Chris gives me a strange look as I casually make my way out into the hall. This place is like a damn castle with a hundred rooms and everything looks like it could be a bathroom door. After wandering the old hallways, with the floorboards creaking at every step, I finally run up to one of the windows, open it, and spit out whatever's in my mouth.

"Wow, that was awful," I say, flicking my tongue against my teeth to get the taste out. I turn around to see a maid standing behind me. She's looking at me like she's just caught me defiling the place. Not knowing what else to do, I apologize and nod my head, trying to casually walk past her as if I haven't just found myself in one of the most humiliating situations of my life.

When I get back, most of the tastings have already taken place.

"Where did you go?" Chris whispered.

"What did I eat?" I ask him.

"Goose liver pâté, you didn't hear the tour guide?"

"Ew, no," I say making a face. "How could you let me eat that?"

"I didn't know your palette was limited to pasta and burgers," he tells me.

"Oh, shut up," I tell him. I take a sip of my wine to get rid of the taste in my mouth.

After that experience, I stick with wine for the rest of the tasting.

"So you want to get something to eat?" Chris asks as we jump back on our bikes.

"Absolutely. I'm so hungry," I tell him.

We settle on a little pizza place. It's the first food place we come up to. Chris treats me to a large slice and we split a glass of lemonade. The owner's twelve-year-old daughter has made it, so of course we can't say no.

When we get back to the picnic tables in front of the place, Chris excuses himself to go the bathroom. I notice him pull his cell phone out again. Who does he keep calling? I'm sitting and enjoying my surroundings when I hear someone behind me.

"Jill?" I hear my name and turn around with my straw still in my mouth.

"Bra-Brady?"

Chapter Eighteen

Then it registers. Oh my God, it's Brady and he's with the twenty-year-old tart! He took her for a weekend in Martha's Vineyard? We always said we were going to come here together ...

"Um, hi," I say, not really sure what else to do except try to hide my devastation.

"Wow, you look great," he says. (Thanks, makeover!) "What are you doing here?" he asks, rather accusingly. What did he think? I followed him or something?

"Well, I always wanted to come here," I say in a tone aimed at reminding him of our talks about coming together.

"Listen," he says, "about everything that's happened—"

"Brady, to be completely honest, I'm over it and I really don't want anything ruining my weekend, okay?" Wow, I think. That was the most courageous thing I've done since the breakup.

"Right, I understand," he says.

"If you're alone here, you're more than welcome to join us for dinner," Jenine, the tart says. Is she crazy?

"We'd love to join you," Chris reappears and puts his arm around me. I'm completely speechless. I'm glad he came to rescue me, but what the hell is he saying yes for?

"Um, great. Then it's settled. We'll do dinner tonight at eight," Brady says, a little uneasily.

"Chris," he says, putting his hand out. Wait for it …

"Brady," he says back, shaking his hand. Suddenly I see it register with Chris.

I try desperately to figure out a way to cancel this awful dinner, but I can't seem to come up with an excuse. Suddenly, my mind has turned to mush.

"Well, I'll let you guys enjoy your lunch, and we can meet at that Le Halles for dinner tonight," Brady says.

"Bye, guys," Jenine says.

"Yeah, bye," I manage with a wave.

When I turn back to Chris, my mouth is so wide it could hit the floor.

"Be cool until he's out of sight before you kill me," he says, taking a sip of lemonade.

"Are you kidding me right now? What's wrong with you?"

"I didn't know who he was," he defends himself.

"Well, if I have to hit you over the head just to be able to cancel this date and take you to the hospital, don't think I won't."

"You can't cancel now. It'll look bad," he tells me.

"Who cares? You really want to sit in on this? Do you know how uncomfortable this is going to be?"

"You're going to go with all the confidence you have, and you're going to show him what a self-assured person you are and how unaffected you are by this breakup."

"We were together for six years. I'm not an ice queen, nor do I want to come off as one. I think the reason we broke up in the first place is because I was a robot."

"You're not a robot," he says, encouraging me to sit down. He softly touches my arm, but I pull away. "I know this will be tough, but trust me, I saw how you handled him when he tried to bring up the situation, and you were great. You're going to show him what he's missing and that will

123

especially hit him when the new college semester starts and this girl is nowhere to be found."

I stare at him. "You *did* know who that was beforehand, and you still said yes to dinner!"

"Okay, so maybe I did know who it was," he admits.

"You jackass." I hit him.

"Trust me. I know you hate me now, but this will be good for you."

"What, are you my therapist?" I hit him again. "What makes you think you know everything about me? I haven't seen you in ten years and suddenly you know what's best for me?" I start to walk away.

"Jill, come back. I'm sorry."

"No. I'm mad at you right now, and I need to cool off," I say.

"Please don't be mad at me. You're right. I don't know what's best for you—I was only trying to help. I know if I was in your situation, looking so hot, with somebody new on my arm, I'd absolutely want to show my ex what he missed out on."

I try not to smile.

"You're right, I don't know you now. But I'll tell you about the girl I did know. She's sexy, confident, and fun. I just thought this would help you get over him. But you're right, I don't know the current Jill, and if you don't want to do this then we can cancel, and I'll never step on your toes like that again."

I fold my arms. Clearly he isn't doing this to torture me.

"I have to think for a little," I finally say. "I'll meet you back at the B&B."

"Where are you going?" he asks.

I throw my leg over the bike. "Shopping."

That's it. Desperate times call for desperate measures. I immediately need to book some me time. I get my hair blown out to fix the frizz of the day, and I realize I need to shop for a new dress at one of the boutique stores on the main street. Being in a state of pure panic, I pull out my phone. I need to call Liz for some emergency advice.

"Don't get drunk tonight," she warns. "You don't want to risk saying anything stupid."

"What else?" I ask, holding up random dresses next to me and then immediately vetoing them.

"Buy a sexy dress, but not too sexy. You don't want to look like you're trying too hard. You want to go for classic beauty. Something conservative but also close-fitting. Accent your boobs without hanging out of them. Think what celebrities wear to charity auctions."

I search hungrily through all the racks, like a desperate animal on the hunt.

As she talks, I visualize a great dress Reese Witherspoon wore to a breast cancer awareness dinner. (I saw a picture in *People Magazine*.)

"So like a scoop neck, tight dress, not slutty, got it," I say out loud to her. As I have her still on the phone, I am now just spinning in circles hoping that this dress is going to miraculously be here and pop out from wherever it's hiding. I let out a huff of panic when I notice the sales woman approaching me. She's a middle-aged woman who looks like she stepped out of the *Real Housewives* series. I guess my distress signals were blasting pretty strong. I then realize she is walking over to me with a white dress, very similar to the one I had in my head.

"I overheard your phone conversation and pulled this out for you," she says with a smile. I immediately hang up on Liz and give this woman the biggest hug. She's a little taken aback, considering I almost knock her over, but laughs it off and pats me on the back.

"You're a lifesaver," I say, almost on the verge of tears.

"Fitting room is open over here," she smiles, and leads me to it. While doing so, I pour out my sob story to her which continues while I'm still the dressing room. I'm half expecting to open the door and she's no longer going to be there, and I'm just a crazy person talking to myself.

I try the dress on, almost afraid to open my eyes because I need this dress to work as I am running out of time before I have to meet everyone at the restaurant. When I finally open my eyes, I let out a sigh of relief. It thankfully fits in all the right places. "Not half bad," I say to myself, while checking out my backside. I open the door, and believe it or not, the saleswoman is still standing there.

"You look amazing," she boasts.

"But not too sexy, right?" I ask hopefully.

"Just the right amount," she says. I'm hoping she means it and isn't just trying to sell me.

Suddenly my phone rings and I see it's Chris. It's the tenth time he's called to apologize to me.

"I told you, I'm not mad anymore," I tell him.

"Good," he says, relieved. "But where are you? We're going to have to leave soon."

"Can you meet me there?" I ask, looking at my watch.

"Are you planning on running away with your ex?" he asks.

I roll my eyes. "No, I'm just running late. My hair and makeup is done, I'm just buying a dress. I'm not far from the restaurant, so it doesn't make sense for me to go back to the hotel. I'll just walk to the restaurant when I'm done."

He hesitates for a few seconds. "Okay then," he says, realizing he has no choice in the matter.

I wrap up my purchases, which consist of new white peep-toe shoes, that killer dress, and a gold chain with a small circle pendant on it. I hand over my credit card and glance at my watch. It is exactly eight o'clock. I want to be late, but not too late.

The woman hands me the shoes I just picked out.

"Your ex is going to drop dead," she says. "And this Chris guy, he's a good guy," she adds.

"Thanks." I smile. She's now the hundredth person to tell me that.

She hands me a bag for my day clothes and offers to keep them behind the counter until tomorrow. I suddenly really love this town; everyone here is so thoughtful and nice.

"Knock 'em dead," she says.

"If only," I call out to her.

Chapter Nineteen

As I walk up to the restaurant, I see Brady, Jenine, and Chris are already there. I stand up straight and do my best un-obvious strut.

Both guys turn in my direction, but I realize I care only about Chris's reaction. I don't even glance at Brady until I reach them.

"Oh, hi," I say casually. Just as I'd expected, Jenine is wearing a tight black skirt that's riding way too far up and a hot pink halter that's too small for her D-cup boobs. I don't want to say she looks trashy, but she kind of does. Especially in this setting.

"You look stunning," Chris tells me.

"Thanks, honey." I smile. I just realize I overdid the "honey" and we exchange a look.

"So since we're all here, should we sit?" Jenine says, looking at Brady for approval. "Brady?" she says.

I look towards him and it's then he seems to come out of his trance. He continues to stare at me when he answers her. "Sure," he says.

We get into the restaurant, and Jenine sits down first, then Brady. Chris pulls out my chair for me. The gesture takes me by surprise because I can't remember the last time a man did that for me. Probably Chris, ten years ago.

"So how do you two know each other?" Jenine asks.

"We went to high school together," Chris says.

"We used to date back then, and when we ran into each other again, I don't know—sparks flew." I look at him.

"Yeah," Chris agrees, looking back at me. I can't tell if he's just putting on an act for them. "How about you two?" Chris asks, already knowing the story. I assume I told him everything the night I cried my heart out to him.

"We work together," Jenine says.

"Wow, you're a lawyer too? That's impressive." Now I see where he's going with this.

"Well, I'm not exactly a lawyer," she corrects him.

"Oh?" Chris presses.

"I'm Brady's secretary," she finally admits.

"Oh, okay, great," Chris says. Mission accomplished.

"So Jill, any luck with the job hunt?" Brady breaks in.

That question felt like a knife. "I've gone on a couple of interviews, but to tell you the truth, I'm sort of reevaluating my life right now," I tell him.

"Oh?" he asks. Is he deliberately mimicking Chris's tone? "Where are you living right now?"

Another knife. "I'm at home right now, but I mean, you remember how miserable I was working a hundred hours a week. I never had any fun. I didn't like being that person."

"So what will you do?" he asks as if this whole concept of me not wanting to be a lawyer anymore is absurd.

"I'm not sure. I'm in the process of figuring that out. Maybe something with kids. Chris is great with them and, I don't know, when I see how happy they are around him, it makes me want to help out and try to do some good too."

"What do you do, Chris?"

"I'm a teacher," he says.

"Oh, okay," Brady says. He's definitely imitating Chris.

"You know," Chris says, "I started off in banking, but I was miserable and I realized life is too short. My father spent his whole life working a million hours a day at a bank. I never saw him." Nice return, I think.

"Surely you lived a nice lifestyle, though," Brady persists.

"Sure, he paid for great vacations, but he was always working on them. He even lived in another country for two years. He just kept saying to me once he was on the board, he would be around more and he could concentrate on being the family man he always wanted to be."

"That makes sense," Brady says defensively. "You have to work hard to get to where you want to be."

"Yeah, but in that process he missed out on being my dad," Chris pushes back.

"Well, did he get on the board?" Brady asked.

Chris nods. "Yeah, he did. When I turned twenty-two and started working for him, he finally made the board. Then two weeks later, he was diagnosed with a brain tumor."

"Oh my gosh," Jenine interjects.

I feel my stomach drop. I know that was a lot for him to say.

"I'm sorry to hear that," Brady says.

I put my hand on his leg. He looks up at me with a half smile.

"It's fine. He's still alive, you know, fighting the fight. He'll spend the rest of his days fighting this, and all he tells me is how much he regrets his life decisions and how he should have prioritized his family."

"Wow, that's unbelievable," Jenine says, putting her hand on her chest.

"Makes you realize what's important in life, that's for sure," he says, putting his hand over mine. I can't help but blush.

Suddenly things now finally start to make sense me. I realize that he's living at home to help his family.

"So shall we order?" Brady asks uncomfortably.

"Sure." I smile, loving what an ass he's made of himself. "Some foie gras?" I joke with Chris in an effort to lighten the mood.

"Oh yes, because you did so well with it last time," he mocks.

"Well, I do need to expand my palette beyond cheeseburgers and pasta," I joke back.

"Oh my gosh, I love cheeseburgers," Jenine says.

"They're good." Chris laughs, not knowing how to respond to a random comment like that.

"Hey, it's the woman from last night," Chris elbows me.

"Who?" Jenine asks, turning around.

"We played this game the other night," I explain. "Where we guessed people's stories."

"Oh, that sounds like fun. I want to play," Jenine says.

Chris and I look at each other. It could be a bit awkward to play a game with another couple, half of which is your ex. Then again, just having dinner with them is awkward.

"Well, let's see," Chris says. "That couple there, the guy owns a winery somewhere in California and he came here to see if there were any investment opportunities. His wife is from France, and he probably met her while he was visiting on business."

"How do you know all that?" Jenine asks, wide-eyed.

"I don't," he explains. "You just make observations and create a story around them."

"Why don't we ever play this game?" Jenine asks Brady.

"Usually we're involved in our own conversation," he says in an even tone.

Clearly, Brady is now in a bad mood and he's not doing a good job of hiding it. Jenine seems to sense it, too, but doesn't seem to care all that much, as she continues to down her cocktail.

Suddenly, Chris's phone rings. "Sorry about that. Please excuse me," he says, standing up and walking away a bit—but not far enough that we can't still hear him.

"Is everything okay?" I hear him ask.

My stomach flutters with nervousness that something might have happened to his dad. The rest of the conversation is too muted to make out. I have this overwhelming sense of guilt for pulling him away from his family.

He returns to the table when he's done. "Everyone, I'm sorry to be rude, but there's been an emergency and we have to go."

"Oh, I hope everything's okay," Jenine says.

"Hopefully," he says, darting his eyes at me and gesturing for me to stand up.

"It was good seeing you again," I lie, practically knocking over my chair as we leave.

When we're just outside the door, I ask, "What's wrong?" My heart is beating uncontrollably fast.

"Nothing," he says coolly. "I had a friend call to stage an emergency exit. Isn't that what you girls do all the time on blind dates?"

I let out a sigh of relief. "Why did you do that? I thought you wanted me to face my fears and show him how great I've been without him?"

"Which you were able to do in ten minutes. We didn't need a whole dinner."

"Well, I'm glad you did that, because dinner didn't look like it was going to go well."

"Brady kind of has a stick up his ass, huh?" Chris asks.

"He kind of does, actually," I agree. I'm surprised that Chris insulting him doesn't bother me. But I really don't see us getting back together. Chris was right. In only two weeks, I've apparently become a whole different person.

"So where do you want to go eat?" I ask him. "I'm starving."

"I made reservations for eight thirty right over here," he says, pulling off to the side.

"You're slick," I tell him.

As we're settling down, I fumble with my napkin before my nerves finally take over and I bring up his dad.

"Why didn't you want to tell me about your dad?" I burst while trying not to sound so upset.

He takes a long deep breath, as if he knew this was coming. "I wasn't trying to lie to you or anything, it's just been rough the past couple of years, and you've been the one person I could just relax and be myself around without worrying about you feeling sorry for me."

"I just feel like a horrible person for never even asking about your life," I tell him.

"Hey, don't say that." He puts his hand on mine. "I just wanted to help you find yourself without all of my baggage."

I can tell he's trying to be funny, but I can't smile. I feel bad, bad for the fact that I looked down on him for living at home. I thought he was unmotivated and lazy. Meanwhile, he's the most admirable person I've ever met. He put his whole life on hold for his family.

"I'm so sorry about everything you're going through," I try to tell him.

"I appreciate that, but let's not talk about it," he says, pulling away.

"Fair enough," I agree. "Just let me say this one thing." I watch him close his menu and look at me. "I understand the fact that you didn't want to tell me about your baggage," I say with air quotes around his use of the word. "But I don't want to be lied to either."

"I understand," he says, nodding and putting his head down. "You're right, I just didn't know how to handle it, and I'm sorry."

"It's okay," I say, reaching for his hand again. He leans in to kiss me. As we pull away, I start to see him in this whole new light. I could care less about Brady.

When we walk home that night, I take his hand. He doesn't resist, just gives me a smile and interlaces our fingers. We didn't say all that much at dinner but we didn't have to. Our bodies seemed to be doing all of the talking and they continued to back at the B&B.

On the drive back home, for some reason we can't seem to do anything but smile at each other. We are both just giddy and laughing about everything.

"I don't want to go back to reality," I groan.

He laughs and runs his hand along my arm.

"It's a new reality," he explains. "You've officially emancipated yourself from your ex. It's like the first day of your new life."

"I guess you're right," I agree.

"And everyone likes the first day of something new."

I start to think of today, as Chris put it, as a new reality. This is an entirely new thing I'm feeling. It's like I've let go of my entire past life. I don't know where this relationship with Chris is going, but at the same time I don't seem to care right now. I'm living in the moment, for once in my life, and I love that.

"You know, I was thinking," Chris says, breaking up my train of thought. "Even after your list is done. We should make a point to do something new everyday. This way we have something to look forward to all the time."

"I like that," I tell him. "You're like a guru."

"Why thank you, young grasshopper," he imitates.

I was starting to really fall for Chris. Most people just get so caught up in their lives that they let opportunities go right past them, like me. Meanwhile, he makes a conscious effort to be happy every day. Considering what he has to go through at home, that seems nearly impossible, but he still manages it.

Chapter Twenty

After I finally get home, I call Liz back, who left me a long message bitching about how I hung up on her at the clothing store and didn't call her back.

"I'm sorry," I say as I close the door to the car with my foot. "I'll make it up to you by telling you all of the details when you get here."

"Deal," she says hanging up on me.

"What's with this shit-eating grin of yours?" she asks me when she sees me.

"Do you have to be so crude?"

"You just yelled at me, but you're still smiling." She laughs.

"Shut up." I try to hide my smile.

"So what happened?" she asks, snuggling up with my pillow on my bed. My room is the only place for any privacy. My parents are watching television, but my mom loves to eavesdrop. I feel like we're having a sleepover party.

"Nothing." I smile.

"You must've gotten Brady back good," she states.

My smile fades. I realize she thinks my happiness came from making Brady jealous. Meanwhile, I've forgotten all about him.

"Yeah, I think I made him jealous," I say. "Hey, did you know about Chris's dad?" I ask, changing the subject.

"No, what?" she asks. I proceed to tell her the story.

"Oh my God, I had no idea," she gasps. "It does make a lot of sense, though," she says, looking up in thought.

"What do you mean?"

"Well, I mean, living at home, trying to bring you back from the brink of workaholism."

"Do you think that's what this is all about?" I ask, feeling my stomach clenching.

"Now I'm confused."

"Do you think maybe he doesn't really like me, I'm just his charity case—and the only person that didn't know about his dad? I mean, it's not like he opens up to me."

"Why would it matter? I thought you didn't even like him. Unless …" She finally puts it together. "You slept with him?" She throws my pillow at me.

"Liz," I yell.

"Explain yourself!"

"Well, why did you think I took him up there?" I admit. "Clearly I was starting to have feelings. I wanted to figure it out."

"Oh, no, what did you do?"

"What do you mean?" I ask her.

"Both of you have some issues right now. He doesn't want to open up to you about his dad or his life, and you're really vulnerable right now."

I take a deep breath and lean back on the headboard. I feel like such an idiot. "What did I do?"

"Don't be hard on yourself." Liz moves closer to me. "It's not like it means the relationship is doomed, but I know you're going to ask more questions about his life, and he's probably not going to respond well to that, thinking you're attacking him. And has he even said anything about exclusivity?"

"No," I mumble.

"Well, I don't really know what to tell you," she says, standing up.

"You're leaving me right now?" I ask, shocked.

"I have to go pick up the kids," she says as she keeps walking. "Thanks for the details."

To avoid overthinking everything, I try to distract myself by writing about my weekend encounter. I type furiously, and while doing so I'm replaying the weekend in my head. Now I'm overanalyzing every detail.

Making my ex jealous gets a lot of quick responses, too. No surprise there. It's every dumpee's dream to make the ex jealous. I then start to pull at my emotions again, like a thread on a sweater slowly unraveling myself into a frenzy. I should've been doing what my list said, which was learn to live without a boyfriend, and here I go jumping into another relationship. If that is what this even is.

I decide to see what I have left:

Get on TV

Save a person's life

Travel the world

Get over my fear of flying

Learn stick shift

Go somewhere without a plan

Get a massage

Go to a drive-in movie

Go skydiving

"Any ideas???" I type into the computer before I head downstairs to make myself some tea. I get to the kitchen and I realize it's eerily quiet. They must've gone out, I think to myself. I open up the drawer and I see that the tea tin is empty. I squish my face up in thought for a second when I realize that my mom had a tea tin in her bedroom. My aunt went to London a few months ago and brought my mom back English Breakfast Tea. For some reason, I remember seeing it in my parents' room. She made a point of telling me it's special Queen tea and that it's only going to be for special occasions. I roll my eyes at the thought of this. She won't know I used some, I think. I fill the teapot and turn the stove on, and then I go upstairs to my parents' room.

All of sudden my eyes start to burn.

"Oh my God!" I scream. I just realized I walked in on the worst thing a child could ever imagine. My parents having sex!

I immediately shut my eyes and turn, before feeling a sharp pain against my head as I run right into the door frame. "Ow," I scream and keep going with my eyes closed and fall right down the steps. I hear my mother call out to me, but I immediately get up and run into the living room.

I run straight for the couch and scream into a throw pillow. I can't get the image out of my head. I can't believe that just happened. Thirty years of my life, twenty of them living with them, and I was pain free. Now I'm back for a week, and I walk in on them doing it. I'm so grossed out I am about to throw up.

"Honey," my mom calls from the hall, hopefully clothed.

"No, I am not talking about this right now," I yell to her. "We are never speaking of this again."

My whole body literally convulses because of how sceeved out I am. The image is forever burned into my brain, and I would give anything for a lobotomy right now. After taking a few calming breaths, I realize I need to think of something else. Like now. I brace myself before I head upstairs to check my blog again. I'm willing myself now to obsess over Chris again, anything to get my mind off of what's in there now.

I open my laptop back up and hit the refresh key literally a hundred times until the screen finally pops up.

I scan for anything to read, anything to look at, just God help me get this image out of my head.

I hear my parents in the bedroom talking and I just pray they don't want to bring it up.

"Okay, let's get my mind off of this," I say. "What are some ideas for my list?"

I can easily get a massage, but getting on TV and savings a person's life seem really out of the realm of possibility, unless, of course, someone decides to choke on their food around me in the next two weeks.

I sit there drumming my fingers on the desk but I really can't think of anything other than the gross image I have in my head.

Then, like a prayer answered from God, Chris calls me. As the phone is ringing, on instinct I answer it. When I do, I suddenly regret it. I don't know what to say to him now. Liz has me all freaked out. All of sudden, I feel I have to know everything, including what we are. Before, I had a go-with-the-flow attitude, and now my old self is bubbling to the surface.

"Hey, what's going on?"

"Hi," is all I manage. "What's up?"

"I wanted to know if you thought up our next adventure," he says

"I don't know yet," I stammer.

"Come on," he presses. "You've gotta have a new experience lined up, like we talked about earlier."

"You know, not all new experiences are good ones," I find myself yelling.

"Whoa," he says taken aback. "Are you okay?"

"Yea," I say putting my hand on my forehead.

"What's happened in a matter of three hours?"

I debate whether or not to say anything, but then it just comes out. "I walked in on my parents," I say.

All I hear is laughing on the other end. "Thanks for understanding," I say angrily.

"I'm sorry, that's just funny," he says.

"Have you ever walked in on your parents?" I ask.

His laughing suddenly stops. "No."

"Well, I want you to imagine it right now," I say.

"You're really mean," he responds. "I gotta go," he says, sounding disgusted.

"Me too, I need to throw up."

"Don't you have a list you need to cross things off of?" my mom asks, peeking her head through the door. She scared the hell out of me. I guess she was eavesdropping again.

"Yes, but I don't know what to do."

"How about I book us a massage," she says, cocking her head.

"Sure," I agree. "Might as well be productive," I say, not being able to look her in the eye. Thankfully it looks like we are going to just drop the issue and never speak of it again.

The spa my mom brings us to looks nothing like Liz's yoga place. It's a wooden building with a koi pond out front and a water fountain. Inside, everything's made of teak, and you feel as if you're in Fiji, not suburban Connecticut.

"Welcome." The woman smiles behind the desk. Even her voice is soft and soothing. I wonder if that's natural or if the spa owners train their staff to talk like that.

After my mom mentions our appointments, they lead us to different rooms.

"See you in a bit." She waves to me.

The soft-spoken woman leads me down the hallway and I see a room with snow coming out of the ceiling and a sauna across the hallway. I've never seen anything like it. Then again, I've never done this before. She leads us through a room with an infinity pool and finally to a dark teak room in which nature music is playing softly.

"Please undress and lie on the bed with your towel at your waist."

"Thanks," I whisper back, feeling that if she has to keep her voice down, so do I.

I get myself situated and finally start to relax. I try not to think of Chris, my parents, or anything else. I just concentrate on the calm music, the warm temperature of the room, and the smell of eucalyptus. I'm in a state of complete calm when I hear the masseuse finally come in. I pick my head up off of the donut I have my head in to greet her. To my surprise, she's nothing like the other petite women. She has to be three hundred pounds and is very scary looking. "Hello," I whisper to her.

"Head stays down," she says in a Russian accent and physically slams my head back into the donut. I'm immediately terrified.

"Deep tissue massage, yes?" she asks. I hear her flipping pages so I assume she's going through my file.

"Yes, but now that you mention it, I think I might—"

But she's already started; I try not to wince in pain as her sausage fingers dig into me like a birthday cake. "Ow," I say finally.

"You're very tense," she tells me.

"Yes, very." I fight to breathe. The music is no longer playing, I no longer smell eucalyptus, and I'm sweating out of fear. "Please," is all I can manage to say.

"I'll try harder," she persists.

"No," I cry. But she doesn't seem to hear me. I'm literally trying not to weep. "Softer," I try to say.

"You have big knot," she responds.

"Softer," I try to say again. Finally, I can't take it anymore and I burst into tears.

This makes her stop immediately and gasp.

"I'm sorry," I manage to say while sitting up and trying to cover myself with the towel. "I'm just so stressed out right now, and I was dumped and fired and now I'm seeing a new guy but I don't know if he really likes me because he doesn't share anything with me, and I just walked in on my parents doing it!"

The shock on her face is priceless. I thought, if anything, this woman would run right out of the room, but instead, she sits down next to me.

"Men are dogs," she says.

I nod in agreement. Then, before I know it, she has me swallowed up in her humongous breasts as she hugs me. Once I can move my head to breathe, I find this very calming—much more so than the massage itself.

"My man leave me for younger slut," she says in broken English while pulling away.

"Mine too," I tell her. We both embrace. Once again I pour my heart out to another stranger and wind up having a long conversation with her. She tells me how her parents caught her having sex when she was fourteen. I guess I'd rather see my parents than the other way around.

"You come by, I give you free massage," she tells me as I get ready to leave. I also leave her a big tip out of fear—and compassion as well.

"Thank you," I tell her as she walks out of the room.

After I close the door, I tiptoe my way down the hallway until I notice the room for the sauna. When I lift open the heavy door, I notice my mom already in there.

"How was your massage?" she asks me.

"Oddly refreshing," I tell her, noticing we are the only two people in here. The air is thick and makes it difficult for me to breathe.

"That's good," she says, leaning back. My mom appears to be in a full relaxation trance whereas I have never been more uptight. I can barely sit next to her right now.

I eventually get over my sickness and take my cue to sit next to her and lean back as well.

"So are you going to tell me what's wrong?"

"What do you mean?" I ask.

"I know my own daughter," she responds without opening her eyes.

Really, like she doesn't know why I'm tense.

I take a deep breath, mainly because I'm trying to adjust my breathing to the atmosphere.

"I think I jumped into a relationship I wasn't ready for." I finally say anything to keep us from talking about THAT!

"I could have told you that," my mom says.

"Really? Then why, of all people, did you encourage this?"

"Well, you told me to only offer advice when asked." She finally opens her eyes to look at me. "I did think it was too soon, but I also think this is the first healthy relationship you've ever been in."

"You hardly knew my other boyfriends," I explain.

"My point exactly," she says.

"What does that mean?"

"It means"—she sits up—"that you clearly were never serious about those guys if you never brought them home to meet your parents."

"I tried with Brady," I start.

"And he never came, so what does that tell you?"

"That he was busy trying to make partner?"

"No, that everything was always going to be about him and on his terms. Were you really all that surprised when the relationship ended?"

Ouch, I can't help but think. This is the first time ever my mom's been so blunt with me that it strikes a nerve. "I don't know," I stammer.

She takes a deep breath and gives me an apologetic look. "I'm sorry to have upset you," she says, closing her eyes again and leaning back. "I shouldn't have said that."

So much for a relaxing evening, I think.

"So what should I do?" I finally ask after a few minutes.

I see a smile creep across my mother's face. This is what she wanted all along, for me to need her help. "I think you should stop worrying so much and just go with it."

Chapter Twenty-One

"I'm so pathetic," I say out loud.

"Who's pathetic, honey?" my dad asks.

"No one, Dad, just me," I say, picking up my phone again. He fortunately has decided to pretend as if I didn't walk in on him and Mom, which makes this whole awful situation a little better. When we got back from the spa last night, he seemed like he had a speech prepared. It started off "when two people love each other," but thankfully my mom stopped him before he could go any further.

"No you're not, sweetie," he says, none too convincingly.

"Thanks." I roll my eyes and lean back in my desk chair.

For a few seconds I see he's still standing in my doorway. "You know I own a Corvette?"

"Oh yeah?" I ask wondering why he's telling me this.

"It's stick shift, and I've been keeping it in storage. I just brought it home. You want to try it out?"

"Sure." I shrug. Then it hits me that it's on my list to learn stick shift. Back in high school, my dream car was an Acura TSX in royal blue, but of course, it only came in stick shift. I told myself that one day I would learn stick shift and buy myself that car. Clearly, that never happened.

"Thanks, Dad," I say, appreciating that he's helping me out. But I also can't help but feel somewhat annoyed that he never bothered to tell me he had this car when I asked him a dozen times to teach me stick shift in high school.

I follow him down the steps and I watch his excitement. He reminds me of a little kid who did something good and runs to show his parents. I follow behind him all the way to the garage until he stops next to this shiny red car with white stripes along the side.

"What do ya think?" he asks me giddily while he knocks on the roof of it.

"It's gorgeous," I tell him.

"Hop in," he says. I watch as he gets in the driver's side.

"I thought I was supposed to learn how to drive it?" I ask.

"You are," he says, putting it in gear and pulling out of the driveway.

"Then why am I not driving?"

"Because you're going to watch me drive first. See how I just went to first and then second?" He points at the shifter like I don't know what that means.

"Isn't there supposed to be a clutch involved?" I ask.

"Yes, but that will come later," he says, slowly pulling out of the driveway. It's a gorgeous summer day so my dad has all the windows open.

After a few whirls around the neighborhood, he has me handle the gears. "Okay, now drop down to second for this turn," he directs me.

After several minutes of this, he finally says, "All right, I think you've got this."

"Enough to try?" I ask.

He hesitates but says, "Sure."

He makes me wait until we pull into the high school parking lot. He clearly doesn't trust me in a neighborhood with small children running around. I can't say I blame him. When we do reach the high school, I suddenly flash back to trying to parallel park between the smallest orange cones I'd ever seen.

"Okay." He slowly gets out of the car. I immediately jump out and grab the keys out of his firm grip.

When he finally gets in the car, he buckles his seat belt and pulls on the strap just for a triple check. Very reassuring on my end.

"Thanks, Dad," I say sarcastically.

"I've always taught you safety first when driving, and that is what I will continue to teach, no matter how old you are," he says in return.

I turn the key to start up the car.

"Not just yet." He pulls the key out.

"What?" I ask, starting to get frustrated.

"It's best to learn first without the car on," he says.

"Which you made very clear by checking your seat belt ten times."

"Always practice safety," he replies unfazed. "Now, I want you to show me where the clutch is." He is speaking very slowly.

Without looking, I hit it with my foot. Showing him what it feels like when he's treated like a kindergartener.

"Good, now try to downshift," he continues in a monotone voice.

I continue to follow his instructions until finally I convince him to let me turn the car on.

Very slowly, I hit the clutch and switch gears. I do this without a single hiccup.

"That was great, honey!" He smiles, relieved I haven't destroyed his car. "Let's try again."

With all the confidence in the world, I try to replicate what I just did, only this time it doesn't go as smoothly.

"Now that's okay—it happens sometimes," he reassures me. "Let's try again."

I try again, but this time I do even worse.

"Just relax and take your time," he tells me. His voice is getting more and more high-pitched.

At this point I'm pretty frustrated. I make one more attempt, and this time the car shrieks.

"Okay, enough, enough," my dad cries until I turn off the car. I watch as he wipes his brow and takes a deep breath.

"I'm sorry, Dad," I sulk.

"It's fine," he says. I'm fairly sure he's trying to restrain himself from checking his pulse.

"We can go home now. I don't want to destroy your car," I say, disappointed and slouching in the front seat.

"We'll try another time," he says, jumping quickly out of the car to switch places with me.

On the ride home, I'm disappointed in myself. I can't seem to do anything right lately.

"You know I bought this thing in 1970?" my dad says. "I spent my entire life savings on it. I worked day in and day out, sacrificing a lot of things so I could get this car to impress your mother."

"Why would you need a car to impress Mom?" I asked.

"That's just it, your mom didn't need the car, but I thought I did. It helped me build up the confidence to even think I had a chance of asking her out."

I'm a little confused. "So you think I'm doing my list only to impress Chris?"

"No," he says. "My point is that we're human and we sometimes do things we think we need to do to impress others or ourselves. This list you have is great, but if you don't finish it, understand that it's never been about the list."

I give him a half smile and look out the window. I know all of this isn't really about the list, but at the same time, it's been the only thing keeping me going lately. So many people helping me out, cheering me on …

Suddenly I realize just how many people have been helping me, and I wonder how, exactly, I've been paying them back?

I start thinking about Liz. She has three small children and a husband who is constantly working. She is always venting to me about her problems, but the truth is I haven't been listening. I've been an ear for her, but I realize I haven't done anything to help her. The same goes for my parents, my mom was right. I hadn't washed a single dish or did anything to contribute. I realize that right now, that needs to change.

"Do you need help with any of the yard work, Dad?" I ask him as we reach our driveway. He seems relatively surprised.

"I don't think so," he says, "but thanks."

We pull into the driveway and I hesitate before I get out. "Hey, Dad. How come you never told me you had a manual car when I asked if you would teach me?"

He shifts uncomfortably in his seat. "I wanted you to perfect driving automatic first," he reasons.

I roll my eyes and head in towards the house. Our laundry room is right near the garage, and I veer right towards it without a word to anyone. I remove all of the clothes from the washer and put them into the dryer. Then I start going through the laundry basket of dirty clothes and sorting them on top of the washer.

"What are you doing in here?" my mom pokes her head in once she hears the washer going.

"I'm doing laundry," I say as if it's no big deal.

I notice my mom's eyes grow wide. "What kind of conversation did you have with your father?" she asks.

"No conversation," I say while continuing to sort. "I just recognized that I should be willing to help those that are helping me."

My mom doesn't say anything but she smiles as she walks away. Giving me a look like that was the lesson she was waiting for me to learn all along. It seems obvious, but unfortunately it did take me a while to get out of my self-pity stage. Now I am ready to move forward with my life.

"There," I say, closing the top of the washer. "Now what?"

I look around for a few minutes and decide to empty the dishwasher and clean the dishes in the sink. My mom comes downstairs in her garden gear shocked, yet again.

"Do you need help gardening?" I ask.

"Well sure," she says excitedly.

"Great," I say, drying the last dish and putting it away. "I'm going to change and I'll be there in a second."

I watch my mom's face continue in a surprised smile as she crosses the kitchen and heads out of the sliding glass door onto the deck.

I take a deep breath and smile. I'm on a roll, I think, pulling my cell out of my pocket. I dial Liz. "What are you and Tim doing tonight?"

"Nothing. Why?"

"Because you two are going to go out on a date, and I'm going to babysit your kids."

"What do you feel bad about?" she asks.

"Nothing. It's just that you've been doing a lot for me lately, and I think you guys deserve a night out."

"Are you sure? They can be a terror," she warns.

"I'll be fine, I promise."

I show up at her house to find her all done up with her hair in soft curls and a black cocktail dress with a black pashmina.

"You look hot," I tell her.

"Tim isn't even home yet," she says, ignoring the comment and throwing her hands up in the air.

I look at my watch; it's eight thirty. It seems all too familiar. "Listen, it's no rush," I tell her. "Whenever he comes, you go out and I'll stay, no matter how late."

"You won't overcharge us?" she says jokingly while putting her hands on her hips.

"Only by the glass," I joke back as I walk into her kitchen and pull out a wine glass.

Then I put my purse on the counter and pull out a bottle of white wine.

"Is this how you babysit children?" she says again in a joking tone.

"It's not for me, it's for you. I had a hunch if he did work late, I'd need to calm your ass down." I pull the cork out of the bottle.

"Any word from Chris yet?" she asks.

"No, but I don't want to talk about me tonight. I want to talk about you."

"Why?" she asks, puzzled.

"I'm always going on about my problems and, quite frankly, I'm sick of hearing them. I don't even know what you must think."

She laughs and sits down at the kitchen table.

Once I pour her a glass of wine, I go over and say hi to Michael, Chad, and Anthony, who are playing in the living room. Between a Disney movie playing in the background and the racetrack mat on the floor full of matchbox cars, they're so involved they don't even know I'm here.

"Hi, guys," I say, getting down on my knees.

They continue to play with their toy trucks. Anthony hands me a car. He's making the engine sounds for everyone.

148

After playing with them for a while, I head back to Liz who's laughing at me. "You should see me try to call them in for dinner when they're playing with that thing," she says. "They should be in bed already, but I want Tim to at least get a chance to see them."

I sit down at the table with her.

"So, how is it being a mom with three kids?" I ask in my best Oprah voice.

She laughs again and leans back in her chair, keeping her hand on the stem of her glass. "Three boys. I can't buy anything nice until they move out of the house at eighteen." She swirls the wine in her glass.

"Yes, but they have to be fun," I say.

"Oh, tons," she says sarcastically. "Just last week I walked in on Chad jumping on top of his bunk bed. Sure enough, he split his lip but still managed to tell his two brothers to do the same thing the next night, insisting it was fun."

"Quite the instigator," I state.

"No kidding," she says. "Then about two months ago, Anthony wanted to create an indoor water slide so they took a bucket of water and poured it down the front steps, which, if you noticed, are re-carpeted now.

I can't help but laugh.

She gives me a hard stare.

"Come on, you have to laugh," I say.

"I would if Tim wasn't so hard on them. He lost his mind and I had to calm him down. The problem is he's not here for the most part, so he only sees the bad stuff and they see him as the punisher." She looks down at her wine. "It's not how I want my kids to view their father. That's how I always viewed mine, and because of it I never had much of a relationship with him."

I lean in towards her. "Have you talked to him about it?"

"Yes, and he agrees, but at the same time he says it's what he has to do in order to provide for us and for me not to have to work."

I notice a look on Liz's face I've seen before. When she really wants to say something but can't, she pulls her bottom lip in and looks down.

"Do you want to work?" I ask her, trying to read her thoughts.

She hesitates. "I would, but we wanted to start a family early, and I don't want to send my kids to daycare."

"I get that," I say. "But there are certain jobs that can work around kids. Teaching, nursing …" I try to think of what else there is.

"I would have loved nursing," she says excitedly. "I went to school for it."

"That's right," I remember.

"Yes, but starting out, you have to do the night shifts, and with three kids and a husband working as much as he is, it just wasn't possible."

"Have you talked to Tim about all of this?" I ask.

She shrugs.

"I'm not saying nag him, but at least tell him how maybe when the kids start school you'd like to go back to nursing. Give him the heads-up. You shouldn't assume he's going to react negatively. He might be encouraging."

"Maybe you're right," she says. She looks at her watch again. "I certainly could stand talking to him about these late hours."

"Agreed, but do you want my advice on something?" I ask, anxious she will get mad.

"Sure," she says.

"Now, like you said, sometimes an outsider's perspective helps," I set up the statement I'm about to make with her own words. "Maybe even though the kids eat mac and cheese, you could still cook something special for you both every once in a while. Even if you don't think you're going to eat it, it shows some appreciation. It lets him know that you don't prioritize the kids over him."

She thinks about this for a second. "I guess you're right," she says. "I could improve on my own diet a bit as well."

"And one more thing," I say wincing, worried I'm overstepping my boundaries. "As crazy as the day may get, maybe start the conversation when he walks in asking about his day. After that then let him ask you about yours, and you can tell him everything you need to. But I have to agree with Tim that if you have a bad day at work and come home to a house full of stress and anxiety, it's not healthy. Home should be the place you are able to relax and unwind. I know when you have a kid that's a whole new thing, but maybe try to keep it like that as much as possible. It might help. I'm sure you dread it when you go out and as soon as you come home Tim or a babysitter is yelling to you about everything bad the kids did and so on."

She is silent for a few seconds while she stares at me. Her initial reaction is always to be upset if she's wrong, since Liz always has to be right.

150

She's become better at letting it settle first and then swallowing her pride and admitting to it. I anxiously wait for this.

"I just know where he's coming from, I've been there," I say. Then I cock my head. "Well kind of," considering I don't have kids.

She takes a breath. "I appreciate your advice," she starts. "Maybe that's something I need to work on."

"Hey, honey." Tim comes through the door. "Sorry I'm late." He kisses her on the cheek while loosening his tie. She's a bit cool, but he ignores the freeze out. Or maybe he's used to it. "You look gorgeous."

Liz finally cracks a smile.

"How was your day?" she asks.

"Good," he says, surprised. "My boss dropped a bomb on me before I was about to leave, but I was able to get Marshall to hold down the fort until I could handle it tomorrow. I couldn't have you look as great as you do waiting for me."

"That's very sweet," she says, putting her arm on his.

Already there seems to be a lot less tension in the room, which I normally get when I hang out with both of them.

He goes in to say hi to the kids, but they're involved with their toys.

"Can you kiss Daddy good night?" he asks Michael.

Michael leans in and smashes his face against his father's cheek. He rubs the backs of the twins. "You boys have a good day today?"

They don't respond since they are wrapped up in their toys.

After a few minutes, he gives up.

"Okay, you two, get outta here," I say.

"Thanks again," Tim says as he ushers Liz out to the car. She waves.

"Okay," I tell the kids after I've closed the front door. "It's nine. Your mom wants me to put you guys to bed. Is that what you want to do?"

"No," Chad says.

"Then how about some ice cream and a horror flick?" I say.

"Yeah!" They all jump up and down.

Chapter Twenty-Two

So I was only kidding about the horror flick. I gave them some ice cream and decide to put on SpongeBob. After only fifteen minutes of running around due to their sugar highs, they crash.

They are already in their pajamas; I just need to take them to bed, one by one.

I might be a genius, I think. Not only did my plan work, but they think I'm fun.

I clean up all the toys and then settle on the couch with my own ice cream to watch some trashy television. After an hour, I'm just about to doze off when my phone starts to buzz.

"Hey," I say, surprised to finally hear from Chris. I'm nervous about saying something to put him off, so I try to act as I normally would.

"How's it going lately?" he asks.

"Pretty good," I say. "I learned stick shift."

"Not according to your blog," he says in a light tone.

"Well, it was taught to me. So I'm counting it."

"So what are you up to?"

"It's eleven at night. Are you looking for a booty call here?" I ask him. "Because my cut off is 10:59."

"Looks like my clock must be running slow," he says. "I just wanted to chat."

"Really?" I say skeptically, considering he doesn't tell me much.

"Hey, if it leads to anything else, that wouldn't be anyone's fault."

I smile. "How can anything else happen on the phone?" I say.

"Oh, there are ways," he says with an insinuating tone.

"Well, don't plan on it, because I'm babysitting right now."

"Oh yeah? Can I come over?"

"I'm under strict orders by the parents that no boys are allowed or I won't get paid."

"Darn. Well, I could always just sneak out before they come back."

"Nope, they have the place locked up like a fortress. I think there are even trip wires around the property."

"Well, what if I told you this call was coming from inside the house?" he says in a creepy voice. I laugh but at the same time, I can't help but look around.

"So what did you want to chat about?" I ask. "Marriage? I want two kids, a fall wedding, and I want a five-carat diamond," I joke. I decide this is the best way to figure out what type of reaction he would have.

"Man, you're demanding for a friendly chat."

"So how were the little leaguers?" I ask.

"Good," he says. "Coaching is the real way to make money as a teacher."

"That's good," I say.

For a while, there's awkward silence. I really don't want to say anything.

"So my dad has been in the hospital for a while now," he starts.

I perk up; this is the first time he's really bringing this up to me on his own.

"We finally got word that he's coming home. It looks like he's out of the woods, for now at least."

"That's great to hear," I say. I feel like a weight has lifted. I can only imagine how he feels. "So any specific plans with him now that he's home?"

"Not really," he says.

"Well, what might be nice is a small welcome home party. Just close family and friends, nothing too overwhelming."

"Wow, that actually sounds like a great idea."

I smile, glad that he's finally letting me in.

"I could help plan it, if you want," I offer. "I apparently have a lot of free time lately."

"Yeah, that would be great," he says enthusiastically.

"Great. I'll get started on the planning this weekend."

As I head over to Chris's the next day, I'm a bit anxious because I haven't seen his mom in so long. I feel like I'm going on an interview. I want to make sure I don't say anything to offend anyone. My mouth tends to run when I'm nervous.

I decide to get up at the crack of dawn to make an apple pie to bring over. I figure it will take me a few attempts, especially the crust, but finally after a few mild burns on my wrists and a curse-out with the apples themselves, I do manage to finally do it.

I'm finally becoming a cook!

I take the pie out of the oven when I hear my phone buzzing on the counter. It startles me and I almost drop the pie.

"Do you have any idea what you could have done?" I bark at Liz on the phone.

"Oh, no, whatever could I have done this time?" she says, unfazed.

"I just spent three hours making a freaking apple pie and I almost dropped it."

"Oh, stop being dramatic."

"What's up?" I ask, ignoring her insult.

"So I talked to Tim yesterday."

"Oh, great," I say, my tone changed. Last night they came home seeming pretty happy, but obviously I wasn't going to ask with him there.

"So you were right, I really just needed to talk to him. He said he always thought I didn't want to work, and he was willing to work hard enough for the both of us so I didn't have to. So next year we're going to put

Michael in a daycare three times a week. The other boys will be in school so I can start working those shifts."

"That's great!" I say.

"And with me working, he thinks he can afford to try to find another job in his department with better hours."

"Oh, Liz, I'm so happy for you."

"I just wanted to let you know I appreciate you talking me through it."

"Hey, you knew what you wanted. You just had to let others know."

"I'm also planning on making him a chicken dish that I've been wanting to try for a while."

"Well, you're a better cook than me, so I bet it'll be fantastic."

"So what are you up to?" she asks, changing the subject.

"Chris actually invited me over today. His father's getting out of the hospital soon and I'm going to help his mother throw a welcome home party for him."

"Wow, that was quite the jump," she says.

"What do you mean?"

"Well, one minute you're upset he's not letting you in, and the next you're throwing his father a welcome home party?"

"I think it just goes to show that you can't let yourself overanalyze things because you might be worrying for nothing."

"When you're right, you're right," she says.

"Oh, how I wish I could've recorded that," I joke.

"Too bad, cuz it will never happen again."

I hang up the phone and try to restabilize the apple pie. "I'm going to get ready. Don't let Dad eat this," I tell my mom, who came into the kitchen while I was on the phone.

My dad, who hears the tail end of that as he comes in, makes a face at the smell, from the three previous apple pies I burned. "Don't worry," he says making a face.

After quickly changing my outfits about six times I finally decide to just relax and go with the dress I have on. I'm as confident in my look as a peacock until I go over and Chris opens the door. He starts to laugh at me.

So maybe I did overdo it a little. I have on a red halter dress and wedge heels, my hair's in an updo, and I'm holding an apple pie.

"Did I just open the door to the 1950s?" he asks.

I hit him with the hand that isn't holding the pie and try to remove some of my red lipstick.

"Did you really make that pie?" he asks.

"Yes, I did, and you can see from the burn marks on my arm." I show him.

He takes the pie and kisses one of my burns.

"Is that Jill?" I hear his mother call from the kitchen. "Oh my God, I don't think I've seen you in ten years!" she exclaims, coming to the foyer. "Look how great you look!"

"Thanks." I smile as she embraces me with a big bear hug.

She has my mom's look, with the pants up to her rib cage and a silk blouse. Her hair is teased as if it was still the 1980s.

"It's great to see you, too," I say as Chris hands his mom the pie.

"Oh, that was so sweet of you, I didn't know you baked."

"Pretty new at it, actually," I say modestly.

"Well, it just looks delicious." I'm sure she's lying.

"Thanks." I smile.

"So," she says as she places the pie down on the table, "can I get you some lemonade?"

"Sure." I nod.

She ushers the two of us out onto the back porch, then goes back into the house to get the lemonade and slice up the pie.

"Here we go." His mom comes out with a tray of glasses and a pitcher of lemonade.

"Thank you, Mrs.—"

"Oh, call me Donna." She smiles and takes a seat. "So Chris says you want to help us throw a welcome home party."

"It was just a suggestion," I say, worried I might come off as overbearing.

"Of course. In fact, I told Chris here that's exactly what Frank needs. I think it's a great idea. I initially talked about one, but with the hospital business, it's just so overwhelming for us to do right now."

I smile with relief.

"So where do we start exactly?"

"Well, I guess the first question is, who would you invite? If you're inviting family and there are a lot of children, we can make sure to plan something that caters to them. If it's just adults, we can do something more sophisticated."

"Well now, let's see." She leans back. "We do have family with some children maybe five to seven years old."

"Okay," I say, taking a mental note.

"Oh, and don't forget the neighbor's kids," she adds.

"So we want to do neighbors, too?" Chris asks her.

"Well, I'm thinking close friends, which include the neighbors."

"Would you want to have an evening party or a daytime event?" I ask.

"Well, with all the nice weather we're having, I would love an afternoon picnic," she says, gazing out into the backyard. "I think it would be nice for Frank to get some sun."

We spend the rest of the afternoon eating my pie, which came out great by the way, and discussing ideas for the party. I see Chris beaming at how well his mother and I are getting along. At the same time I realize this selfishly helps me with my list because it forces me to become more organized if I'm planning a party. At the same time though, I'm also just trying to help those who've helped me.

"So I'll pick Dad up from the hospital Saturday morning and you two can finish up the last of the arrangements and host the early guests," Chris says.

"I can handle all the food," I volunteer.

Chris stops writing and gives me a look.

I shoot him one back. "Caterer," I assure him. "I'm just letting you know, anything you want me to do before or on that day, I'm fine with. I know you guys will have your hands full, so anything I can take off your plate, I have no problem with."

"Oh I just love you." Donna wraps her arms around me and gives me a hug.

A few hours later, I leave Chris's house, and decide to run to the party store with my mom. I tell her I am going to go shopping and want to see if she wants me to stop at the food store while I am out since I noticed we are low on milk. She gets so excited I offer, she decides she wants to come too. We pick out all the decorations we can find—some balloons, centerpieces, and a few other things I think would create a nice atmosphere for Frank.

"I think that's so sweet, what you're doing," my mom says as we walk down the aisles.

"Thanks," I smile.

When we get back to the house, my dad comes out to help us unload the car.

"Seems like you had quite the busy day," he says.

"Yup, pretty productive," I tell him.

He's about to walk away and I find myself following him. "Can I ask you both something?" I say when we reach the kitchen.

My mom, who is in the refrigerator, closes the door.

"Sure," she says, taking a seat at the kitchen table with my dad. I sit down to join them.

"I'm probably going to regret this for the rest of my life, so please don't go into detail about certain things," I press.

They both look at each other confused.

"Okay," my dad says.

"How do you guys do it?"

"You mean do it?" my dad asks terrified.

"No, no, not that," I say putting my fingers over my temples. "I mean, life, marriage."

"Well, what do you mean?"

"I mean," I begin. "You are both very happily married and content with your lives and jobs. I'm a product of you both, yet I find myself to always be restless. Things are going well with Chris, but I can't help but think of greener pastures. Not saying he's not great, but he's not the life I had planned for myself. I love living in the city and being a lawyer. I don't know if I'm just dealing with culture shock, or if maybe I'm worried that I'm falling short of what I want. I just want to know the key to a successful relationship and how you know it's the right one?" I sit back and wait for them to respond. My father looks like I just spoke another language to him. Fortunately, it looks like my mom gets it.

"First of all, communication is key," she says.

"Well, you can't tell Chris you think you're settling for him," my dad interjects.

"Well, not that," my mom agrees. "What I mean is yes, you do need to know what you want first. From there you communicate that to your partner. Right now I think you're going through a bit of culture shock. I feel like one minute you love the slower paced life, but then the next minute you're restless again," she says. "When your father and I first started dating, we made the mistake of expecting certain things right away. We were kids and we didn't have life figured out just yet. Your father expected that I would stay home once we were married, but I didn't want that, I wanted to work. We talked about it and I went part-time at the hospital. Then of course your father was initially traveling a lot in his job, which is another reason I wanted to work. I didn't want to sit at home all by myself just waiting for him to get home."

"The key is to know that jobs and lifestyles aren't going to be the same forever," my dad says. "So if you think that Chris is the guy who would be willing to move into the city, or if you would be the type willing to move here permanently," he drifts off. "I mean, does that seem worth the effort to be with him?"

It was such an obvious question but it hit me like a ton of bricks. "You know something, I do want to be with him," I realize. "No matter where I go, I want Chris to be there, not just someone like him, but I want Chris."

"Then honey, I think you have your answer," he says, smiling.

Chapter Twenty-Three

Come Saturday, I'm freaking out. I've been so involved in trying to get this party together that I've neglected my list and my blog readers.

Chris and Donna are getting the house in order for Frank and making everything accessible. I've taken over the beer/wine delivery and the platters I picked up from the deli. I've had a small pop-up tent delivered to the house so Frank wouldn't have to worry about the sun.

"You didn't have to do all this," Chris says.

"I wanted to," I insist.

"This is turning out so great," Donna says, looking around. "Chris, I think I'm going to pick your father up, okay? You stay here with Jill and help finish up."

"Sure," he agrees, while lighting the fuel for one of the chafing dishes. He then puts his arms around me. "This is perfect," he says, kissing me. I can't help but melt.

Once the guests start to arrive, my nerves are shot. I run around to make sure everyone's helped themselves to food and drinks.

Chris spends a good twenty minutes introducing me to everyone.

"Look who's here," I hear Donna yell from the back porch. I turn to see Chris's dad. He's frail and walking on a cane, but he looks good, considering. I watch as his face lights up with delight.

I stand off to the side as Chris greets his father and helps him to the tent area. Donna grabs a plate of food to bring to him while giving me a thumbs-up. I respond with a modest smile.

Everyone lines up to see Frank and welcome him home. Normally, I would feel out of place at this point, but I don't. I'm fascinated by how happy Frank looks, and I feel great that I helped with that.

When the crowd starts to subside around him, I notice Chris pop his head up to look for me. Immediately, he makes his way towards me.

"Ready?" he asks.

I nod in agreement.

"Hey, Dad, you remember Jill, right? She helped put this whole party together for you."

"It's so nice to meet you, finally," he says, grabbing my hand and pulling me in for a kiss. I didn't expect him to remember me. He's very weak, but you can still see the liveliness in his eyes.

"Thanks," I say.

He ushers me to sit next to him, which I do.

"So tell me about yourself," he says.

"Jill recently decided she was overworked at her old job and just moved home to figure out what she wants to do," Chris chimes in.

His father gives a slight laugh that turns into a cough. "Sounds familiar," he says. "Jill, that is the best thing you could ever do. Never overwork yourself. Take it from me, you need to enjoy life and be happy."

I smile in agreement. The advice really resonates for the first time.

The music is streaming through the speakers and I watch as people start to dance around.

"Chris, can you help me get your father some more potatoes?" Donna asks.

"Sure thing," he says, standing up and looking at me to make sure I'm okay. I nod to him I'm fine.

"So when did you move home?" Frank asks me.

"A couple of weeks ago."

"Sometimes you just need a break," he says understandingly.

"Yes," I say, taking a sip of my Chardonnay. I look over to see Donna bringing Chris over towards another woman his mom's age. Shortly after, another girl our age approaches them. He leans in and awkwardly hugs her. She looks familiar to me. Then it hits me. It's Sarah Young! She was the bitchy girl in high school that I humiliated myself in front of when I went to the golf club in a matching outfit with my dad. What is she doing here? I can't help but think. Then I see her playfully reach for his hand but he pulls away and nervously looks up at me. At that point she turns around. I try to look quickly back at Frank and hope they didn't notice me staring, but I can't help but see a smirk grow across her face.

I suddenly get a nervous jolt in my stomach.

"You've got yourself a fine girl, son," Frank says, patting Chris on the back as he comes back towards us. Sarah seems glued to his hip.

"I know. Thanks Dad."

I take another sip of wine.

"Oh, are you two together?" she asks, pointing her finger rather accusingly at both of us.

"Sarah, my girl," Frank smiles.

"Hi Frank," she says charmingly while giving him a hug like they have been friends forever.

"So how do you two know each other?" I ask, trying to be casual about this.

"Well, I mean we all went to high school together," Chris starts.

"We dated," Sarah cuts him off.

I feel the wind knocked out of me. He dated Sarah? Really? How could he have not told me?

"Few years back," he interjects.

"Oh come on, we aren't that old, has it really been that long ago?" she smiles while putting her hand on his arm and sipping her wine. I feel my blood start to boil.

"So how is everything, my dear?" Frank asks her.

"Oh you know, everything is well," she says. I take it as my cue that he's done talking to me, and I tell everyone I'm going to refill my wine.

When I turn back around, Frank, who can't really get up, dances in his seat while he watches everyone. I notice he always has a crowd around him, and yet he's not overwhelmed. He is full of great stories and every five minutes or so I hear an outburst of laughter from his table.

"You really outdid yourself," Chris tells me after the party's calmed down.

"Thanks," I say. "I enjoyed planning it."

"Did you ever think of becoming a party planner?"

"I never thought about it seriously before, but I did really enjoy it," I say, trying to forget about my jealous tendencies and focus on the conversation at hand.

"Maybe you could give that a shot," he suggests.

I smile. "I don't know. I mean, this was one party. I can't just go ahead and start a company off of that."

"Well, maybe it's not enough to open your own company, but you could work for a party planning service. And the best part is you can do that anywhere."

"Chris, when you get a few minutes I'd like to talk to you privately," Sarah says as she approaches us.

Suddenly I feel that now-familiar tightening in my stomach.

"Maybe later," he says, brushing her off.

"Okay," she says looking like a hurt puppy dog. It makes me want to slap her.

"Look, about that," he says, taking a deep breath once she's left.

"We can talk about it later," I force a smile.

"Great, thanks," he says relieved.

Later that night, I give up and leave the party when I realize that I'm probably not going to outlast Sarah. It's probably best if I let her say her piece anyway. I am exhausted and I can't wait to settle down and relax with my feet up. I no sooner get home when I notice my phone ring. Assuming it's Chris, I smile figuring now that everything has quieted down he can further explain this Sarah situation to me.

"Hi," I say right away.

"Hi, Jill." I stop breathing for a second and my eyes grow wide.

"Brady?"

"How have you been?" he asks. I hear in his voice he's nervous.

I'm completely shocked he's calling me considering he hasn't bothered to this whole time. "I'm-ugh-I'm fine," I manage, swallowing hard.

"I really want to talk to you," he begins. "I want to tell you how sorry I am for everything that I put you through. You have no idea how upset I am over it."

I swallow hard again and feel my hand shaking. I don't say anything; what does he expect me to say?

"I really want to see you, face to face, to talk," he says, stuttering a bit. "Can I come see you?"

Now is the first time I start to breathe again, but this time it's a gasp. He wants to come here? "I don't want you to," I tell him, still shaking a bit. The last thing I want is for him to come here, how would Chris react? What would my parents say?

I can tell he is taken back by this. "Well, will you come into the city tomorrow night so I can take you to dinner, to, you know, talk?"

I take another deep inhale. I know I should just cut him out of my life after everything he's done, but there is something about hearing his voice. This familiarity, that sends a sense of comfort through me. I'd missed that feeling of security, especially after everything that has happened.

Despite what anyone might say, six years with someone is a long time, and it's hard to just cut the cord and be done with him. I feel my eyes start to well up with tears.

"Sure," I say, trying to keep my voice steady as I wipe a tear from my eye. "What time?"

"Let's meet at 6:30 tomorrow at the Aqua Grill."

I nod my head.

"Are you there?" he asks.

"Yes," I say still nodding my head. "I'll be there."

Chapter Twenty-Four

The next morning I don't hear from Chris still. I realize I need to know if *I'm* still on board with whatever it is we have, especially before I go see Brady.

By the afternoon I sit on the back patio and stare off into space. I've purposely left my phone upstairs and I'm holding the list in my hand.

"Can I offer any assistance?" my mom says, sitting down with a glass of water in her hand for me.

"Thanks," I say, taking it from her.

"How was the party?" she asks me.

"It went really well," I say.

She stares at me for a second. She can tell something is wrong. "Yeah, life is not easy," she says, sitting across from me, "but there just comes a time in your life when you're forced to make tough decisions."

"I know," I say, looking down at my water.

"So do you love him?"

"What?" I ask, surprised, not sure who it is she's talking about.

"Do you love him?" my mom repeats, and I realize she means Chris.

"I don't know." I shift in my chair. "It's only been a few weeks." I also can't help but think what might be going on with Sarah as well.

"It doesn't take long to know how you feel about someone," she tells me.

"I just don't know what I should prioritize."

"I know, you really got thrown for a loop here," she says. "I know I told you your whole life to prioritize your career because I did what I thought was best for you. I never wanted you to put your life on hold to follow around some guy who doesn't treat you well."

I give her a look, urging her to make her point. "The thing is, at the same time, sometimes you do have to make sacrifices for the people you love. If your father told me tomorrow we had to move, I would quit my job and move for him. Your career is important, but it's your relationships with people that mean the most. This is what your father told you yesterday. You spent ninety hours a week at that office. Have any of your coworkers called to see how you are?"

"No," I say, looking down again. Not wanting to tell her about Brady.

"You have a lot of support here, not just from us but from Liz and Chris, too. You need to be sure to surround yourself with people who love and support you. I'm not saying give up on your dreams, but remember that there's more to life than work." After she says her piece, she gets up. "Sorry for offering advice when it wasn't asked," she says as she goes inside.

I smile, continuing to look out into the backyard.

"Where are you off to?" my mom asks when I come down stairs later that afternoon. I'm dressed in a blue chiffon dress, one of the many clothes Liz had me buy, and my hair is swept up.

"I got a call from a couple coworkers today, oddly enough," I lie. "They invited me to this happy hour so I could maybe get some potential job opportunities."

She stares at me for a couple seconds. I stiffen a bit, worried she's figured it out and is going to give me a speech. But surprisingly she doesn't. "Have fun," she says.

I take the opportunity to give a quick wave and head out the front door.

The whole drive up I am trying to figure out why I'm even going. I didn't want to tell anyone because I knew what the response would be. They would tell me I was crazy for doing this, that I'm only going to get my heart broken again, that I shouldn't jump just because he called. I knew all of this, but the truth was I couldn't stop myself.

I arrive at exactly 6:20 at the restaurant and I notice that Brady is already there. He looks more nervous than I am at that moment. This gives me the confidence to keep a straight face as I make my way towards the table. He stands up as I approach and hesitates in his gesture to hug or kiss me. I ignore both attempts and just sit. He gives an awkward smile and sits down, putting his hand over his tie. Once again, cautiously monitoring his every move. I suddenly realize how much that really irritates me.

I clear my throat and nervously take my napkin and place it on my lap. I am trying desperately to keep myself busy at the moment to avoid eye contact, even though I know I will eventually have to.

"I took the liberty of ordering you a glass of wine," he says, pointing at it.

"Thanks," my face softens a bit.

"It's Pinot Grigio, your favorite," he gives a hopeful smile.

I smile and look down at my plate. Then I take a deep breath.

"So what do you want to talk about?" I ask.

I watch as he plays with his napkin that is still on the table. Then he reaches for his scotch and takes a big gulp. When he's done, he looks up at me. "I've been a mess without you, Jill," he finally says as if he just opened the floodgates and now everything is going to come pouring out. "I took advantage of you, and I took you for granted, and it makes me sick to my stomach every day," he says, looking back down at the table, afraid to look up. "I miss you," he eventually says as he looks back up to meet my eyes.

I swallow hard. Trying to hold back tears. "What exactly do you want from me?" I ask in almost a whisper.

"I just want to talk. I want you to do whatever makes you happy, but I just wanted to talk about us. About what got us here and hope that maybe we could rebuild from it."

"Where's Jenine?" I say, looking down at the floor and scratching my neck.

"I fired her," he says. "As stupid as I was, I finally realized she would never make me as happy as you did. I miss our intelligent conversations, I miss when we would challenge each other, I miss when I could talk to you about something and you knew exactly what I was going through. I realized I could never have that with someone like Jenine. The truth was, the reason I went towards Jenine is because as much as I loved what we had, it had all stopped."

I finally look up at him.

"When you started to really work towards partner, everything fell to the wayside, including me. We never saw each other anymore. We barely even spoke, let alone challenged each other." I see him get frustrated, but then calm himself. "You never wanted to talk about your day to me, and usually when I told you about mine, I could tell your mind was elsewhere. I felt like I had lost you a long time ago."

I still can't bring myself to say anything.

"Jenine would then hang on my every word, and I thought that there was a connection there, because to be honest, I had forgotten what that had felt like."

I start to bite my upper lip. I guess this is what I subconsciously realized brought me here. That it really wasn't entirely his fault.

"I'm not saying that excuses at all how I acted," he continues. "I just wanted you to know how I felt. I had been trying to tell you for months, but you were always too busy."

I look down and start to nod my head, my eyes starting to tear up. I take a deep breath to calm myself. "You're right," I manage. I notice his eyes get big as he leans back in his chair. I can tell he clearly wasn't expecting that.

"The truth is, Brady," I exhale. "Is that I can't completely blame you for what happened. I made my work my life. I let it take me over and consume me, and no matter the goals I set for myself, one thing I've learned is that you have to learn to respect those around you that are trying to help. You have to recognize the people that will always be there for you and never take them for granted. So in that sense, I want to apologize."

"Really?" he says surprised.

I nod my head. "I want to apologize for neglecting you in more ways than one. I want to apologize for not listening to you, to not letting you listen to me, to stressing out and taking it out on you. To be honest, I think you had been more than patient with me on that."

I see him relax a bit and reach for my hand. I let him grab it, but rather than feel a tinge of excitement, I feel nothing.

"The truth is, though, how you handled it was very childlike and very hurtful. I don't really know how I'm expected to recover from that."

This time he grabs both of my hands. "Jill, we don't have to figure it all out tonight. I just knew we both had some unfinished business that we needed to talk about. I don't even want you to make a decision tonight. I just want tonight for us to just be, well, us," he pleads.

For the first time I feel my shoulders relax.

"Okay," I say. "Tonight let's just be us."

"Crab appetizer," the waiter says, placing a plate of crabs on the table between us, causing us to release our hands.

"These are the best," Brady says, relaxing a bit. He pulls a claw off of the plate and tightens the crab cracker around the shell. I notice him stick his tongue out as he cracks it before pulling out the meat. I can't help but smile, as this was a joke of ours that I always called him out on.

"Why do you feel the need to stick your tongue out when you do that?" I ask, smiling.

"I don't know," he says sticking his thumb in his mouth to suck off the juice. "Maybe the same reason you feel the need to open your mouth when you put mascara on," he smiles, remembering our banter. He hands me the plate of crab meat.

I laugh, taking the plate from him and picking at it. I have to admit it is the first time in a long time that I feel this old familiar feeling. It is nice to feel so comfortable. I can't remember when I was at this much ease with him.

After dinner, Brady invites me for a glass of wine at our old apartment.

"I'm not sure," I say, a bit hesitant. Although I am having a great time, I can't exactly just forget what happened between us.

"I'm not going to try anything, I swear," he says. "Just one drink."

Walking back with him, I feel a sense of nostalgia. It amazes me how I know this neighborhood like the back of my hand, but now even though it's only been a few weeks, it feels like I was here ages ago. When we reach the building, I notice the doorman who I had my meltdown with. He looks at me as if he might recognize me, but thankfully I can tell he isn't able to place me. I give him a quick smile and put my head down as Brady puts his hand on my lower back and leads me into the elevator.

When we reach the apartment, I get this completely overwhelming feeling. Almost like déjà vu. I know where everything is, but it's not really my apartment anymore.

"Can I get you another glass of wine?" he asks me, heading towards the kitchen and pulling out a bottle that he had in the refrigerator.

"Sure, thanks," I say, looking around, possibly for any signs of Jenine. Surprisingly, nothing looks different. Everything in here is all Brady and a little bit of me. The pictures I had taken of the New York skyline were still framed in the hallway and the throw pillows I had picked for the couch were still there.

I take a seat on the couch as Brady hands me a glass of wine. Then he comes around and sits next to me with his own glass. We both take a long sip like it's our first date again and neither one of us knows what to do.

"So any luck with finding a job?" Brady asks me.

"I was thinking about maybe going in another direction, like party planning."

Brady lets out a laugh. "Come on. You? A party planner?"

"What's so funny?" I ask him.

"Nothing's funny, Jill, it's just you. You're a lawyer. You live, breathe, and die for it," he says, leaning back and crossing his leg so his ankle is resting on his knee.

"Well, that was my problem, I let it consume my life and I don't want that to happen again."

"Jill, I know you too well. You aren't going to be happy unless you're a lawyer. I mean, come on, you have to be going crazy living in the suburbs, with your parents no less. You're not that person. You're a hard-ass lawyer, fast-paced city girl," he says, taking a break to sip his wine.

I look at him for a few seconds. "Maybe that's not who I am anymore," I respond. "Maybe I do want a bit of a slower-paced life where I can actually appreciate the world around me."

"Sweetie, I didn't mean to upset you, I just feel that no one ever really changes. You are who you are. When I saw you in Martha's Vineyard with that Chris guy, I mean, come on, a teacher? That's not you. You need to be challenged more, the same way I do."

"Well, one thing I have realized in our couple weeks apart is that people can change. I like the new person I've become," I stiffen and take a sip.

"Who brought up the idea of you being a party planner?" he asks me.

"Chris," I hesitate.

"Exactly. Chris wants you to stay home like him. He doesn't know you like I do. He may seem like he wants what's best for you, but what's best for you is getting your life back. Him asking you to stay is more about his selfish needs." He puts his hand on my knee. "I know you better than anyone, Jill. Let me make you happy again."

I look up at him. He stares back at me intently. Then he puts his hand on my cheek and pulls me towards him. I feel his soft lips touch mine, and I let him kiss me.

We pull away from each other, and he looks at me oddly. I immediately reach for my wine off the coffee table and take big gulp.

"I have to go," I say to him.

"I know," he says, understanding.

When I get home, I notice my mom is still awake. She isn't sitting in the dark, thankfully, but she did have a lamp on next to her while she sat on the couch reading. I walk in to greet her.

"Did you have fun?" she says, taking her glasses off to look at me.

"I had to go," I say, shaking a bit.

"I know," she tells me.

Before I realize it, my eyes have overflowed and I begin to cry. She puts her arms out to me and I crawl onto the couch putting my head onto her lap.

She realized that she didn't have to say anything, and I was glad that she didn't. She just sat there and stroked my hair until I fell asleep.

The next morning I muster up the courage to call Chris.

"Hey," he says. "I was getting worried about you."

"Sorry, yesterday was a little crazy," I say.

"Yeah, I stopped by your house and your mom said you had gone into the city to take care of some things."

"Chris, I want to be honest with you," I tell him.

"Okay," he says a bit nervously.

"Brady called me, and I went to see him last night. We both wanted to get closure."

"And did you?" he asked, not saying anything more.

"Yes," I reply. "I really see things clearer now than I ever have before."

"That's good," he says, becoming more muted.

"You see, the thing is," I begin. "I realized that what I have with you, I never had with Brady. I never got the excitement that I get whenever you call me. I never felt that chemistry that you and I have when we just hold hands. I realized most importantly is that he could never be you."

"I agree," he says. "I've never felt what I had with you with anyone else before."

I smile. "So, last night Brady and I just went out to dinner. He wanted to apologize and try to justify his actions. Though I do agree that some of it was my fault, I realized he's never going to change. And the new me doesn't want to be with someone like him."

"So what are you saying exactly?" he asks.

"I'm saying that I'm in love with you, Chris." I feel my stomach jump as I say this. "I have never said that to anyone before, not even Brady."

I feel like I'm out on a ledge while I wait to hear him reply.

"I've wanted to say it for a long time now, I just didn't know if you were ready," he responds, his voice seems relieved.

"I'm ready," I say, "probably more than ever."

"Then, I want to be honest with you as well."

My whole body feels as if it's going to collapse.

"It's about Sarah."

"Oh," I say, anxiously waiting for him to go on.

"We dated a few months after you and I broke up. We dated for a few years, but once my dad got sick, she bailed on me. She was upset that she wasn't getting the attention she needed, and even though she wouldn't say it, I knew she couldn't handle what my dad was going through."

"What you were going through too," I say.

"Yeah. Well, anyway, I haven't seen her in a few years, but the reason she was at the party was because our parents are friends and, well, I guess my mom told them that Sarah could come too."

"So what did she want to talk to you about?" I ask.

I hear him hesitate for a moment. "She wanted to tell me how she was sorry for how she reacted about everything."

"That was nice of her," I say. "Was that all?"

"She wanted to get back together. I told her it was too late for that. She is only coming out of the woodwork because my dad's better. But the

172

truth is, I don't want to be with someone that's going to bail anytime anyone gets sick. Then here you are throwing my father a party."

I can't help but smile.

"So are we okay?" he asks.

"Of course we're fine," I smile. "You know, I think I might really look into this party planning thing," I say, getting comfortable on my bed. For the past ten minutes I've just been pacing my room.

"That's great," he says. "Do you need my help?"

I smile with relief. "Not right now. I think I'm going to call Liz and see if she knows of any functions that she can hook me up with."

"Cool, good luck with that. I'll look around on my end as well."

"Thanks," I say. "Well, I better get going, but do you want to get together later?" I ask. "I missed you a lot yesterday."

"Definitely," he responds. "I missed you too."

"Well, I better get going," I tell him. "Call you later?"

"Sure."

Chapter Twenty-Five

"Well, the twins' birthday is coming up," Liz says when I call and tell her about my newfound revelation. "Do you want me to let you throw them a party? I guarantee if you can please a bunch of six-year-olds, you can please the most pain-in-the-ass bride.

"You think?" I ask.

"Just give it a shot. If you really enjoy it, then maybe it's something you pursue. If not, then you figure something else out."

"When is their birthday?" I ask.

"This is what will really make you a true planner," she says. "It's in two days."

"You've got to be kidding me!" I say, shocked. "Procrastinate much?"

"What can I say? I'm a busy woman. I've been helping this crazy lady cross things off a list she made when she was eighteen."

"Fair enough," I tell her. "Give me the details."

Two days later I'm running around town with two large clown cakes. The boys refuse to share a cake because each wants to blow out their own candles.

I've made sure to have two identical cakes so they can't argue over which one is better.

When I walk into the house, I see the kids running around like crazy, but Liz is nowhere in sight.

"Liz?" I ask, putting the cakes down on the counter. I check on the boys who are watching television, and I begin to search the house. "Liz?" I say again as I walk into her bedroom. She is sitting on the bed with her back to the door.

"Liz, are you all right?" I ask, noticing her hunched shoulders.

"Tim and I are over," she tries to say while keeping her composure, but of course the phrase makes her burst into tears.

I immediately run over to her. "Liz, I'm so sorry," I say, holding her tight. "What happened?"

After a few sobs, she pulls away from me to talk. "You remember when you told me to tell him how I felt? You know, about how I wanted to go back to work and he was going to work less hours?"

I nod my head as I feel my stomach drop. When a friend is getting divorced and the explanation starts with something you told them, you know it can't be good.

"Well, he promised me he would go to work this week and he would tell them to either allow him to work less hours or put him in another position where he would be allowed to do so. He promised me," she starts to tear up again. I hand her a tissue from the end table.

She takes another deep breath. "When I asked him this morning if he had ever done it, he told me that he couldn't bring himself to do it since he didn't want to jeopardize his success."

"Oh Liz," I say, rubbing her arm.

"So I told him that he's selfish and cares more about his career than me and this family. I told him that if he wanted to live his life like that then we can't be together."

"What did he say?" I ask.

"He didn't say anything, Jill," she says, looking at me with her red, watery eyes, her mascara actually still intact. "He just left." She puts her head back down and starts to sob again.

"It's going to be okay," I tell her, hugging her and rocking her back and forth. "You're a strong woman."

"I can't do this on my own," she says with her head still buried in my chest.

"You won't have to," I reassure her. "I'll be here. That's a promise."

The phone begins to ring, and I see her jump a bit. I know she's hoping for it to be Tim, but the caller ID shows it's one of the vendors coming to the party.

"I've got all this covered," I assure her. "You just concentrate on yourself, okay?"

"Thanks, Jill," she says smiling. "You really are my best friend."

I smile and give her one more hug before I answer the phone.

"Hi. This is the Happy Clown Service calling," I hear.

"Yes, hi," I say with relief, walking out of the bedroom to give her some privacy.

"Unfortunately, our clown had an unexpected emergency and will not be able to make it."

"Are you freaking kidding me?" This is sooo not good. "He had an emergency ten minutes before he was supposed to arrive? What, did he lose his magic red ball nose?" I say, trying to keep my voice down as not to upset Liz any further.

"I apologize, ma'am. You will be refunded."

"Try telling that to a bunch of six-year-olds," I bark back.

Since the clown was supposed to bring a bouncy castle, it looks like we are getting neither, and the guests are going to be arriving in an hour. In desperation, I call Chris.

"Relax, I've got you covered. And I'll be there in a half hour."

"Thank you so much," I say with relief.

"Hey," I hear one of the boys yell. I look over and both of them are covered in one of the cakes.

"No!" I yell, running over. I immediately pick Chad up and put him out on the deck, closing the sliding glass door. "Stay," I yell to him like a dog, while running back to Michael and bringing him over to the sink. After he's cleaned up, I let Chad off of the deck and wash him under the sink as well. Once they are relatively clean, I take them upstairs to change them into the party outfits that Liz has laying out the bed. Hopefully, they can stay unsoiled for the next hour. At that point, Anthony hears the boys and wakes from his nap. I quickly try to get him ready too so that Liz is not disturbed. "All of you please promise me you'll be good for Mommy," I tell all of them. While I got everyone ready, I corralled them all into one room and didn't let them out of my sight.

"Where's Daddy?" Chad asks.

I feel my chest cave in. "I'm not sure, but I'm sure he'll be here soon," I say hopefully. I know obviously things are bad with him and Liz right now, but would he really miss his sons' birthdays?

After I bring them all downstairs, I begin to clean up the destroyed cake. At least there was a second one to go off of. Just as I'm wiping down the counter, the garage door opens and I see Tim standing there. He looks like he just came back from war.

I stiffen a bit. I don't know what I should do.

"Hi," I manage. "Liz is upstairs."

"Thanks," he gives a weak smile. He stands there for a second before the kids all come running up to him.

"Hey, happy birthday, guys," he says while trying to sound excited.

"Boys, let's let your dad get ready for your party," I tell them while leading them back towards their car mat on the living room floor. I don't look up until I realize that he's left the room. I debate whether or not I should've taken the kids outside in case they start yelling at one another.

I decide I should probably call Chris and see where he is, but I realize that I left my phone in the garage when I went to throw out the cake.

I walk towards the door in a rush.

"Ahhhh," I scream and hit whatever is in front of me.

"Jill, relax, it's me." I recognize Chris's voice.

"Chris?" I ask. He's dressed up in a clown outfit.

"Yeah," he said.

"You scared the hell out of me," I say, looking at his goofy rainbow wig and white makeup. He looks like Ronald McDonald.

"I figured that when you started hitting me and screaming," he says.

"Thanks for doing this," I say, "and sorry I hit you."

"It's okay," he laughs.

"I can't believe you dressed up for this," I say smiling. Brady would never do something like this.

"Of course," he says. "Where's Liz and Tim?" he asks, looking over me.

I shake my head.

"Oh," he says, seeming to get it. "Well, I guess I'll go set up the bouncy castle."

"You got a bouncy castle too?" I asked surprised.

"The rec center has one," he explains.

"You're the best." I smile. "I'm not going to lie. I wouldn't have been able to pull this off if it weren't for you."

"Well, it's not over yet," he says.

Just then, a swarm of kids comes running through the door and disperses throughout the house, screaming.

"It's only just begun," he says dramatically while staring into the distance.

So party planning may not be my thing, I decide while I'm helping everyone clean up. My feet hurt from chasing thirty kids around all day, I have bite marks on my arm, and I'm convinced I'm going to get a nice shiner on my face after getting kicked by a kid in the bouncy castle after some snot-nosed kid ran off with my cell phone.

"I don't know what I'm going to do," I tell Chris.

"Hey, it's not your thing. It's fine."

"But I mean, what am I going to do? I don't have anything but my law degree and ..." I trail off.

"What?"

"I don't want to lose you," I finally admit. "I see what Liz and Tim are going through, and I don't want to be that."

"Hey." He leans in and kisses my cheek. "I'm not going anywhere. Figure out what you need to do, and we'll figure out a way to make us work."

"Really?" I say, surprised, thinking about what my dad had said earlier about making sure we were both willing to figure everything out together. "I don't think anyone has ever been that supportive before, especially anyone in a clown outfit."

"Of course," he says. "And I have this outfit for another few hours if you have any kinky fetishes," he jokes.

"Wow, that's okay." I laugh.

Just then Liz walks past me looking for anything to keep herself occupied. I look over at Chris who says he's going to get going.

"Bye, thank you so much for everything, you saved the day," Liz says, wrapping her arms around him and squeezing him tightly. He looks at me surprised, but I motion to him to just go with it. When he does finally leave, I ask Liz to help me with the garbage outside.

"Are you all right?" I ask her, sitting on one of the pop-up chairs.

"Yes," she says, sighing while taking a seat next to me. "I know I'll be fine."

"Did you and Tim get a chance to talk?" I ask.

"No," she shakes her head. "But that's just it," she says. "He never wants to talk. So I just have to accept that and move on with my life," she says, holding back tears again.

"Well, let me help clean and then I'll get out of your hair," I say, standing up. "Liz."

She looks up at me.

"Make him talk to you," I tell her.

Chapter Twenty-Six

The following morning, I do another load of laundry and tell my mom I'll head to the food store. I grab my dad's Corvette keys off of the counter. In my head, I start to run through all his instructions. After a few seconds, I say to myself, *Screw it and do what comes naturally.* Fortunately, that works. I pull smoothly out of the driveway. Well, almost smoothly. I stall at the end of the street and quickly turn my head around in the hope that no one noticed. I start it up again and pull away.

I drive around town for a good two hours, up and down every street. I take in suburban life and think about whether or not I could do it. I look at the shops and doctors' offices and finally I come across a law office. I'm somehow compelled to pull in.

"Hello?" I ask once I'm inside, whispering as if I've just walked into a library. The place looks just like an old municipal building. Come to think of it, I think it was the old municipal building. The interior is old mahogany, with a strong scent of wood polish. The place looks as though it's in the middle of a renovation—one geared more to conservation rather than modernization. This is probably considered a historic landmark at this point. There are these dark Corinthian columns and an oversized secretary desk that almost make you think your approaching a judge in court.

"Can I help you?" A woman in her mid-sixties with gray hair raises her eyes to me above her bi-focals.

"Hi." I smile. I'm trying to think why I came here. Was I going to just come in from off the street and ask for a job? Before I can say anything more, a man about my father's age walks out of one of the offices. He looks so familiar to me, and I don't know why.

Then it hits me that this is Mr. Tracton. Mr. Tracton worked on a case with my mom. As a nurse, she noticed that one of her leukemia patients was wrongly diagnosed. With no one to fight for him, my mom decided to step in.

"Mr. Tracton." I smile at him, not knowing if he'll even recognize me.

"Ms. Stevens, I haven't seen you in so long." He smiles, making his way towards me. He has silver slicked back hair now and thick crow's-feet along his eyes. When he reaches me, he gives me a hug. "How have you been?" he asks.

"Good," I lie. "How about yourself?"

"I'm great. He smiles again. Without even knowing why I'm here, he's already offered me coffee and opened his office door for me to take a seat. Once I'm situated, he makes his way behind his desk as if he had an appointment.

"So what brings you in?" he asks, taking a seat.

I can't find the words to lie, so I just come out with it. "To tell you the truth, I'm not sure why I'm here." I laugh nervously.

He seems a bit confused but doesn't push me. "How's your family?"

"They're great," I say. "Mom's still a part-time nurse and loves her job, and my dad's getting ready to retire soon."

"Good for him," he says. His smile is genuine. "I haven't seen you around town in a while."

"I know. I moved to the city for a few years," I say. "I was working for a law firm out there."

"So you became a lawyer." He smiles as if I'm his own child. "I knew the way you would sit at the kitchen table and listen to your mother and I talk about that case that you had a knack for it."

"Well, what you and my mom did really stuck with me."

"What kind of law do you practice?" he asks.

"Malpractice," I say.

"So are you home for good, or are you just visiting?" he asks, making his way towards his bookshelf. He opens one of the cabinet doors to a silver tray with a coffee maker. He pulls it out and gives me a look. I nod. He pours it in a mug and sets it in front of me. I accept the drink with a smile and we raise our mugs to one another before I take a small sip and try not to react to the strong aftertaste creeping up my throat. I swallow hard.

"I just recently moved back home," I say.

He nods as if he knows what that's code for, and says, "You know, I used to work in the city as well. Every young kid does when they get out of college. You graduate, move to the city, and suddenly you're up there with the big boys, working insane hours, commuting to a tiny apartment that you're never in. It's a blast—don't get me wrong, I loved it. But eventually the thrill wears thin and you realize you can't keep doing that forever." He gets up and starts to walk around the room. "When I was your age I worked at Goldman and Blum. Big time law firm, all the corporations would come to us when they were in a jam."

"You started out in corporate law?" I ask, trying not to sound so shocked. Corporate law is pretty much the hardest on a lawyer. I just think about all the oil spills that happen because corporations don't bother to take the necessary precautions, and then after all the disaster it causes to the environment, you still have to defend them.

"I know, pretty heartless, huh?" He laughs, his crow's-feet growing deeper as he smiles.

"I wouldn't say heartless," I backtrack.

"It's fine," he says. "I did it for the money. Eventually, though, nothing about it made me happy. I was working a hundred hours a week, I was living in a shoebox, and when I realized I didn't even like what I was doing, I decided change things up."

"So what did you do?" I ask.

"Well, unfortunately, my job knew I was getting restless, so they worked me to the bone until I finally cracked."

"That's awful," I say.

"Yup, and I bet you know better than anyone it's pretty hard to sue a law firm."

I nod in agreement and take another sip. This time I gag a little. He laughs and goes over to his mini refrigerator, pulling a half and half pack.

"Thanks." I smile.

"So I'm going to go out on a limb here and say that you just left your job, either fired or quit, but now you don't know what to do with yourself?"

I give him a dumbfounded look, which seems to amuse him more.

"Here's what you do," he says, and then puts his hand up in defense. "If you're asking for my advice."

I nod eagerly.

"More than anything, you need to find out what you love, whether that's being a lawyer or not. To tell you the truth, I was in that exact predicament. I hated corporate law so much, I thought I was going to have to quit the profession altogether and start my life over. I started working here because I didn't know what else to do at the moment, and your mom came to me with her case. It was because of her I realized I could use my skills for good."

I look at him. I knew I loved and respected my mother for what she did for that boy, but I'd never known what she had done for Mr. Tracton as well.

"Your mother saved me," he says bluntly. "I thank her for it, and my wife thanks her for it. Heck, I was a mess until that case came along. I think my wife was ready to divorce me. Almost went into divorce law in preparation," he jokes.

I laugh with him. "Mr. Tracton, I think I'm in exactly the same place you were."

"I know you are. I had that same look on me then as you do now. Tell you what—" he stands up and makes his way around the desk towards me and sits on the edge with his arms folded. "How about you come in a couple times a week? I know it's not much. It'll be almost like an internship. I'll rotate you around the office. We do everything from malpractice suites to divorce law."

"You know, I think that would be great." I smile genuinely.

"That's great to hear," he says, opening the door for me. "I could use the help. Now that I'm thinking about it, maybe you could do something for me?"

"Anything," I say.

"My daughter just graduated and she doesn't know what she wants to do with her life. I tried talking to her, but you know how kids never listen to their parents' advice."

I nod, thinking of all the fights I had with my parents.

"If you wouldn't mind, she might want to come in and meet you."

"Absolutely." I smile.

As I walk out of his office, I feel as if a weight has been lifted off of me. I'm so thankful to have a man like Mr. Tracton to help me through this. This is exactly what I needed. Everything that's happened to me has suddenly been completely worth it.

I immediately want to call Chris up and tell him the good news.

"That's unbelievable," he responds, seeming just as thrilled as I am.

"I know! I'm so excited right now," I say, bursting.

"I think this is the best I've ever seen you," he says.

"I'm not sure if I'm getting paid or anything, but at least it's a good place to start."

"That shouldn't be your focus right now," he says.

"I know," I agree.

"So what are you up to tonight?"

"Hmm," I say, pulling out my list. "Maybe skydiving?"

"I'll do that with you," he says. "But not at night."

"I was kidding," I tell him.

"Why, though? Clearly it's something you want to do."

"I don't really know why I put that on the list, I think just because it's one of those stereotypical things."

"Trust me, if you didn't on some level want to skydive, I don't think you would ever in a million years write that on a to-do list."

I try to dig deeper into my subconscious. I still can't figure out what state I had to be in at the time to actually write this on my list. Then it hits me. "You've got to be kidding me," I say out loud.

"What?" he asks.

"I wrote this on my list because of you."

"What do you mean?"

"I overheard you in class say you wanted to do it, and I felt if you could do it then so could I."

"So it's only fitting that we go together," he says, unfazed by the fact that I copied off of him out of spite.

"Damn you, you're going to make me do this at some point, aren't you?" I say.

"Oh, yes, I am," he says.

"Have you done it before?"

"No," he says, "but I always wanted to do it."

"Well, if you always wanted to do it, then what's been stopping you all these years?" I ask smugly.

"No one to do it with," he responds instantly.

After I hang up with him, my excitement is put on hold when I realize I want to tell Liz the good news. I still hadn't heard from her, and I am nervous that this fight of theirs really did turn into something serious. And it's because I told her what to do. I never meant to get in the middle of their marriage.

I muster up the courage to call her.

"Hi," I say hesitantly.

"Hi," she says, sounding a little better.

"How are you?" I ask.

"I'm sorry I didn't call you," she says.

"I understand."

"I'm still waiting for him to get home."

"So he's coming home?" I ask hopefully.

"He says he doesn't want to lose me or the kids and that we are more important than his job."

"That's great," I tell her. "Of course, you already knew that."

"Well, he promised today to talk to his boss, so when he comes home we'll find out if he did it. And if not, I have the window open ready to throw all his shit out of."

"Believe me, Liz, he loves you more than anything."

"Thanks."

"How about we go to yoga together? Get your mind off of things."

"You'd better not embarrass me this time," she says.

"I promise, my mom and I have been practicing. I'm much better now, I swear."

When we're finally at the yoga studio and we get out of the car, Liz shoots me a warning look. I roll my eyes at her. She has no idea how much better I've gotten at this.

We step inside and, of course, Fern the instructor is at the front of the room. She immediately recognizes me and tenses up, probably debating if she should toss me out now or not. I look over at Liz who seems just as uneasy. I try to pretend I don't notice and go right to the closet to pull out a yoga mat.

"All right, everyone, I need you to become fully relaxed," she says. Everyone takes a seat and crosses their legs.

"Breathe in," she says. You can hear everyone in the room take a loud, obnoxious breath. "And out." I find people breathe out even more obnoxiously.

"And in," Fern says.

Seriously, no one else finds this annoying? I remember how Liz might kill me if I get us thrown out again, so I just take a deep breath and try to join in.

"Please get into the child's pose."

Everyone moves to rest on their shins. "S'il vous plaît me prendre à l'aéroport," I whisper. I now associate every yoga pose with a French phrase. I giggle a little, knowing I just said to myself "take me to the airport."

"What?" Liz whispers.

"Nothing." I smile.

"Vinasa," Fern says.

Laisse nager au fromage.

I stifle a giggle. I just (mentally) said "Let's swim to the cheese." I've forgotten how to say "beach."

By the end of class, I actually do feel more relaxed than ever. I don't know if it's from doing yoga in a calmer setting, or just my revelation with life in general. Even Liz looks like she's lightened up.

I check for missed calls and notice a number I don't recognize. When I listen to voice mail, I realize it's from Francine, Mr. Tracton's daughter. It turns out she's finishing up at NYU and asked if I can come meet her tomorrow in Bryant Park. I call back to agree immediately. She seems really sweet and part of me still wants to make sure that I'm officially ready to leave the city …

"So are you getting together with Chris tonight?" Liz asks me bringing me back.

"Hmm, I guess so," I say.

"You don't sound really enthused," she says.

"I am," I assure her, "I'm just thinking about the list and what else I can get done this afternoon." I feel as if I'm on such a high I can do anything right now and I want to.

"Well, didn't you have a drive-in movie on there?" she asks me as she turns onto my street.

"Yeah, but I haven't seen one of those since we were kids," I say. "I think it's abandoned now."

"I've got a cool idea," she suggests. "Tim and I did this once."

Chapter Twenty-Seven

I pick Chris up a few hours later. I tell him I have another surprise for him.

"So, looks like you're doing well with the stick shift," he says, noticing my improved skills.

"Well, tell that to my dad. You should've seen the tears in his eyes when I pulled away."

"That scared, huh?"

"I fixed him a strong drink before I took the keys from him."

"So where are we going?" he asks while looking out the window.

"I told you already, you'll find out when we get there."

Fifteen minutes later, we pull into the abandoned drive-in theatre. The screen's still there, and a few remaining metal posts where the speakers used to be. The snack shack has been boarded up with "No Trespassing" signs on it and it looks as if this place has just been left to rot.

"I know I'm the guy and I'm supposed to be tough, but this place is a little creepy," he says as the sun starts to set.

"Oh, relax," I say, putting the car into park.

"So I get this is part of your list, but how is this going to work?"

I ignore him and hand him a basket from the backseat equipped with wine, popcorn, and sandwiches.

"Does your dad know you're eating in his car?"

"No, and I suggest you don't tattle on me."

"Scouts honor," he says, putting his hand up.

I hand him two cups and he puts them in the holders and pops the wine bottle.

"Is this from our Martha's Vineyard trip?" he asks, reading the label.

"Indeed it is." I smile. "A nice bottle of Chablis," I say, purposely mispronouncing it.

He then puts a sandwich for me on the center console. "So, now what?"

"Well," I say, pulling my purse up onto my lap. "I figured since scary movies are the big thing to watch in drive-ins, that we would watch *The Omen*." I pull out my iPad and set it up on the dashboard.

"Oh, nice," he says, impressed.

"I have to warn you," I say. "I'm a big baby and I scream and cry through everything."

"Well, don't judge me if I do the same," he jokes. "So why a drive-in movie?" he asks, taking a sip of the wine.

I shrug. "I'm not really sure," I trail off, trying to think back. "It just always seemed like something cool to try. You know, you watch the movie *Grease*, and everyone hangs out there, it just seemed like it would be a fun thing to do."

"You wanted to hook up at a drive-in," he starts giggling.

I hit him and roll my eyes. "Shut up, it was never like that," I say, pulling my hair behind my ears and settling back in my seat.

"Admit it, you saw it as the scene for a Harlequin romance sort of thing."

"I did not," I say blushing.

"So is this your way of seducing me?" He lowers his brows and licks his lips.

"It wasn't the plan, but how can I resist that?" I smile, nudging him with my elbow. "Let's just watch the movie."

Two minutes into the movie, Chris leans over and locks both doors. I can't help but laugh.

"What?" he asks sheepishly.

"Nothing. You're just funny," I say.

"What, I've got to be the tough guy all the time?"

"No, but I mean, come on, nothing scary has even happened yet."

"The music alone is creepy."

"So you get scared when you hear music?"

"You know, I really don't think you're as tough as you think you are," he tells me, biting into his sandwich.

"I'm not saying I'm tough, I'm just saying you need to relax a little."

With that, he leans in. Before I know it we have forgotten all about the movie.

All of a sudden we hear tapping on the window and we both start screaming at the top of our lungs, expecting to see the demon child in the flesh.

"What are you two doing here? This area is closed."

We quickly realize a police officer is talking to us and it's not some psychotic killer.

We can't help but laugh. "I hope he doesn't tell our parents," I whisper to Chris as the officer takes our licenses.

"So what do you think, can we still count this?" I ask Chris.

"I say we got the full drive-in experience," he smiles mischievously.

"Oh, I have to call Liz," I say, grabbing my phone.

"You want to wait until the cop leaves?" he asks.

"What, the car is not on, I'm not driving," I say, anxious to hear what happened with her and Tim.

"It's all good," she says when she answers the phone.

I feel like a weight has been lifted off of my shoulders. "Thank God," I say, slouching in the seat.

"He went to his boss today and told them that he needed more time with his family."

"That's great to hear," I say, trying to keep my voice down so the cop doesn't hear.

"Yeah, it turns out he's more valuable than he originally thought, and they're willing to work with him."

"Oh Liz," I can't help but say. I'm like a proud mom. I'm so happy for her that everything worked out.

"So if you wouldn't mind, do you think your mom could look into any openings at her hospital for next year?"

"You got it," I tell her.

"Hey, lady, off the phone," the cop knocks on the door.

"Sorry, gotta go," I say, biting my lip and hanging up the phone.

The following afternoon, I make my way into the city. The trains are crowded because of summer tourists. As I sit there watching the city fly past me, I suddenly get a sickening feeling. What am I going to say to her? What makes me a mentor when I don't know what to do with my own life?

By the time we pull into Grand Central, my stomach is in a complete knot. I have no idea what to expect. I take slow, deep breaths as I walk over to Bryant Park, where I promised to meet her. I have no idea what she looks like, and I'm mad I didn't at least glance at the family photo he had on his desk. Once again I prove to be more about my own problems than other people. Although maybe I shouldn't be so hard on myself. I'm here, right?

I already have beads of sweat running down my forehead. I don't know if it's nerves or if it just happens to be one of the hottest days of the season. It's weird to be in the city on a weekday and not in work clothes. I'm wearing loose jeans and a pink blouse. I suddenly feel way too casual. I'm convinced people are looking at me and know I don't have a job to go to. It makes me self-conscious.

Bryant Park is always full of interesting people on a hot summer day. You have the suites, the uber-fashionable magazine employees, and your eccentric people who creep everyone out. I've been here thirty seconds and already a shirtless, bald man has asked if I have any sunscreen.

Within a few minutes of settling down at a table, I spot some of my coworkers and I stiffen up. I'm nervous about them seeing me. Will I get the awkward, "Hi, we used to work with you," or even worse, sympathetic looks because my boyfriend cheated on pathetic moi with his secretary? I notice that one of them, Brian, is looking at me. I watch as he leans in to say something to the others and they all nonchalantly try to look my way.

That's it, though. No one says hi or so much as waves at me. They pretend as if they never knew I existed.

"Hi, are you Jill?" I'm so lost in a trance over what just happened, I don't even notice Francine trying to get my attention.

"Oh, Francine?" I ask, standing up to shake her hand. "Hi, nice to meet you." She's in a sunflower dress with a hot pink cardigan. Her blonde hair has a sunflower in it as well and she's wearing Jackie-O sunglasses.

"Nice to meet you, too." She smiles. "I hope you don't mind doing this. I know my dad probably forced you."

"Not at all. He's a great man," I say. "Believe it or not, your father was the voice of reason for me."

"Funny how his advice will work out better for you than for me," she says, sitting down.

"Well, it's because he's your dad," I say. "I never want the advice my mom tries to give me, but apparently she helped your dad."

"I guess," she says. "I don't know. I decided to be a fine arts major, but now I don't know what I want to do."

"I wish I could say that feeling will change, but I'm almost thirty and I still don't know what to do with my life."

"It's just frustrating because I started off doing an undergraduate degree with courses that would help me get into law school, but I realized I did that more for my dad than myself, so then I went the opposite way with fine arts. Now I'm not sure I want a career in the arts."

"Well, I wouldn't worry too much about that," I tell her. "It's interesting to see how many people graduated with a certain degree but end up doing something completely different."

"Really?" she asks.

"Oh, yeah," I assure her. "Do you know what else you might want to do?"

She suddenly seems to get more comfortable and leans back in her chair. I notice my coworkers are staring at me.

"I kind of wish I'd gotten into broadcasting," she tells me.

"That's interesting. I think you can still manage to do that," I encourage her.

"Really?" she says hopefully.

"Have you thought about getting your masters in communications?"

"I can't see my dad going for that," she says, biting her nails. "And I feel so stupid for changing my mind all the time."

I give her a reassuring smile. "You're young, and you haven't wasted any time. Your undergraduate arts degree can get you into a master's program in communications. And based on the conversation I had with your father, he just wants you to do what makes you happy. As long as this is something you really want to do, I can't see why he wouldn't encourage you to continue."

I see her smile hopefully for the first time. Then she surprises me by leaning in and giving me a hug. "Thanks, Jill, I really appreciate it. I just hope it works."

"I'm sure he'll be supportive, but if he really doesn't approve, you can always take out loans," I tell her.

"I guess you're right," she says. "How did you know what you wanted to do?"

"Well, actually, from your father, I now realize. But I was working in too intense of an environment. Your dad's just offered me a part-time job at his office, and I think that's really going to help me decide what to do next."

Then it hits me. "I have an idea. I have a friend whose husband works as an executive at a big network. I could ask her if he'd be willing to take on any interns."

"Really?" She's even more excited than before.

"If he is, you can try it out for the rest of the summer and make sure it's something you really want to do."

"Oh my gosh, thank you so much," she says.

"I'll get back to you," I say smiling.

"Are you turning into one of those goody-two-shoes now?" Liz asks me at a late lunch that day. "Are you going to start a damn charity?"

"All I'm saying is you say Tim's overworked, so what's wrong with him taking on an intern? Just let her see what the place is like for a few weeks."

"Can we please remember what happened when your boyfriend had an intern?" She glares at me.

"Secretary, and ouch," I say. "But Tim is a family man who loves you to death. He's too mature for that crap, and if I didn't believe it, I'd never put you in that position. Besides, you really have nothing to worry about with this girl. I met her and she's really sweet. She comes from a great family, and I owe them a favor."

Liz rolls her eyes at me and asks to see a picture. I pull up Francine on Facebook and show it to her.

"I'll talk to Tim. When do you think she can start?"

"Thank you, and I love you." I smile.

"If something happens, I'm giving you all three kids to raise," she tells me.

"Oh how I love your dry sense of humor and how you try so hard to be heartless," I say to her sarcastically.

She scrunches up her face at me. "Don't ruin my reputation here."

"Oh, stop."

"So are things starting to turn around for you?" Liz asks, changing the subject.

"I guess so," I say, taking a sip of my water.

"How are you doing with the list?"

"Well," I say, putting my fork down. "I need to go somewhere without a plan, figure out my life's purpose, travel the world, get on TV, go skydiving, and, oh yeah, save a person's life."

"So only a few things left." She laughs.

"It's like my dad said, it was never about the list, it was more about getting my life on track, which this list helped me do."

"What do you mean?"

I decide to tell her my dad's Corvette story.

"So let's break this down," she tells me. "Number one. You can easily go somewhere without a plan. Hell, I could put you in the car now and not tell you where we're going or what we're doing."

"Is your life that easy that you can afford to just get up and go?"

"That's what babysitters and mothers-in-law are for," she says. "Figure out your life's purpose," she continues. "Well, I think you're on the right track for that."

"I don't think I'm anywhere close, though," I counter.

"Look, that whole figure-out-your-life's-purpose deal is more of a philosophical thing, anyway. No one knows what their life's purpose is until they're a hundred years old, looking back on their lives. All you can do is find something that makes you happy and pursue that, whether that's a career or a family," she says, rubbing her stomach.

"You're pregnant?" I squeal.

"God no, three's enough for me," she says, winking and taking another sip of her vodka. I shake my head at her.

"Get on TV," she continues. "How easy is this when Tim works in television?"

"He's an executive, and why would he put me on TV?"

"We'll figure something out," she says, leaning back and crossing her arms.

"We just asked him to give Francine an internship. I can't ask him for this, too. And do you really control your husband that much, you can make career decisions for him?"

"Yup," she says without missing a beat. "Hey, we could film you skydiving!" She claps her hands.

"If anything doesn't get done on that list, that will be it."

"Well, we'll just have to see about that."

"And how am I going to save a person's life?" I ask, ignoring her.

"Well, we are at a restaurant. Anything can happen."

With that, she stands up and starts to walk away.

"Where are you going?"

"The bathroom. I'll be right back." She rolls her eyes. "Jeez, can't you trust me?"

"You're right, you've given me so much reason to trust you."

She flips me off.

"And there's the friend I adore so much," I call out to her.

Chapter Twenty-Eight

It's the first day of my new job. I can't help but feel like a dork. I'm sitting in what I think is a suburban firm's version of the human resources department with two other people. Both look like they're about sixteen.

"So which department are you working in?" the baby-faced boy asks me. I can't help but look at his face, which, clearly, he hasn't had to shave yet. His big boy suit is slightly too big for him. It's probably a hand-me-down. Ha. I felt so mature and professional during my city internship. Now I realize I must have seemed like a baby to the lawyers.

"Malpractice," I say, trying to be friendly.

"Well, I'm glad they're not having me do that," he says.

I just shrug.

"I'm in Management and Governance," the other girl chimes in. She's the spitting image of one of the female characters from *Law and Order*. I think I actually saw that outfit in an episode. She's got her blonde hair pulled back into a bun and she's wearing glasses.

"Cool, I'm in Structure and Performance."

"Oh, have fun with that." They exchange flirtatious looks. Sitting between them is now very uncomfortable.

Thankfully, my name is called and I submit my filled out forms to the balding, overweight man behind the counter and smile for my ID picture.

"All right, you're all set," the man says a minute later. He hands me my ID card, which I see immediately has something sticky on it. Whether that's from him or the machine, I have no idea. I try to hold back my look of disgust.

"Thanks," I say, picking up my card by the corners.

I make my way to Mr. Tracton's office; only someone calling my name stops me.

"Mom?" I say. "What are you doing here?"

"Well, I wanted to come by and say hi to Lou and thank him for helping you out."

"And you had to do that on my first day?" I say.

"Oh, stop it." She waves a hand at me. I reluctantly lead her up to his office.

"Marilynn, what a lovely surprise." He stands up to give my mother a hug.

"Oh, Lou, it's great to see you," she says, handing over a plastic bag of cookies she pulls out of her purse.

"What's this?" he asks.

"It's just a little something to say thank you. I wanted to stop by and let you know how much I appreciate you helping my little girl here," she says, putting her arm around me.

I feel like I'm in elementary school again.

"Don't worry, she's got a phenomenal resume, and I'm sure she'll have no problem fitting in here," he says.

"Besides, Jill here made a point of meeting my little girl and showing her the ropes. She has an interview with a morning TV show that Jill apparently has a connection with."

"Oh, isn't that great." My mom smiles. "Well, Lou, it was great seeing you. You and Beverly have to come over for dinner some time."

"Absolutely, Marilynn." He smiles. They exchange cheek kisses.

"Oh, honey, here's your lunch," she says, pulling a brown paper bag out of her oversized purse. I swear she could store an entire supermarket in there.

"Thanks, Mom," I say through gritted teeth.

Once she leaves, I can see he senses how completely mortified I am.

"Parents," he says, closing the door. "If we can't embarrass you, then what are we here for?"

I let out a nervous laugh.

"Take a seat," he says, pointing to the chair in front of his desk as he makes his way towards his. "So what departments do you think you want to explore?" he asks me, sitting down.

"I think I'd like to look into the medical malpractice—you can probably guess why. And that way I'd get a chance to work with you as well."

"I like it." He smiles. "And I'm very flattered."

smile back. Although I don't know Lou Tracton that well, he feels almost like a father figure to me.

"I've got just the assignment for you," he says. He reaches into his filing cabinet and hands me a file. "A doctor failed to remove a surgical sponge during surgery causing ongoing abdominal symptoms in the patient."

"I'm on it," I smile. It feels good to be back.

A few days in and I already feel like a pro, and I am amazed by how impressed everyone is with me.

"You're doing great here, kid," He tells me.

"Well, I'm sure, for a part-time associate," I say modestly.

"No, I'm serious. Everyone here thinks you're a gem. Your experience has made you a big fish in a small pond. You say the word and I'll give you a permanent job here."

I'm floored. "Thank you very much, Mr. Tracton, that's great to hear." I'm flattered, but still hesitant about staying here and working permanently for him.

"Call me Lou," he says.

"Sure," I smile. It's great now, but what will I think that in about six months?

"So would you take the job?" Chris asks me as he pours me more wine at dinner that night to celebrate.

"I don't know," I say nervously. "I mean, it's great and I'm really enjoying it, but I don't know if it's because it's great to work again or because it's something new."

"You know you need to stop analyzing everything as much as you do."

"What do you mean?" I ask, wiping my mouth with my napkin.

"I mean," he says, putting his glass down, "anytime you're happy, you seem to think there's a catch to it, and you're constantly waiting for the other shoe to drop."

I think about this for a second. Do I really do that?

"I mean, don't get me wrong, given what you've been through, I get your reasons for being hesitant, but sometimes you need to live in the moment, and if it feels right, you just have to go with it.

"You're right," I admit. "I don't know why I do that."

"I know why." He puts his hands on mine. "And it's okay. I just feel like you don't know when you have something great right in front of you. I don't want you to miss out on great opportunities."

"I know," I say. "I think you're absolutely right. I just feel as though I've wasted years of my life and I'm afraid to do that to myself again."

"Don't believe for a second that you've 'ruined' your life. You've accomplished a lot of great things, and you'll continue to do that. Don't be so quick to write your whole life off because of a few bad moments."

I give him a smile. "Thanks," I say.

We head back to his house after dinner. He's holding my hand and I can't stop the tingling sensation running through my body.

"Mom, Dad, we're home," Chris says as we walk in.

"Your father's sleeping," his mom whispers and points upstairs.

"Still really out of it?" he asks.

Donna nods.

"I can go," I say.

"Not at all, honey, stay." She pulls my arm and leads me into the kitchen.

"Can I get you two some coffee?" she asks, pouring herself some.

"Sure," I say, taking a seat at the kitchen table.

"Sugar?" she asks.

"Sure," I whisper, remembering Frank's upstairs. I notice some of the pills that are on the table for Chris's dad. There seem to be a lot of them. I know battling a brain tumor you need some serious medication, but there are more here than I've seen my eighty-year-old grandma with. One drug in particular catches my eye. Zipiltore? Why does that drug seem so familiar to me?

"Here you go." Chris hands me my cup.

Thanks." I smile, slightly distracted.

"So, Jill, I heard you started up at that law firm downtown."

"Yes," I say.

"How do you like it so far?"

"I'm actually really enjoying it, and the commute's not too bad."

"I bet." She smiles, taking a sip of her coffee. "So is that permanent?"

"Right now I'm technically a part-time associate, but if I decide I want to stay they have offered to hire me if I want to."

"Well, isn't that great news," she smiles at me.

"Just after a few days, Jill made her mark there," Chris says proudly as I smile at him.

"Well, I bet you have that affect on everybody." She smiles.

Later that night, I'm tossing and turning. I can't figure out what's bothering me. I grunt in despair and throw my covers off. It's now two o'clock and I'm not even close to falling asleep.

I start to pace the house trying to figure out why I'm so restless.

"Wow, I feel like I'm becoming a schizoid," I say out loud.

Then it hits me. "Oh my God!"

I immediately race over to my computer. I type in the name of the drug I saw on Chris's kitchen table.

Now I know why the name struck me. I read about it in the *New York Times* a few months back. After being on the shelves for a year, it was recalled for its massive side effects.

After a few hours of research, I decide to go into the office at six. By the time Lou has come in, I've already had about five cups of coffee and I'm racing around the office like a roadrunner.

"Mr. Tracton!" I yell to him as he walks past.

"Ms. Stevens, what are you doing here so early?"

"I've been here since six. I have to talk to you."

He ushers me into his office, a little frightened by my hyperactivity, I think, and I don't really blame him.

I proceed to tell him the story of Chris's father, his condition, and the drug I found on their kitchen table. I then tell him about the article I found on the drug and the additional research that I've done.

"Wow," he says, completely stunned. "You've done all this, and when did you notice this in your boyfriend's house?"

"Last night," I say.

His eyes get wide and he makes a whistling noise. "You've got some work ethic," he says, laughing. "Well, the next thing you have to do is talk to Chris's family about it."

All of a sudden I feel my stomach clench. I hadn't thought about that. I certainly don't want to rock the boat, but if he's on a drug that's been recalled, I obviously want to let them know.

I have Lou help me with my plan of action.

That afternoon, I leave work early and have Chris and his mother meet me for a coffee.

"Chris, Donna, I wanted to talk to you about Frank and his progress over the past year, if you don't mind me asking."

"Well, sure." Donna seems hesitant and looks at Chris.

He's staring at me, confused.

"I'm asking because when I was over your house last night, I noticed a familiar drug name on one of Frank's pill bottles. I couldn't remember why it was familiar until late last night. It turns out Zipiltore has been recalled by the FDA because of its severe side effects."

"Oh my God." Donna grabs Chris's arm. "He's been taking that since he got home."

"It's probably nothing permanent," I assure her. "But obviously, the sooner he's off it, the better. It can make patients very weak, disoriented, and can cause severe vomiting."

"So what do we do?"

"Well, Lou and I would like to speak with Frank's doctor as to why he was given this drug, since one, he should already know about the recall, and two, there shouldn't even be any more to distribute, so who's supplying it?"

Donna lets out a gasp and Chris holds her hand for support.

"I apologize for coming to you like this, but I wanted to bring it to your attention."

"No, I appreciate it immensely," Donna, says, reaching for my hand now.

"Thanks, Jill," he leans in to hug me. "We have to go though," Chris says while he stands up.

"Of course," I say, standing up.

"We'll call you later, okay?"

"Of course," I nod.

"So how did everything work out?" Lou asks that Friday morning.

"Good, I guess." I put my files down on his desk. "I spoke with Chris this morning. His mom tried to call the hospital and got nowhere, so I suggest we contact them today, make them talk to us and go from there."

"Absolutely." He smiles. "This one's all yours, kid."

Walking back to my desk, I can't help but feel nervous. What if I put Chris and his family through pain and upset for nothing?

I haven't been this nervous about a case since my very first one at Weinstein and Morris.

"This is all you, Jill," I repeat to myself. "Here goes nothing."

That night, Chris comes in to the office to meet with me. He comes with a couple cartons of Chinese food.

I realize no one's ever done that before. Brady always made me feel guilty when I was too busy to eat with him, but it never occurred to him that he could sit with me while I worked.

"How'd ya know I was in the mood for Chinese?"

"Because I'm psychic," he replies, placing the bag of grease on my desk.

"Thanks. I'm starving," I say.

"So how did you make out?" he asks while opening the cartons.

"The hospital wasn't calling us back, either, so I went down there threatening legal action. We finally got a hold of Dr. Petral. He's actually a great guy. He prescribed a completely different drug to your father—the right drug. We went to the pharmacy and it turns out the pharmacy was passing off the Zipiltore as the generic version of the drug Dr. Petral prescribed just so they could unload the pills."

"So what happens now?"

"Well, with Dr. Petral's testimony, we've got ourselves one hell of a case that we're going to win."

"That's great," he says, relieved.

"So how's your dad?"

"Well, just twenty-four hours off those pills and he already feels a lot better. He's less woozy and is still a bit weak, but not as out of it as he was before."

He still seems upset. I put my hand on his. "Everything's going to be fine. He's getting the right care, and we're going to clean out those pharmacists for all they're worth."

"It's not that," he says, shaking his head. "I just feel horrible that we didn't know any of this, that he was being mistreated, and we had no idea."

"Chris, it's not your fault, you're not a doctor. How were you supposed to know?"

I stand up and give him a hug; no one's ever held me so tight. It's nice to be needed, I think.

"You saved my father's life, Jill."

"I don't know if I did that," I say modestly.

"It's true," he insists. "I really don't know what I would do without you." He then leans in and kisses me. Afterwards, he looks back up at me and laughs a bit.

"What's so funny?" I ask.

"You just managed to cross that off of your list."

Chapter Twenty-Nine

The next morning, I get a screeching phone call from Liz.

"Oh my God, you wouldn't believe what I just did for you."

"Oh no, what did you do?" I ask her. I'm still half asleep. I had to work until two in the morning to get everything ready for the case. Chris helped me with the time line and the history. When he couldn't help, he was just there for moral support.

"I figured out a way to accomplish everything on your list."

"I'm not sure I like this."

"Oh, but you'll love it!" she squeals. "Sunday morning, dress in your very best and don't make any plans."

"What are we doing?" I ask.

"Well, if I told you, then I would have to kill you," she says.

"Damn you."

"Oh, and I spoke with Chris so he knows too, but trust me, he will not give it up."

"Why do you bother telling me that?"

"Because I know it drives you crazy! Happy birthday, girl!"

"Don't force me into old age yet, I'm still a week away."

That afternoon is incredibly productive. My mom and I do our yoga routine, and she and my father quiz me on my French. At this point, I'd say I'm at the college level. I'm starting to read and speak pretty well—not great, but I can get by.

After begging my father, he agrees to let me drive his car with him to the grocery store. He's surprised to see how easily I get it started and drive it around town.

"How did you get so good?" he asks me.

"I memorized your directions," I say innocently.

"Or practiced when I wasn't looking?"

"Something like that." I smile.

When I get home, I update my blog. I have Chris's permission to talk about the case, not in full detail, but the gist of it. I also give my readers updates on my life.

I can't believe the number of followers I'm starting to get. Everyone wishes Chris's dad the best and congratulates me on coming back to life. There's even a post from someone who says I've helped with her outlook on life, and even if I don't finish my list, she still finds me to be very inspiring.

That night I cook dinner for my family—beef bourguignon, no less. After six hours of slaving, I serve an exquisite meal to my parents.

"I have to say, this is a new Jill I'm seeing, and I love it," my father says as he cuts his meat and shoves a piece into his mouth.

"I agree," my mom says. "I haven't seen you look this relaxed in a long time. You look ten years younger."

"Thanks, Mom."

"So, Jill," my father chimes in, "did you finish your list?"

"No. I have a few more things left to do, but Liz claims she has a way to help me finish it for tomorrow."

Just then the phone rings.

"Hello?" my mom answers. "Oh, hi, Liz, we were just talking about you."

Did Liz really just call my house? I stop mid-bite.

"Oh, my, what a wonderful idea," I hear my mom squeal. "Thanks for the heads-up. I'll keep an eye out. Buh-bye, dear. That was Liz," she says unnecessarily, sitting back down and taking a sip of water. Then she starts to grin at me.

"Great. Now you know about it, too—whatever 'it' is."

"Honey, this is so sweet of her to do. You ought to appreciate her for it."

"I've known Liz my whole life. She never does anything good unless she can get some sadistic pleasure out of it."

"Oh, stop being so negative and just go along with it for your own good."

That night, knowing I have to rest up for God knows what, Chris comes over and we hang out at my house to watch a movie with my parents from my mother's collection: *Roman Holiday*. Audrey Hepburn plays a princess who escapes her palace for the night and pretends to be a regular person to experience normal life for once.

I can't help but relate, in that way. Even though I had a position at a high-end law firm, I often (all the time) found myself overworked, overstressed, and longing for a weekend to myself just to do something fun.

By the end of the movie, I actually feel inspired. Sure enough, the princess has to go back to her life, but that doesn't mean I have to!

What am I waiting for? I ask myself. I'm loving my life here. I love Chris, my family, and my new role at the law firm. Even suburbia is growing on me.

"Look at you, not even crying," my dad jokes with me.

"No need to cry," I say. "I was fortunate enough to get my life back."

The next morning, I'm freaking out. It's four o'clock and I have no idea what Liz has planned for me, but I know I'm probably not going to like it.

Then I hear Liz honking the horn (it's only the middle of the night—who could she really be disturbing!). I race to the car to avoid her waking the neighbors, and she hands me a coffee.

"Ready to go?"

"I guess," I say.

"Here's her secret bag," my mom says, coming out with a duffle bag.

"What's this?" I ask Liz.

"You can just put it in the trunk—thanks," she says, ignoring me.

"Where are the kids this morning?" I ask.

"I had my mom sleep over," she says.

"So do I get to know now?"

"Nope, but don't worry. Eventually you'll figure it out."

An hour later we've made it into the city. I'm still clueless as to what's going on until I see Tim standing in the middle of the street, waving us on. I look up. We're at his office.

"Oh my God, what did you do?"

I'm quickly ushered out of the car and into the studio, where I'm told to sit in a chair in front of a mirror. Immediately, I have people swarming me with curling irons and makeup brushes.

"Liz, please tell me what I'm doing here? I take it that I'm going to be on TV, but for what?"

"You guessed it, you are going to be on TV," she says. "You know, you're too smart to fool."

I stare her down through the mirror.

"You're being interviewed about your list."

"Why would anyone care about my list?" I ask.

"Because of what you've accomplished. I ran the idea by Tim, who spoke with his boss, and they think it's a great human interest piece."

"Liz, I don't know if I can do this," I say, my palms sweaty all of a sudden.

"You can and you will," she says, looking down at her phone. "It's five thirty, the kids are up, and I already have five missed calls from my mother." She walks away groaning.

There are butterflies in my stomach. I don't know how I am going to be able to do this. Doing a client presentation is one thing, but being in front of millions of viewers?

"Miss. Please try to calm down. You are sweating and smearing the makeup," the makeup artist tells me.

"Sorry," I say. I really want to hit him in the face. Calm down? Is he serious?

"Okay, Jill, we're ready for you," a woman with a clipboard and headset tells me. It's now almost eight and I've been sitting in the green room for who knows how long. I can't believe how long it took them to do my makeup and hair. Did I look that bad before?

Liz has been in and out of the room. Apparently Michael knocked his front tooth out while riding a pillow down the steps.

"They're baby teeth, Mom, he'll be fine," I hear her say. "As long as he's not bleeding, you're okay."

For the past hour, though, I've been trying to think of a way to escape without anyone noticing. But now Clipboard Woman has come in and there is suddenly no escape.

"Here we go," I say to myself.

After being ushered down the long hallway, I'm introduced to Gregg Martinez, the host. I take a seat across from him on the couch.

"Don't be nervous," he says. "I screw up all the time."

Is that supposed to make me feel better? I don't know how to respond except with a nervous smile.

"In five, four, three, two," we hear from behind the camera.

I immediately lock up.

Chapter Thirty

"Good morning, everyone, and welcome to *A.M. Morning*. I'm here today with a very special guest, Ms. Jill Stevens. Last month she was fired from her job at a prestigious law firm and found her boyfriend cheating on her the same day. She was forced to move back home with her parents, all a month before her thirtieth birthday."

Wow, I think to myself, if that doesn't make me sound pathetic, I don't know what does. Sure, I exploited my story on my blog, but this was a bit much.

"Now, Jill, what went through your head the day you were fired and found your boyfriend cheating on you?"

"Um, well, Gregg, I mean, what would anyone think? Everything you've worked so hard for, everything you've dreamed of, just falls apart and there's nothing you can do to stop any of it. It's a horrible feeling. At first, none of it seems quite real, and then you're just devastated."

"Well, the hardest part must have been to move back in with your parents right before you turned thirty."

I suddenly have a strong loathing feeling for Gregg. "Yes, that was difficult," I say.

"So tell us what happened once you moved in?"

"Well," I start, "I was cleaning out my room when I came across a list."

"A list with thirty things to accomplish by age thirty," Gregg chimes in. Every time he talks, he feels the need to sit up, and each time, the yellow leather couch makes a squeaking sound. A parody show once mocked him for this.

Does he want me to tell the story or not? "Yes, that's correct. It was a high school assignment."

"And would you mind telling everyone what was on the list?"

"Well, I mean, it was like any other list someone might write at eighteen. You have crazy dreams like getting on television and writing a book, and other things that are easier to accomplish, like learning to drive stick shift," I say, even though the stick shift wasn't all that easy.

"Well, we have a copy of the list here, and we're going to read it to our audience," Gregg says.

With that, he proceeds to read the list, and then says, "You actually did graduate from Columbia, you did get a job at a great law firm, and you've made it to TV. Let's see—" he scans the list. "Why don't you tell us about your experience kissing a total stranger?"

Everything in me wants to kill Gregg and Liz too.

"It certainly was a unique experience that I intend never to repeat," is all I say.

"And when we come back, we have some special guests who have helped Jill work towards accomplishing her goals. That's right after a word from our sponsors," says Gregg.

"Cut," I hear.

"You're doing great," Gregg says, patting my arm. I try to hold back a scowl. I will never watch this show again.

Then I see Liz and Chris appear. As mad as I am, I feel a sense of relief.

"So how much fun are we having?" Liz asks, rubbing my arm.

"I'm going to kill you later," I tell her.

"You're doing great, and you look super hot," Chris tells me.

"Thanks," I smile.

"Back in ten seconds," we hear.

"And welcome back to *A.M. Morning*. I'm here with Jill Stevens, who, when down on her luck, turned to a list she made over ten years ago and has made it her goal to accomplish everything on it."

Well, that was a lot better than his introduction, I think.

"We are here with Chris Mathews and Liz Rosenberg, who are Jill's very good friends. Can you tell us a few of the experiences you have had while helping Jill with her list?"

"She got us kicked out of yoga," Liz says. "I thought I was never going to be able to show my face in there again."

"That was the first time, and I've gotten a lot better since," I say defensively.

"You did do much better the second time," Liz admits.

"And you were no prize with that karaoke number," I jab at her.

"I rode a roller coaster with Jill, and she did a better job on that than I did, and I've been riding them for years," Chris says.

"And fortunately, we have that picture here," Gregg says while I notice the screen switch over to it. I wince as the picture of me with my mouth full of blood is displayed for the world to see.

"That looks like it hurt a bit," Gregg comments.

"A little," I agree, secretly wanting to kill him.

"So, Jill, what's left on this list that you haven't accomplished yet?"

I try to hide my panic. "Well," I say, looking at the list that is in the screen in front of me. "I haven't traveled the world or gone skydiving, which would also assist in getting over my fear of flying."

"Well, have we got a surprise for you," Gregg says.

"We're giving you four tickets to Paris, where you can perfect your French, and from there, you'll take a week-long tour that will take you to Spain, Italy, and Greece."

"Oh my God, thank you so much," I say, my hand over my mouth. I'm literally gasping. I jump up to give Gregg a hug. All those offensive comments he has made are suddenly forgotten.

"And stay tuned, because at the end of our show, we're going to watch Jill here go skydiving."

"And cut," I hear.

I slowly let go of Gregg and stare at him. My heart has stopped. "Excuse me, what?" I ask.

"This way, please," the Clipboard Woman calls out to me.

"Where am I going and what the hell am I doing?" I ask. Then I remember Liz's throwaway comment (at least, I thought it was) about filming me skydiving.

"Relax, I'm going with you," Chris says, standing up.

"But—"

"You can do this," he says, holding my shoulders.

"Hurry up and get changed," Liz says, throwing my duffle bag at me.

A little while later, I'm standing on top of the *A.M. Morning* building while a helicopter is spinning its propellers waiting for us. I'm frozen.

"Come on, let's go." Chris pulls me across the roof. In seconds, the helicopter is in the air. I can't help but scream.

"Are you all right?" Chris yells over the engine. The pilot urges him to press a button on our headphones to talk.

He repeats himself.

I shake my head nervously. "It'll be all right," he says, reaching for my hand. "If you can do this, you can do anything!"

I force myself to smile. It actually isn't so bad right now. It isn't as bumpy as I had expected it to be, and the view of the city is pretty exceptional. What I'm worried about is jumping out of the plane.

Twenty minutes later, we are at a small airport somewhere in New Jersey. We land, and before I know it, I have on a jumper and a man is quickly running me through the safety course. I know we have to be aware of the time because of the show, but I don't appreciate them racing through the part in which I learn how to save my life if I need to!

All of a sudden, we're on a small plane. Now I feel as if I'm going to throw up.

"Just don't think about it," Chris says.

"If you can't think about it, then why do it?" I ask.

He doesn't know how to respond to this. He just rubs my back as I keel over with my head down.

"Okay, okay, time to go." An oversized muscleman I hadn't even noticed slaps me on the back. "Let's see what you've got," he says to me. Tears start to fill my eyes.

"You'll be fine," Chris assures me. "I'll go first."

"Okay, hurry up," the man says to him. He obediently stands up and another man, who looks like he's done this a lot, straps himself to him. Chris smiles at me as if nothing is wrong, but I can tell he's a little nervous. How could he not be?

"Okay, everyone ready?"

"Ready," Chris yells.

"Go," the man instructs, and with that, Chris and this man jump out the plane.

"Chris, oh my God," I can't help but yell.

"Your turn. Hurry up," the man instructs. The cameraman films me as I'm being strapped to another diver. I try hard not to cry.

"Don't worry. I've done this a thousand times," the pro tells me.

"Ready?" the guy yells.

I take a deep breath and close my eyes. "Ready," I yell.

All of a sudden I feel my feet dragging as the man hurls him and me out of the plane. I'm screaming and freaking out the whole time. My stomach feels as if it's in my throat. After what feels like an eternity, the man pulls the chute and I'm jerked back—and then we're floating. When I do open my eyes I see a mini-camera in front of me. This guy's been filming me the whole time.

I hope not for the whole time, but I'm sure it was.

"Having fun?" he yells.

I can't even speak since I'm still trying to catch my breath, but I can't help smiling.

"Oh my God, this is insane!" I finally say. I'm so completely overwhelmed.

When we get on the ground, a camera crew and Chris are waiting for me. Chris runs up to hug me. "You did it!" he says, spinning me around. "I'm so happy for you!"

Then the cameraman, who hands me an earplug and a microphone, interrupts us. Immediately, I hear some static and then Gregg's voice.

"Jill, are you still with us?"

"Yes, Gregg." I'm still smiling.

"How'd it feel?" he asks me.

"Amazing—best experience of my life," I tell him.

"That's great to hear. Well, that's all for today. Tune in tomorrow for a very special show. We'll be cooking with Chef Gordon Ramsey."

With that, I hand back the microphone and earplug.

"So how does it feel to have accomplished everything?" Chris asks me as we make our way back to the helicopter. I eye it nervously. Even though I just went skydiving, the thought of getting back into that thing isn't pleasant.

But I'm still smiling. "Feels pretty great," I say.

I watch his smile turn huge, and then he kisses me.

Chapter Thirty-One

A few days later, Chris and I start looking at condo apartments. We decide we want to stay in the area to be near our jobs and families, but of course we need to get out of our parents' houses. Now that Chris's dad is doing better, he feels his mother will be fine.

I agreed to come on board full-time at the firm. I love it, and I'm doing more for myself and other people than I ever have before.

"Jill, I came to drop off your lunch," my mom says, smiling as she walks into my office.

"Let's go to lunch," I suggest.

"Sure," she agrees.

"So I got a call from a publishing company today," I tell her, once we are seated at a restaurant across the street.

"Really?" she asks curiously.

"An editor saw my story on Sunday and decided to read my blog. She told me she wants to turn it into an actual book."

"Oh, honey, that's so great! Congratulations!"

"Thanks." I smile. "Everything seems to be going pretty perfectly."

"So, are you loving your job?"

"Yup," I say.

"And Chris?"

"I love him, too," I say.

"Like I was telling you, you can have it all as long as you're with the ones you love."

I roll my eyes. "Yes, Mom, you were right. I'm happy with my job, my family life, and my love life—all of it, is now finally back on track."

"Good," she smirks. "I'm very happy for you."

"Thanks," I say genuinely.

"So when are you going to get married, and when am I going to get some grandkids?"

"Mother!"

"I'm just kidding." She smiles.

The next morning, I wake up to my parents singing "Happy Birthday" to me the way they did when I was six. Half awake, I pull the pillow over my face in an effort to mute the sound of the off-key rhapsodizing.

After dragging myself out of bed, I head downstairs for some much needed coffee.

"So what's the plan for the big day?" my dad asks me while my mom hands me pancakes that spell out 3-0. Some things will never change.

"I didn't make any," I say, taking a sip of my coffee.

"No plans, huh? You spent all month with a schedule of stuff to do, and now that you've accomplished it all, you don't make plans anymore?" my dad asks.

"Well, we are all flying to Paris tomorrow. I have to get ready for it," I tell them. "Not to mention the surprise party you're trying to not tell me about."

"There's no party." My dad laughs nervously. "We've supported you at home for a month now, and you want a party for it?" He fake laughs again and walks out towards the garage. He was never good at secret keeping.

I smirk as I take a sip of my coffee and look at my mom, who's standing at the sink.

"What makes you think there's a party?" she says while wiping down the dishes and avoiding my eyes.

"Because you told me not to make any plans for my birthday," I say. "Either you're throwing me a party, or you're an awful mother."

"You hush now," she says to me.

I roll my eyes.

"By the way, your birthday present is outside," she says.

I smile as I follow her out to the garage. I see my dad waxing up the Corvette.

"Happy birthday, sweetie," he says.

"Are you seriously giving me the Corvette?" My jaw drops practically to the floor.

"Just promise me you'll only put premium gas in it and make sure you get it washed once a week."

Before he can finish his speech, I have my arms wrapped around him.

"Thank you so much," I say. "For everything."

"You're welcome," he smiles.

I then pull away and proceed to jump up and down towards my mom and give her a hug. "Thank you both so much!" I yell, more excited.

"Just be sure to drive safe," she says.

"I'm going to take a shower, pack, and then I'm driving this baby around town!"

After spending the morning packing for my trip, I call Chris to let him know not to pack a hair dryer because I'll have one.

"Do I look like the type who uses a hair dryer?" he asks.

"Well, I'm just saying."

"Stop worrying about tomorrow and let's celebrate your birthday today."

"What do we want to do?"

"I don't know. What have you done for your other birthdays?"

"I worked late and ate a crappy cupcake the office gave me."

"Okay, well, we certainly won't be doing that," he says. "I'm coming to pick you up."

"Forget that, I'm driving!" I say, telling him about my new car.

"Where are we going?" I ask him while we are driving around town.

"Back to high school," he says, pointing for me to pull into the parking lot.

"What are we doing here?" I ask.

"We're starting a tradition," he says, hopping the fence of the football field and unlocking it for me.

"And what's that?"

He leads me over to the bleachers and pulls out a blank piece of paper and a pen.

"What's this?"

"It's your new list."

"My new list?" I repeat.

"Yup, forty things you want to do before you're forty."

"Uh, I just turned thirty and I already have to worry about turning forty?"

"Yes, and this is something I want you to keep doing. It will remind you to live every once in a while."

I smile and lean in to kiss him. "What about your list?" I ask him.

He pulls out another piece of paper from his back pocket and hands it to me. It's all crumbled and looks like it's barely survived whatever it's been through.

"Is this that old list from high school?" I ask. "I thought you had lost this."

Yeah, well, turns out I did have it," he says.

I start to scan it.

1. Lose my virginity

2. Get into college

3. Get over my fear of public speaking

4. Score a goal in lacrosse

5. Drive a Ferrari

6. Take dance lessons

7. Drag race

8. Skydive

9. Go to a baseball game with my dad

10. Meet Derek Jeter

11. Get Terry back for dying our dog blue

12. Coach a team

13. Be man enough to watch a horror movie

14. Be able to grind a rail on a skateboard

15. Learn photography

16. Go on a safari

17. See the Great Wall of China

18. Learn to play golf

19. Win in a fight

20. Build up my body mass

21. Visit California

22. Learn how to surf

23. Be an extra in a film

24. Hang out with a celebrity

25. Go cliff diving

26. Invent something

27. Go to the Playboy mansion

28. Finish a book

29. Learn to fly fish

30. Throw a raging party

"Huh," I say, reading through the list. "So have you accomplished anything on this?" I ask.

"Very funny," he says, taking the list back. "I've actually done a lot, but considering my birthday's a month and half behind yours, maybe this can be our new project."

"Absolutely," I tell him. "This is such a guy's list." I can't help but laugh.

"What?"

"Come on, go to the Playboy mansion?"

"So?" He laughs. "I can have dreams, too, you know."

"And you weren't kidding when you said you never finished reading a book?"

"That's what Cliff Notes were for."

"Again, such a boy."

"Wow, reading through this list again, I'm not sure I can do some of this stuff. Like be able to grind a rail. When you fall as a kid you heal faster than you do when you're my age."

"Hey, never say never. We are going to do all of this."

"You know, I never did score a lacrosse goal."

"Well, you might still be in trouble there because I was an amazing goalie back then."

He looks down at the school field. "Care to accept a challenge?"

After picking the locks and breaking into the old gym, we grab a few sticks, balls, and a goal net.

"Let's see what you've got!" I call threateningly from the goal line while waving my stick around.

"Are you sure you don't want to warm up a bit? I don't want to hurt you."

"You couldn't hurt me. I'm made of steel!" I yell back, pounding my chest.

"Are you sure?" he asks again.

"Just throw the ball, you damn girl!"

"Okay."

Within half a second, I see a white ball come flying at me. I try to stop it but it flies right underneath my arm.

"Goal!" Chris starts screaming and running around the field.

"Cheap shot!" I yell back, laughing.

"I finally scored a goal!"

"You did! Congratulations!"

He comes up to me and starts to spin me around.

"Well, that one was easy," he says, taking a pen out of his pocket and drawing a line through his list.

"Now, I would love to stay, but shouldn't we be getting to my party?"

"Hey, this whole month's been about you. Today is about me. I don't care if it's your birthday," he says.

"Well, fine then," I joke back. "Just wait to see what I've got planned for your birthday. It's going to be foot rubs for me, and backrubs …"

"Oh, shut up," Chris says, kissing me.

When we get back to my house, Chris leads me inside. "Happy Birthday, sweetie!" My mom comes up and hugs me for the fifth time today.

"How was your day?" she asks me, walking towards our front closet.

"It was good," I say, eyeing her suspiciously. "What are you doing?" I ask.

"Getting you ready for tonight," she says, pulling out my pink prom gown that I had thrown out.

"What the hell is that?" I ask.

She smiles mischievously, "I told you that you would wear this again."

"I'm not wearing that," I argue.

"Oh yes you are, and I'm wearing this," he goes next to my mom and pulls out a blue tux. I can't help but laugh.

"What is this, prom night?" I laugh.

"Just because you're a grown-up, doesn't mean you have to act grown-up all the time," he smiles, handing me the pink poofy dress. "Come on, have fun with it."

I try to pretend to be mad, but I can't help but smile. Just then I see my dad come down in a ruffled burgundy tux.

"Are we ready to go or what?" he asks. I burst out laughing along with everyone else. "I love you guys," I can't help but say as I hug both my mom and dad before I head upstairs.

Twenty minutes later we arrive at Charlie's.

"Surprise!" everyone yells.

"This was all me, just so you know." Liz hands me a glass of champagne and hugs me.

"Love the side ponytail you're rockin'" I tell her.

"An 80's prom theme requires going all out," she says while displaying her neon rubber bands around her wrists.

"Oh, I know no one can pull this off better than you," I say laughing.

I look around and I can't get over the number of people I see: my parents, Lou, his daughter Francine, close relatives, and Chris's parents, all dressed up like 80s prom geeks for me.

"So good to see you," I say to Frank after I've said my hellos to everyone.

"It's great to see you with my boy here," he says, slapping Chris on the back. "He got himself a great girl."

"Well, thanks," I say, blushing.

"Happy birthday," he smiles.

"Thank you." I smile back. "He's looking great," I say to Chris when we walk away.

"This is from all your blogging fans." Liz hands me a box.

"What is this?" I ask.

"It's a Karaoke machine," she says.

"Wow," I laugh. I put the box down, lean in and give her a hug. "Thank you so much."

Just then Francine comes up to me. "Happy birthday," she says.

"Thanks," I respond.

"I wanted to tell you I've been enjoying my internship so much."

"That's great," I tell her.

"And it turns out there's a position opening up that they want to interview the interns for at the end of the summer, so we'll see how it all goes."

"That's so great, Francine! I'm so happy for you." I give her another hug.

Just as she and I are catching up, we're interrupted by the squeal of a microphone. Everyone jumps.

"Excuse me," Chris says, tapping the microphone. It looks like he grabbed the karaoke machine when we weren't looking. "Sorry to interrupt, but we wanted to thank everyone for coming and supporting our Jill here turning the big three-oh. Everyone give it up for her," he says, clapping. Everyone joins in. "Now I know there might be a lot of great things you got Jill for her birthday, but I'm about to give her a gift that I'm sorry will top every single one of yours. In order to accomplish this, I'm going to have to ask Liz to get up here and sing some Irene Cara for the crowd."

Everyone applauds.

"Nothing will make Jill happier than to get Liz back for everything. Everyone give it up for Liz!"

The crowd starts cheering, and I see Liz's face turn completely crimson.

"I'm not doing that," she tells him.

"Do it, do it!" Tim starts the crowd chanting. I watch as she hits him. He's really turned around in the past few days.

Finally, Liz manages to peel herself off the barstool and slowly make her way up there.

"I'm getting all of you back," she says. "Remember, just because I'm going to be a nurse doesn't mean I have to save you."

The crowd burst into laughter.

As the music starts, I see her face get all flushed again. She gives me a terrified look so I go up and join her, which gets the crowd going.

Then the music begins for "What a Feeling," and I burst into laughter as we begin singing. "First when there's nothing, but a slow glowing dream, in a world made of steel, made of stone …"

The crowd starts cheering us on and singing, "What a feeling, bein's believing. I can't have it all now I'm dancing for my life. Take your passion, and make it happen. Pictures come alive, you can dance right through your life … what a feeling."

When the song's over, Liz gives me a hug. We're laughing hysterically.

"Happy birthday, girl," she says. "You know I wouldn't do that for anyone else but you."

"I know," I say, hugging her back.

As I look around, I realize for the first time in my life how grateful I really am for everyone I have as part of my life.

"This is for you," Chris says, leading me over to a quieter area of the party.

My face flushes when I notice it's a small ring box.

"Open it," he urges.

I slowly open the box and I see a diamond ring.

"Oh my God, Chris," I feel my eyes begin to water.

"So is that a yes?" he asks me.

I shake my head. "Yes," I say hugging him. "Of all the decisions I have had to make over this past month, I never been more sure," I smile.

"She said yes!" he screams, picking me up and swinging me around.

Everyone begins to cheer, and my parents come over to hug me.

"I'm so happy for you," my mom begins to cry.

"Congratulations." My dad shakes Chris's hand. "I know you'll take great care of my little girl."

"Welcome to our family," Donna and Frank hug me.

I'm so overwhelmed with happiness. A month ago I would've never thought I'd be where I am now. I am in such a better place in my life. It just goes to show it's never too late to start living your life.

"So what do you want to do when we get to Paris tomorrow?" Chris asks, coming up from behind and putting his arms around me.

"Hmm, I'm not sure," I say. "Maybe we should make a list."

About the Author

Courtney Psak is a New Jersey native who grew up with a passion for reading and writing. After traveling the world, she settled into New York City where she earned her Masters in Publishing. She is a member of the National Writer's Association and the Women's Fiction Writers Association. She currently resides in Hoboken with her husband. She spends her weekends seeking adventure through hiking, skiing and traveling.

Connect with Courtney Psak

I really appreciate you reading my book! Here are my social media coordinates:

Friend me on Facebook: https://www.facebook.com/courtneypsakauthor

Follow me on Twitter: https://twitter.com/CourtneyPsak

Favorite my Smashwords author page: https://www.smashwords.com/profile/view/courtneypsak

to my blog: https://courtneypsakauthor.wordpress.com/

Visit my website: http://www.courtneypsak.com/

Made in the USA
San Bernardino, CA
28 December 2015